BOOKS BY SUSANNE DUNLAP

*The Musician's Daughter*

*Anastasia's Secret*

*In the Shadow of the Lamp*

# *Anastasia's Secret*

❧ SUSANNE DUNLAP ❧

**BLOOMSBURY**

NEW YORK BERLIN LONDON SYDNEY

First published in the United States of America in March 2010
by Bloomsbury Books for Young Readers
Paperback edition published in March 2011
www.bloomsburyteens.com

For information about permission to reproduce selections from this book, write to
Permissions, Bloomsbury BFYR, 175 Fifth Avenue, New York, New York 10010

The Library of Congress has cataloged the hardcover edition as follows:
Dunlap, Susanne Emily.
Anastasia's secret / Susanne Dunlap. — 1st U.S. ed.
p.    cm.
Summary: As world war and the looming Russian Revolution threaten all they hold dear,
Anastasia, the youngest daughter of Tsar Nicholas II, and her family are being held
in captivity, where she falls in love with one of their captors.
ISBN 978-1-59990-420-7 (hardcover)
1. Anastasia Nikolaevna, Grand Duchess, daughter of Nicholas II, Emperor of Russia, 1901–1918—
Juvenile Fiction. [1. Anastasia, Grand Duchess, daughter of Nicholas II, Emperor of Russia,
1901–1918—Fiction. 2. Princesses—Fiction. 3. Interpersonal relations—Fiction.
4. Russia—History—Nicholas II, 1894–1917—Fiction.] I. Title.
PZ7.D92123An 2010        [Fic]—dc22        2009018257

ISBN 978-1-59990-588-4 (paperback)

Book design by Donna Mark
Typeset by Westchester Book Composition
Printed in the U.S.A. by Quad/Graphics, Fairfield, Pennsylvania
1  3  5  7  9  10  8  6  4  2

*To my mother,*
*who never lived to see me an author,*
*and to my father,*
*who reads my books for both of them*

## ⸎ CAST OF CHARACTERS ⸎

The life of Russia's last imperial family was full of people. Running the court that resided at five or six different palaces and on several yachts, and caring for the five children—one of whom lived with a debilitating disease—required an army of courtiers, servants, and doctors. Most of them don't appear in this novel.

But a vivid picture of their existence and all they went through would not be complete without some idea of the many people who devoted themselves to the Romanov family, some choosing to share their privations to the very end. It can be confusing keeping track of everyone, especially because the imperial family gave nicknames to all the people who surrounded them. Given the way Russian names and titles were constructed, it's hardly surprising.

A quick word about those tricky Russian names: if you know the function of each part of a name, it's not very hard to understand who's who.

1. **First name or Christian name.** This is the name your parents gave you when you were born.

2. **Patronymic.** A Slavic tradition, this name follows the first name and literally means son of or daughter of [father's first name]. Since Anastasia was the daughter of Nicholas, her patronymic was Nicholaevna. Alexei, the boy, was Alexei Nicholaevich. Acquaintances and friends might easily have called Anastasia Anastasia Nicholaevna.

3. **Family name.** The same as a last name in English, except that names are altered to be gender specific. Romanov was the imperial family's last name, but the girls were all Romanova, while the boys were Romanov.

## THE IMPERIAL FAMILY

**Tsar Nicholas Alexandrovich Romanov**—Called Nicky by the tsaritsa, otherwise Papa or Father. The people often called him Batyushka, which means "Little Father," a term of combined affection and reverence.

**Tsaritsa Alexandra Fyodorovna Romanova**—Her nickname was Sunny, given to her by the tsar when he first met her.

**Grand Duchess Olga Nicholaevna Romanova**—Always referred to as Olga.

**Grand Duchess Tatiana Nicholaevna Romanova**—Always referred to as Tatiana.

**Grand Duchess Maria Nicholaevna Romanova**—Called Marie by her mother and relatives and Mashka by her sisters.

**Grand Duchess Anastasia Nicholaevna Romanova—** Called Anastasie by her mother and relatives, Nastya by her sisters, and sometimes Shvybz.

**Tsarevich Alexei Nicholaevich Romanov—**Called Baby, Sunshine, Alyosha, or Alexis.

## THE SUITE

Sometimes referred to as the Household, these are the ladies and gentlemen with court appointments, who had specific jobs to perform to help the court function in its ceremonial and practical way. There were dozens of suite members, but this story features only those who were closely involved with the family immediately before and during their captivity.

**Anna Alexandrovna Vyrubova—**The tsaritsa's closest friend, called Anya by the family. She did not at first have a court appointment, but was later made an honorary maid of honor.

**Countess Anastasia Vasilyevna Hendrikova—**Maid of honor to the tsaritsa, but also a good friend. She was called Nastinka or Nastenka by the family.

**Baroness Sophie Buxhoeveden—**Maid of honor, called Isa by the family.

**Catherine Adolphovna Schneider—**Known as Trina by the family, she originally joined the court to teach Alexandra Russian when she became engaged to Nicholas, and remained as a friend, tutor, and general helper to the family.

**Lili Dehn—**Maid of honor and friend to Alexandra. She remained with the family during their captivity in

Tsarskoe but stayed in her own house under arrest because her son was dangerously ill.

**Count Paul Benckendorff**—General aide-de-camp and grand marshal of the court. Served as "gatekeeper" for those who wished to have an audience with the tsar, and a very loyal member of the suite through their imprisonment at Tsarskoe Selo. He was quite elderly and did not follow the family into exile.

**Count Vladimir Borisovich Fredericks**—Chief Minister of the court and old friend of the family. Called the royal couple *mes enfants*, "my children" in French. He did not go into exile with them because of his age.

**Prince Vasily Alexandrovich Dolgoruky/Dolgorukov**—Most commonly he seems to be referred to as Prince Dolgorukov. He was another aide-de-camp to the tsar and marshal of the court, and went into exile with the family.

**General Ilia Leonodovich Tatischev**—General aide-de-camp to the tsar and marshal of the court, also went with them into exile.

**Colonel Grooten**—One of the palace commanders of the guard, friendly with the family, and responsible for commanding the Composite Infantry Regiment of the Household Troops, also known as the Composites, the elite corps of guards that protected the imperial family.

## THE TUTORS AND DOCTORS

Lessons continued for all the children throughout their captivity at Tsarskoe Selo, Tobolsk, and Yekaterinburg. Several of those responsible for educating these spirited and sheltered young people were eventually considered privileged members of the family. The tsaritsa suffered from a heart condition, and the tsarevich was a hemophiliac. Two different doctors became the devoted caregivers of the imperial family.

**Pierre Gilliard**—Called Zhilik by the children and others, he taught them French at first, then became the primary tutor to the tsarevich, eventually taking on more responsibilities for all of them when they were in exile.

**Sidney Gibbes**—English teacher. The children called him Mr. Gibbes; the tsar and tsaritsa called him Sid.

**Alexandra Alexandrovna Tegleva**—The children's governess, more of a supervisor than a teacher. She and Gilliard eventually married and returned to Gilliard's native Switzerland.

**Eugene Sergeevich Botkin**—Doctor to the imperial family.

**Vladimir Nicholaevich Derevenko**—Also sometimes spelled Derevanko, doctor in charge of Alexei's care. His son, Kolya, often served as a playmate to Alexei.

## PRINCIPAL SERVANTS

The army of servants that attended to the Romanov family before the revolution was vast. The twenty or so who went with the family into exile in Tobolsk must have seemed to them like a fraction of what they needed. The ones named here are those who have relatively important roles to play in the Romanovs' exile. In general, the servants are referred to by last name.

**Anna Stepanovna Demidova**—The tsaritsa's personal maid.

**Alexei Ivanovich Volkov**—Valet to the tsaritsa.

**Magdalena Franzevna Zanotti**—Madeleine Zanotti, who was in charge of the jewels and gowns of the tsaritsa and the grand duchesses.

**Klementi Grigorievich Nagorny**—Alexei's servant, who carried him whenever he was ill.

**Ivan Dmitrievich Sednev**—Valet to the children.

**Ivan Mikhailovich Kharitonov**—Chief cook.

**Terenti Ivanovich Chemodurov**—One of the tsar's valets.

## THE CAPTORS

Another changing cast of characters, from people who were once loyal to the tsar and his family, to those who wished them only harm. This is a roughly chronological list of the people primarily responsible for their imprisonment.

**Alexander Fyodorovich Kerensky**—Second prime minister of the Provisional Government and also minister of war.

**Colonel Korovichenko**—Commander of the palace guard, in charge of the family's imprisonment.

**Colonel Eugene Kobylinsky**—Commander of the palace guard after Korovichenko, accompanied the guard to Tobolsk.

**Damadianz**—Assistant commander who took over after Korovichenko.

**Vasily Pankratov**—Commissar at Tobolsk.

**Alexander Nikolsky**—Commissar at Tobolsk.

**Vasily Yakovlev**—Bolshevik official in charge of transferring the imperial family to Yekaterinburg.

**Nikolai Rodionov**—Last commissar in charge of the family at Tobolsk.

## FAMILY PETS

The imperial family had more than its share of animal companions. Several dogs, including the tsarevich's spaniel, Joy, and Tatiana's French bulldog, Ortino, went into exile with them. While they were in Tobolsk, apparently Anna Vyrubova sent them the gift of a King Charles spaniel puppy, which became mainly Anastasia's and was called Jimmy. Olga had a cat, and the tsaritsa had a Scottish terrier named Eira—who was evidently fond of dashing out from behind things and biting peoples' ankles.

The only pet that had any real part to play in the actual drama, though—and therefore the only one mentioned often in this book—was Joy, who survived the tragedy at Yekaterinburg and was taken back to England to live out her life.

# Anastasia's
# Secret

## ❧ PROLOGUE ❧

*May 20, 1918, on the steamboat* Rus

We are surrounded by guards. Not the nice ones; the ones we don't like, who make us bow to them, make us show our identity cards and take a long time to examine them, even though they know perfectly well who we are and that we haven't been anywhere outside of the Governor's House in Tobolsk for months.

Worst of all, one of the guards is Sasha.

*Sasha! Look at me!*

He won't. He stares straight ahead. The corners of his mouth are turned down slightly. The scar that extends from beneath the patch over his eye is red. He must be angry. But why? I don't know, but I can guess. If I took a photograph of him, the color of his scar wouldn't show, and it wouldn't tell the story.

The only good thing is that soon we will all be together at Yekaterinburg: Papa and Mama, Alyosha, Olga, Tatiana, Mashka, and I. I left Sasha's balalaika behind because they would not let me take it, and then it was stolen by the soldiers. Now I have nothing to remind me of the old days.

Oh where is *that* Sasha! The one I love, the one who loves me. This Sasha, who turns away when I look at him, is not the same. Merciful God, bring him back! Let me have my friend again. Make him remember all we have been. Then I'll be able to survive anything.

## ☙ CHAPTER I ❧

I was very small the first time someone told me the story of the day I was born. There were no terrible storms. No comets flew across the sky. Mama had an easy birth—I was the fourth child, so she was used to it. All that happened was that my father left the palace and went for a long walk alone in the gardens at Peterhof. He probably smoked while he walked. He enjoyed cigarettes and often gave them to us as a treat when we were older. He had to compose himself so that he would be able to smile and tell my mother he was glad that he had a fourth daughter instead of the long wished-for son, a tsarevich to continue the Romanov line. A tsarevich to continue three hundred years of history.

But three years later Alexei was born, and everyone was happy.

My childhood—what I remember of it now that so much has changed—was tranquil. Idyllic, even. I had no real cares, except to do my lessons and learn to knit and sew, making things for the poor children at first, then the soldiers later.

When I think about it now, most of the years merge into one another, with the same events occurring over and over again. The same hours in the schoolroom. The same annual cruises on the *Standart* to the coast of Finland. The same picking up the household and going from palace to palace—the Alexander Palace in Tsarskoe Selo in the spring, Peterhof in the summer, Livadia in the Crimea late in the summer, Skernevizi in Poland for hunting in the autumn, and the Winter Palace when we had to attend official functions at any time of year. The year 1913, when all of Russia celebrated the three-hundredth jubilee of Romanov rule, would have been just like every other, with a few more parties and boring events, except that I met Sasha. That is where everything began.

My whole family and all the court had been forced to attend the most tedious celebrations. I wore clean through three pairs of shoes in one month. It wouldn't have been so bad if I had been in long gowns like my sisters Olga and Tatiana, but my coming-of-age on my sixteenth birthday was still four years off. Four years and a lifetime, it seems now.

I had wandered into the gardens, complaining of a headache so I wouldn't have to go with my mother and her friend Anya Vyrubova to inspect yet another nursing home Mama had endowed with money from her own purse. I heard the distant sound of a balalaika, and it drew me toward a garden wall. In the street celebrations for the jubilee it was common to hear someone playing this three-stringed guitar. The sound always made me feel sad and happy at the same time. It brought to mind pictures of the onion domes of Moscow and the Crimean peasants in their colorful costumes. I loved to play the balalaika.

My brother, Alexei, had one that he also liked to play when he was well, but I knew it wasn't Alyosha strumming now. He was with his tutor, M. Gilliard—Zhilik, we called him—trying to learn French.

As I walked into the garden I realized that the music wasn't coming from over the wall, but from a corner inside the garden itself. It sounded like a lovely instrument and the player was very skillful.

I crept up slowly and quietly. One of the gardeners was a fearsome fellow we were all afraid of, and if it happened to be him playing I would let him be and slip away before he saw me.

But it wasn't. In fact, it was someone I had never seen before, dressed in the uniform of the Semyonovsky Guards. He made a nice picture in his crisp uniform with its brass buttons and braid. He was leaning against a tree, gazing at nothing, and strumming his balalaika. I wished I had my Kodak camera with me.

I was so wrapped up in my thoughts that I stood there for a long minute before I spoke, waiting for the young soldier to finish his song. When it was over, I asked, "Who are you?" The words spilled out before I thought about being polite.

He jumped up and fell backward, tossing his balalaika aside. It landed in a flowerbed with a *twang*.

"Oh! I ..." He stood quickly and dusted himself off. "I beg your pardon. I'm with the Composites. I'm supposed to be ... guarding ..."

The Composite corps was the guard of the palace, made up of elite representatives from all the different regiments. Yet this fellow hardly looked like a battle-proven soldier. His face was smooth and young, a nice shape, with full lips and a nose that turned up slightly. Freckles dotted his cheeks and brought out his startlingly blue eyes. At first I caught my breath when I saw him, curiously attracted to this complete stranger. I quickly recovered, though, and decided I couldn't resist the temptation to take advantage of the situation.

"Did you think to frighten people away by playing, or were you planning to attract the rabble with a tune and then turn them over to the police?"

"Forgive me. Are you one of the grand duchesses? Please don't tell . . ."

"Oh heavens, you don't need to worry about me. I'm only Anastasie. No one heeds me very much. I won't say a word to anyone."

His face relaxed into a smile that turned his blue eyes up at the corners and wrinkled his nose slightly. "I'm Alexander Mikhailovich Galliapin, but everyone calls me Sasha."

"How did you come to be here, Alexander Mikhailovich, whom everybody calls Sasha?" I asked him.

A nervous twitch tugged one of the corners of his mouth down slightly. "I . . . I couldn't help . . . I—walked in."

I should have told him just to walk out again. We weren't allowed friends Mama and Papa didn't approve of, and there were few enough of those. But something told me I was in no danger from Sasha. And so instead of sending him away, I asked, "Why?"

I think it was that question that began our friendship. He could not believe a grand duchess—a princess, the youngest daughter of the ruler of all the Russias—would be interested in the comings and goings of someone as lowly as he was.

Sasha looked down at his feet, a slow flush creeping up from his neck to his face. "I don't know exactly," he said.

Something told me he did know, that perhaps he had come here to escape from something, as I had. "You can tell me, you know," I said. "I'm not going to turn you in."

He smiled again. What a smile! "You're right. I came here for a reason. To get away from someone."

"Who?"

"My sergeant. He's a drunk. He beats me because he knows I'm really too young to be in the regiment."

"How horrid," I said. "Why don't you have him punished?"

Sasha laughed. "That's good! Have my sergeant punished!" He continued laughing, a sound that bubbled like a fountain and made me smile too. "Well, I'm used to it, I suppose. That's why I joined the guards. To get away from my father's beatings. He was always drunk too."

It struck me that the poor fellow hadn't really managed to escape at all. "My father is very kind to us. I've never been beaten." I didn't know what else to say.

"Well, you wouldn't be, would you? I expect everyone has to bow three times to you when they see you, and would be whipped for forgetting to address you by your proper title." He crossed his arms over his chest, daring me to notice that he had done no such thing himself at that moment.

I was shocked. Although no one treated me very specially, no one ever spoke to me rudely—except my sisters and brother, and that was different. Then it struck me that here was someone completely outside my own world. He might be able to teach me what real life was like, outside the palace. I took a chance, and decided not to notice his rudeness.

"Is that what people think?" I asked, genuinely curious. "Mostly everyone calls me Nastya. Or Anastasie. Or Anastasia Nicholaevna, if they want to be formal. Mama says using a title is only appropriate on state occasions."

"It is said your mama has views that the Russian nobility does not appreciate."

"Really? What else do people think about us?"

He opened his mouth to speak, then closed it again. "Are you sure you want to know?" he asked. "You might not like it."

I shrugged. "What could they say? Mama and Papa are good and kind, and my sisters, brother, and I—we are just like other children."

"Listen." He took a step closer and lowered his voice to a whisper. "If you really want to know, they think the tsaritsa doesn't care for Russia, the tsar is afraid to do anything that will mean change, and the rest of you are aloof and spoiled."

"How odd." I suppose I should have been offended by what he said, but instead I was fascinated. If I had never seen Sasha again after that, he would have given me a gift already, a view of my life from a completely different perspective, and it was a view that was not very flattering.

I decided I had better change the conversation. "So how do you remain in the guards if you are too young?"

"I thought I'd grow, but I didn't. My commanding officer guessed, but he finds me useful, I suppose. I'm not allowed to parade because I ruin the line. Mostly I polish boots and buttons, sometimes I fetch swords and guns. I know how to clean a rifle now, and many of the officers ask me to do it for them before a parade. Oh, and they like to hear me play the balalaika." He looked toward his instrument, as if he needed my permission to retrieve it from the flowerbed. I saved him the trouble by getting it myself. It was a plain wooden instrument with only a little carving on its triangular body and frets of brass up the slender neck. I handed it to him.

"If there is war, will you fight?" I asked him.

"What do you know of war?"

"Everyone speaks of it. I don't know much." I tried to shrug casually, realizing that I might have given away more than I should have. I had a way of overhearing conversations I wasn't meant to. It was the one advantage to being "just Anastasie." Recently Papa and his advisers had been speaking about Prussia and Austria. But I didn't want to let on to a guard I had only just met that I knew anything in particular. "Besides, when one sees soldiers everywhere, one naturally thinks of war." It was a feeble explanation and I was certain he saw through it.

"Then no one has told you that the Germans are arming, and making rather unpleasant noises that are upsetting all of Europe?"

Fortunately, I didn't have time to answer him. I heard Mlle Schneider—Trina—calling my name. "I have to go. My tutor is calling me. May we speak again?" I asked, not sure why, except that I hadn't found out everything I wished to from this young man with the upturned blue eyes and freckles across his nose, who had dared to steal into the tsar's garden to play the balalaika.

"All you have to do is command it!" he said loudly, and bowed with a great flourish of his hand.

"Ssshh!" I said. "I want to be able to talk to you without anyone knowing. The police record everything we do, you know. I can't go to the water closet without someone writing a note about it. They say it's for our safety."

"How tedious. Well, I'll look for you in the garden again, just here," he said, slapping the trunk of the oak tree near where we stood. It was spring, and the leaves were still small and pale green, and the light from the sun shimmered through them.

"Will you bring your balalaika?" I asked.

"You like this peasant instrument? I thought you royals were too proud for that."

"Wrong again," I said. "I love it." I decided not to tell him yet that I too knew how to play it.

"Then I'll bring it."

"All right," I said, then ran off to find Trina.

## ❖ CHAPTER 2 ❖

After our first encounter, I didn't see Sasha for a while. He came once more that season and brought his balalaika. The quiet ballads he played made me sigh and reminded me of Livadia, our estate in the Crimea where the Tartars often had festivals, playing their balalaikas and beating their tambourines all day long and into the night.

But we were busy with the jubilee, and Sasha was occupied with his guard duties. I didn't expect to see him much, but I was vaguely disappointed anyway.

Our life as the imperial family went on almost as normal— or what felt normal to us, at any rate. Marie and I shared a room, and Olga and Tatiana had theirs. We slept on simple camp beds without pillows. We all rose early, had cold showers, and ate breakfast at eight. My little brother Alexei joined us if he was not ill. He was born with a terrible disease— hemophilia—that made him bleed inside and suffer abominably. Although he had been well for long stretches of time, he would never be entirely cured. We thanked God daily that he had been better since that awful time at Skernevizi and then at Spala, our Polish estates, when he nearly died. The doctors had given up hope, and then Mama received the letter from Grigory that said Alexei would survive, and to tell the doctors not to bother him. She did, and he did, and after that Mama and Papa believed more than ever that Grigory Efimovich Rasputin was a saint.

Personally, I thought he was just odd and harmless. He was very kind to all of us children, although he sometimes made me uncomfortable, the way he looked at me with his startling blue eyes, so pale they were almost colorless. Now I can't believe he ever did half what they say he did.

After breakfast every day except Sunday we tidied our rooms, then Mashka and I went to the schoolroom for our lessons, while Olga and Tatiana did other things until it was time for theirs. We had French and English, mathematics and geography, art and drawing. I loved my drawing lessons—anything to do with pictures, really—and the music and dancing. I didn't care for German at all, and Mama gave up trying to make me learn it after a while. Once the war started, no one spoke German if they could help it anyway.

I think my first premonition of what lay ahead came that early summer of 1914 when we were traveling to Tsarskoe Selo from our holiday at Livadia. We had come back early on the imperial train because there were "troubles" abroad and at home. Also, Alexei was not well, having slipped on a chair in our schoolroom. He had his nurse and Mama looking after him in their private car.

At first, at every station along the way there were crowds

to greet us—waving and cheering, some people in tears, hands clasped in front of them as if our train were the holiest of icons that could perform miracles. "For Tsar and country!" I heard all around me. I was surprised. We were normally treated with respect, but this seemed out of all proportion. Had something happened that we did not know about, or at least that Mama and Papa had chosen not to tell us?

"Papa, what is all this?" I asked him.

Mama answered, "Oh, there has been an unfortunate incident in the Balkan states. The Archduke Ferdinand has been . . . assassinated. I'm sure it will come to nothing, but there is such an outcry against the Germans now."

Mama did not look up from her sewing, but her lips were pressed together in a tight line, and Papa reached over and put his hand on her knee.

"The people adore your mama and papa," said Mme Vyrubova, Anya, who was traveling with us even though the other maids of honor had been sent ahead on their own. That always made them jealous.

"It is so foolish," Mama continued, her voice a little shaky. "Your papa has determined that we are to call St. Petersburg 'Petrograd' from now on, just so it does not sound German."

Of course, Mama is German by birth, although she was brought up mainly in England and is now wholeheartedly Russian. Her brother is the Grand Duke of Hesse. It would be her worst nightmare to go to war against her own family.

My sisters and I excused ourselves from the luncheon table and returned to our parlor in another car. I wondered if Mama was right, that it would all blow over. I wasn't so sure.

Cities did not change their names over trifles. I thought then of Sasha, and wondered what he knew. I had not seen him since the spring, when we were at Peterhof. He had told me then that unsettling events were occurring on our Western frontier. When I had brought this news back to Tatiana and Olga they laughed it away. No one was laughing now.

But that was not the worst of it. Later that day, as we drew into another station, I saw a great crowd gathered, just as they had gathered at many such stations along the way. Only this crowd was not cheering and waving.

"Look, Mashka," I said. She left her book and came over to peer out the window with me.

"I expect they have bread and salt to present to Papa," she said, then shrugged and went back to reading. It was a tradition to give the tsar bread and salt on a gold tray when he came to your city. Papa had decreed that only wooden trays should be used, though, when he found out that the poorer villages could not afford gold.

But this crowd appeared different from the others. They were not simply quiet, they were silent. And the silence was filled with something tense and hostile. It was warm at that time of year, and I had opened the window to get the fresh breeze, but I decided to pull it back down almost all the way as we drew nearer to the crowd and I could discern flashes of something like anger in their eyes.

We were not scheduled to stop, but as our train approached, the crowd swarmed the tracks so that the engineer had to pull the brakes and, amid much screeching and scraping of metal on metal, we ground to a halt. The people pressed up against the cars. Because the platform was low, they were nearly the height of a man beneath us. They turned their sullen faces up to stare. I drew back a little from the window.

Suddenly a guard threw open the door to our carriage and ran through, closing and latching the protective metal shutters. "Don't open them until I say!" he barked.

As soon as the guard left, I unlatched the shutter nearest me and raised it a little so that I could look out. It all seemed unreal from inside our train, up above the heads of the common people outside.

"Don't, Nastya!" hissed Olga. She and Tatiana had been playing a game of bezique, but stopped abruptly when the train came to a halt. Their game was as orderly and tame as their hair, which was always neatly arranged and smooth. I ignored my oldest sister, who was nineteen and quite grown up, and peeked out. Local guards had come with their bayonets fixed and tried to push the crowd back, but the people held fast.

"Come, brother, join us! Your life is as hard as ours," a man quite close to me said to one of the guards.

I thought he sounded very friendly and wondered if the guard would agree. Instead he lowered his rifle and plunged the bayonet through the man's stomach.

My hands flew to my mouth. I thought I would vomit. I concentrated hard to stop the bitter saliva from flooding my mouth.

The next thing I knew the entire crowd had erupted in screams and shouts. I felt our train car being jostled. Then, Papa himself ran through our car, his eyes wild with fear.

"We must go! Start the train!" he called as he ran up to the car behind the engine.

Just before the door slammed shut behind Papa, I heard a voice from up ahead respond, "I can't! The people are blocking the way!"

I didn't hear what Papa said next, but I felt the great steam engine rumble, and we began to inch forward. I peered out again. Most people scattered as we picked up speed, spitting and cursing and shaking their fists at us. I was relieved to be in the safety of the carriage instead of standing among them. Something Sasha had told me stuck in my mind, something about the anger that was barely hidden beneath the surface of most Russians. I was beginning to understand what he meant when I looked into the eyes of those people.

I must have been holding my breath, because as the train started up again, I let out a long sigh. I could hear the blood rushing in my ears. It was a strange sensation. I don't think I was ever really frightened before that time. I have been frightened many times since, though.

But the tragedies weren't over for that day. One very angry person must have stood his ground when everyone else stepped aside to let the train pass. Just as we began to pick up speed, the engineer pulled the brake and all of us were thrown from our seats.

He had not pulled it soon enough. I heard my father cry out, "Stop! Stop! We have hit some poor devil! We must see to him."

"It is too late, Your Majesty," said a guard. "We can do nothing, and there is great danger behind us."

My father passed back through our car, this time sobbing. We all stood and dusted ourselves off, then went back to our seats. Olga and Tatiana tried to recommence their card game. Maria picked up her book again, but I saw her hand shaking as she turned the pages. I went back to staring out the window, wondering how many more people like that there were in Russia and what would happen if they all gathered together and attacked us.

## CHAPTER 3

Once we were back in Tsarskoe Selo, at the Alexander Palace—the one of our many palaces we really thought of as home—I sent word to Sasha that I wanted to meet him. I was eager to ask him about the incident at the station, to find out if he knew anything about it and what it all meant. Sasha and I couldn't simply send letters; everything that came and went from the palace was read by the secret police. It was for our protection, they said, to prevent attacks upon us. But I sometimes wonder if the Bolsheviks had members among these same police and were storing up information about us for later.

So instead of letters, to keep our friendship secret we devised a way of communicating through the girl who brought in the eggs, and who was happy to earn a few extra kopecks. These Sasha supplied, because I never had any actual money. Everything we wanted was purchased from our personal accounts, which were managed by the palace staff. It is funny now to think that I had no idea what things really cost, only that there was always enough money for everything that we wanted.

✦

Sasha and I sat at the foot of the oak tree in that protected glade of the garden where we had first met. High shrubs nearby kept out prying eyes, and the thick foliage of the oak protected us from the summer sun.

"Why were those people at the train station so angry? So hostile?" I asked.

"You really don't know, do you?" Sasha had his amazed, superior look.

If someone else had acted that way, I would have been angry. But in my meetings with Sasha, I dropped all formality and decided that it was worth his friendship to tolerate whatever he said or did. Something about the way he looked at me made me forgive him for anything. And it was unsettling to think how little I really knew about what went on in Russia. "Did you hear of it?" I asked him, steering the conversation back around to the pursuit of information.

"No," he answered. "I expect no one will. The Okhrana hushes up everything that casts a bad light on the tsar, if they can. What's the life of one peasant, after all?"

Now he had gone too far. How could he imagine that we thought any person's life was not sacred? But I didn't want to show my anger and risk sending him away. Instead, I pulled up a clump of grass and threw it at him.

"Be careful, Your Imperial Highness Grand Duchess Anastasia!" he said.

"Oh!" When he wanted to provoke me he called me by my title. I had to resist the temptation to fall upon him and pummel him with my fists. It would have done my white dress no good at all, and I would have had to offer some reasonable explanation later. I satisfied myself with sticking my tongue out at him.

He laughed silently until the tears streamed down his cheeks. "You can't be serious. You're just like a little girl, yet you're a grand duchess."

"I am just a normal person, like you or any of Papa's subjects." I refused to think of myself even then as a little girl, and it infuriated me when Sasha said it.

Sasha grew serious. "It's true, they have not spoiled you and given you high and mighty airs. But do you really know what it's like to be what you call a 'normal person'?"

"I know the servants, who are not wealthy, and the sailors on Papa's yachts."

"They all receive costly gifts from your parents at Christmas or Easter, or at the end of a cruise. They have long since feathered their nests with the proceeds from imperial presents that they sell in the marketplace."

I didn't want to tell Sasha that I hadn't any idea which gifts were costly and which were not. I had seen peasants working in the fields, seen shopkeepers and tradespeople in the streets of Petrograd and Moscow, seen the Tartars in the Crimea, with their red and gold costumes and their horses. But I couldn't really claim to know any of these people, or to have any idea what kind of lives they led. "Nonetheless, the people have a good life here. If they do not, it is because they are lazy and refuse to work."

Sasha's face darkened and I realized I must have gone too far in repeating something I had heard Mlle Tutcheff, a governess we had for only a short time, say when I was younger.

"That way of thinking is what will ruin your family and all of the Russian nobility as you know it," he said.

It was hard sometimes to stay calm when Sasha told me things. I was getting tired of not knowing anything, always having to accept what he said as the truth. "If you think I am so uninformed, why don't you show me what the real people are like? For all I know, they're like you, sleeping in comfortable barracks with three meals of meat a day!"

I knew I had stung him. He was silent a moment. I was sorry, but I couldn't take back my words. After a pause, he replied, "All right. If you think you can manage it. I'll show you. Be here tomorrow before dawn, and I'll have you back in time for breakfast."

I hesitated, but not for long. What harm could it do? Even if the secret police knew where I was going and with whom, I could make sure that Sasha was not blamed for anything. And I didn't think the Okhrana had infiltrated as far as our bedroom, in any case, to spy on when we went to bed and when we got up in the morning. They were more interested in Mama and Papa. "What should I bring?" I asked.

Sasha shrugged. "Some food, if anything. And dress as plainly as you can." He said this with a critical look up and down at my starched white dress with its bright red sash.

Almost all my dresses were white, but I had coats that were not. I wasn't worried that I could look plain.

We said our good-byes, and I returned to the palace with my head full of how I would manage to sneak away before dawn without letting anyone know, even Mashka. I decided that if she woke up, I would say that I was going to the toilet, that my stomach was bothering me a little. She would believe me. I often had such complaints.

First, though, I had to secrete away some food, for the purpose, I presumed, of distributing to some worthy, hardworking family. What would be appropriate? And how would I get it? I knew there were vast stores of provisions in the kitchens, and I knew my way around the bakery from when I was younger and would sneak down there looking for pastries. But what excuse would I have now that I was thirteen and no longer a child in search of treats?

The good thing about being the youngest daughter is that no one expects you to act very grown up. Even though by that time I had already started bleeding every month, I could run and play and be as rough and tumble as I was at ten and everyone would simply smile. That's what gave me the inspiration for going down to the kitchens. "Let's play hide-and-seek," I said to Mashka, who, as usual, was reading a book of romances.

"Nastya, you really mustn't be such a child now," she said, although I could tell she wanted to say yes.

"Aren't you bored with having everything the same every day? It's been so tiresome since we came back from Livadia early. My legs need to run."

She cocked her head to one side and closed her book with

an exaggerated sigh. "Well, I suppose if you must. But I'll hide, and you look for me!"

Mashka jumped up in a flash, and I laughed aloud to see her. "Count to one hundred!" she called over her shoulder as she skittered off in the direction of the public apartments. Our favorite place to hide was in the hidden access ways and cubbies where servants could duck away as the imperial suite or noble guests approached. Perfect, I thought. She would be waiting a long time for me to find her.

When I went down to the kitchens, I discovered that it wasn't hard to coax dainty pastries and biscuits from the French pastry chefs. But the things that would be really useful—bread and meat—were shut away in locked pantries. Pastries, I thought, would be better than nothing, and so I took a basket and filled it with confections: marzipan and chocolate, mille-feuille and crème, little gateaux in the shape of flowers and animals.

I had been so caught up in amassing my treats that I nearly forgot to look for Mashka. In the end I found her in a window seat in the small library, where she had pulled out a pile of books and was making her way through them.

"I wouldn't exactly call this hiding!" I said.

She glared at me. "I wouldn't exactly call what you were doing 'seeking.'"

At first I worried that she had seen through my deception. "It's a big house," I said, although the Alexander Palace was actually the smallest place we stayed.

"You used to be able to find me in minutes. What were you doing?"

"I simply forgot all the secret ways. It's been a while."

"We played last year." She snapped her book shut. "It's time for tea."

Mashka marched off like an angry nursemaid. I was a little sorry that I had used her for my own purposes, but I somehow felt I was justified.

It wasn't hard to wake up early the next morning. I was so full of anticipation I barely slept. Which was a good thing, because although the dawn came all too soon at that time of year, the day turned out to be rainy and the sunrise was barely noticeable.

I wore the coat I hadn't wanted and that I was hoping would be given to the orphanage the next year, the one that had been handed down all the way from Olga and was beginning to show signs of wear. Armed with my basket of treats, I crept through the secret passages and turnings that I hadn't, in fact, forgotten, and made my way to the garden to meet Sasha.

He was there, waiting for me. His outline was indistinct in the mist, as if he had moved when his photograph was taken. Even though it was the middle of the summer, the rain and damp made me shiver. "You're not afraid, are you?" whispered Sasha when I reached him.

"No, I'm fine. Just a little cold."

"This way."

He took my arm and steered me firmly toward a towering yew hedge, and for a moment I panicked that perhaps instead of being my friend he actually wished me harm. And I had ensured that there would be no secret police or their spies around to rescue me if that were the case. But soon enough I discovered that the hedge hid a low gate in the iron palings that I had never noticed before. We crept through it and pulled it shut behind us. The gate led to an alleyway behind some small houses. I knew where these were; we passed them often enough on our way to visit the local hospital.

Soon, however, we were beyond the part of the town that I knew, and the houses became poorer and shabbier. Some looked as though they might fall down. Their wooden sides had been propped up with rough poles leaning against them. I thought at first that they must only be sheds for animals—they had no windows, and gaps that surely let the wind whistle through in the bitter winter.

"A family of ten lives in that one," Sasha whispered. He was so close to my ear that he startled me, and I frowned at him.

"Don't exaggerate!" I snapped. He shrugged and gestured for me to follow him again.

I was sure we would soon leave the town altogether, as the houses became more sparse, and here and there a goat or some chickens scratched about in the mud for a bit of food. We climbed a hill, beyond which I thought would be nothing but open fields. Yet when we reached the crest, I gasped.

Spread out from the sides of the hill, sloping away for about a mile and a half was a filthy campground dotted with fires. People in rags slept on the open ground, curled up against the rain that fell steadily. A few had constructed lean-tos out of discarded blankets and old broom handles. I covered my mouth and retched. Even from this distance, the stench was abominable. Clearly there was no place for human waste other than among the people themselves. When I recovered myself enough to talk, I asked Sasha, "How many of them are there?"

"It depends on the time of year. Two or three thousand just now I think. In the winter, more people try to come into town for shelter."

"I cannot believe that my papa and mama have any idea that this"—I swept my arm in an arc—"could possibly exist."

"I don't blame them specifically," Sasha said, "but I blame their ignorance of what's really going on in this country. People are starving in the countryside and being worked to death in the factories."

I looked down at my pathetic little offering of cakes and pastries. "I don't suppose these will do much good." But I was at a complete loss as to what else I could do. Papa would be able to order the engineers to construct a field of stout, dry tents and dig latrines. But I was only the youngest grand duchess, hardly ever spoken to except to be congratulated on making everyone laugh, or for performing a piece well on the piano or the balalaika. My father would never believe I had seen such a thing; perhaps he would attribute it to my active imagination. And he had other more important things to think about, including a possible war. "Tell me. What would fix this?" I asked.

"I don't know. The Bolsheviks say giving people the power to decide things for themselves would be a start."

At that time, I couldn't really imagine what that would be like. Papa decided everything for the whole country. It would be Papa who would soon say that Russia would go to war. It would be Papa who would send thousands of young men away from their families to be killed. At that moment, I was very glad I wasn't Papa. And yet, he also had the power to make things better for thousands, even millions of Russian people. Why would he not do that if he could? And if the people had all the power, would they use it for good or not? I had read enough history to know of many examples where the people took revenge when they tumbled a monarchy—the French, for instance. The Reign of Terror was bloodier by far than all that preceded it, and the French people ended up with another emperor in Napoleon.

I put my basket down on a flat rock, hoping that someone would find it before ants or stray dogs did, but too embarrassed to go any farther and give it to one of those unfortunate souls down below. "Take me back," I said. Sasha pressed his lips together in a hint of a satisfied smirk. I was annoyed at him for being right about me.

# CHAPTER 4

A few days after that, Papa was late coming in for supper. It wasn't like him to be late. Mama, who was beautiful, tall, and graceful with soft eyes and a straight nose, looked more tense and anxious than usual, even though Alexei—her Baby, her Sunshine, our Alyosha—was reasonably well; well enough in fact, to be sitting next to her in his military uniform, looking very self-important.

"Tatiana, go and fetch your father," Mama said. She always asked Tatiana to do things like that. We all knew that Tatiana was her favorite daughter, despite her attempt to pretend she had no favorites.

Tatiana had just risen and taken two brisk steps toward the door when Papa entered. We froze when we saw his face, knowing that something had happened.

"It's war," he said, standing next to his chair. "There's nothing to be done. The Germans have violated Belgium's neutrality, and we must honor our commitments—even if they hadn't already declared war on us."

"Don't worry, Papa," Alexei said, standing and walking to his side. "I can help you with this war." He looked so thin and frail in his uniform, which had been specially made to fit him. But he stood as tall and straight as he could, despite the lingering pain in his ankle. Alyosha could be a little brat when he wasn't sick, but I supposed that was because he knew how important he was.

Tears welled up in Mama's eyes and rolled down her cheeks, and soon Mashka, Olga, and Tatiana were weeping too. Only I did not. Perhaps, because of Sasha, I knew more than the others, I don't know. But far from a surprise, it seemed the logical next thing to me.

From that day forward we barely saw Papa. He was too busy meeting with the generals and the ministers. When I passed by his chambers, hoping to hear details that were lacking in what Anya and the other maids of honor and the servants told us, I heard voices raised in anger and fear.

"Your Majesty, you cannot lead the troops yourself! Leave it to your generals and remain in safety where you can govern." I recognized the voice of Sukhomlinov, the minister of war.

"How can I expect my loyal Russians to risk their lives if I do not share their suffering?"

"But there are concerns here too. If you leave, who will take charge of everything?" That was Count Witte, an old friend and adviser of Papa's.

"The tsaritsa is my companion and shares my power. I trust her completely."

Silence. What did it mean?

"But, Your Majesty. The tsaritsa . . . the people . . ."

"What?" Papa's voice was sharp. "What are you trying to say?"

"You know what the rumors are. You have seen the cartoons." The voice was Count Witte's, soft and placating.

"Nonsense. All of it! No one believes it. No one who has the slightest knowledge of Sunny would believe it for a second." Although his words were strong, I thought Papa's voice held an edge of uncertainty.

"But that is just the point. No one knows her. The people think she is aloof and uncaring." The old general was pleading. "You kept the tsarevich's illness a secret for so long, and the grand duchesses are sheltered away. They could do much if you would only permit it."

"I will not parade my little girls in public until they are of age! Olga and Tatiana do their share. And as for Alexei, he may come with me to the front. He has been quite well for some time thanks to . . . our friend."

I gasped. The idea of Alyosha going anywhere near a battle horrified me, despite his uniform, and I knew my mother would be distraught.

"Please, I beg you, Nicky." That was the voice of my uncle and Papa's only living brother, the Grand Duke Michael.

Silence again. Then Papa sighed aloud. "Very well. I will bow to your wishes for now. I shall let my uncle, Grand Duke Nicholas Nicholaevich, command the armies. But I make no promises for the future."

"You must go to Moscow. It is important, to ask God's blessing for the war."

Moscow! I loved Moscow. It was so different from

Petrograd. The onion domes and colorful buildings, the ancient history from the days before the tsars. If Papa went, then we all would. We always traveled together.

I heard footsteps approach the door, so I quickly ran down the corridor and around a corner. Grand duchesses were not supposed to eavesdrop. But my head was buzzing with everything I had heard. I didn't dare share it with my sisters because they would go straight to Mama. I needed Sasha. But I had not been able to see him since the declaration of war. I wondered if he would be sent to the front.

Sasha at the front, being shot at by Germans. The idea sent a knife into my stomach. At the time I thought it was because he was my only friend outside of the family, and the only person who could make the idea of war real to me. I didn't realize it was the beginning of something else, that there might be more to my caring about him than friendship.

Besides, when it came to things such as this, things that were far outside our life in the palace, I suspected that Sasha was the only one I could count on to be honest with me. I wanted to know what people were saying about my mother. What cartoons had been drawn? What did they have to do with her? And who had allowed them to be published?

I ran down to the kitchens and left a note for the egg girl, Varenka. I hoped Sasha would get it.

❦

Varenka managed to find Sasha, although he had moved from the guards' barracks. His note began: "We cannot meet in the gardens. You'll have to find a way to get to camp."

Leaving my family for more than an hour—it sounded impossible. But something told me it was important to try. Maybe I took it as a challenge, a dare. Or maybe it was a chance to become closer to Sasha, who was still a mystery to me. He had come into my world, but I knew nothing about his. So I made a big decision, and took my first step alone out of the closed circle that had kept me safe and secure for my entire life.

## ❧ CHAPTER 5 ❧

So it was on a hot, sultry morning at the beginning of August, 1914, that I found myself wearing Varenka's rough scarf and brightly colored skirt, carrying her empty egg basket through the streets of Tsarskoe. I was certain someone would recognize me. Varenka and I looked nothing alike. But I was surprised to find that the passersby hardly noticed me. Although I felt very much like a normal person, I assumed after my conversations with Sasha that I would stick out like a mountain peak wherever I went. Of course, my parents had been very careful to keep us out of the public eye. The only photographs taken of us were for family albums, except the occasional official portrait. And for those, we were so dressed up and posed that none of us looked like ourselves.

Of course, in those days when status and rank mattered so much, no one looked very far beyond clothes. Dressed as I was in Varenka's simple skirt and blouse, a mere glance was all it took to label me insignificant. And since my basket was empty, I didn't have to worry that anyone would approach me to buy eggs.

I did attract a few whistles as I walked by the military barracks, however. I was well aware that, clothes or not, women and girls could be the object of unwanted attention. The whistling told me right away that these were not the elite guards to which Sasha had been attached in peacetime. His note had said: "I'm with Thirteen Corps now. You won't believe what's happening. I can't get away. If you want to see me you must come to me."

I realized from his tone that more than his location had changed, but I was unprepared for what I found. It was almost like the makeshift campground for the poor, only here were all men, mostly peasants, some younger than Sasha, some who looked too old to fight. The only things that made them look like soldiers were their coats and boots, and the fact that they all cradled rifles in their arms or leaned on them like pitchforks. It was still early. Most of them were scooping porridge into their mouths, and a man with a wooden leg passed among them, distributing rations consisting mainly of hardtack.

"Excuse me, I'm looking for Junior Officer Alexander Mikhailovich Galliapin," I said to the man with the rations.

"Over there." He jerked his head in the direction of a tent. Its flap was closed, but I walked over until I could hear what was going on inside.

"You've had your training. All you have to do is receive orders and follow them." It was the voice of an older man, and it sounded stern, reproachful.

"But I never intended to be an officer!" It was Sasha. His

voice was tearful and if I did not know him I would have thought he was little more than a boy.

"There are not enough trained officers to manage our army. Everyone with experience is being called upon to head a platoon. Count yourself fortunate to have only one. The officers with real training get several."

Sasha was to command a platoon? He had been a mere private soldier, the lowest of the low, in the Semyonovsky. I glanced back at the motley crowd behind me. They looked as if they had been called up in the midst of plowing their fields or building something. What kind of army were we sending into battle?

The tent flap flew open then and startled me out of my thoughts. A man wearing the uniform of a sergeant swept out. He looked right through me, and I might have thought he hadn't seen me except that he swerved neatly to avoid crashing into me.

"Sasha!" I whispered hoarsely as soon as the sergeant had vanished behind a supply wagon.

"You might as well come in. I'm not ready to come out just yet."

I didn't like the bitterness I heard. Still less appealing was the sight I beheld when I stepped beneath the flap of the tent. Items of clothing were littered around. A kit bag had fallen open and its contents—including a safety razor—tipped out onto the dirt. Sasha himself sat upon a camp bed. He looked like a soldier from the waist down with his smart trousers and polished boots, but like a frightened animal from the waist up. He wore only his undershirt, exposing his thin, pale arms, and his long neck looked vulnerable without the stiff, military collar he normally wore. Above that, contrasting with the boyishness, his unshaven cheeks were dark with a few days' growth.

"Sasha!" I cried. "What does this mean?"

"They have promoted me," he answered, sounding more as if he had been telling me that he had been sentenced to prison.

"Isn't that what you wanted? To be a real soldier, not just polishing boots and cleaning guns?"

He stood, putting on his uniform jacket and buckling his belt as if I were nothing more than a fellow soldier or a valet, accustomed to seeing him in a state of undress. "But that's just the point. I'm not a real soldier. I haven't had the proper training. They've shown me how to read the telegraph tape, the forms I should expect for getting orders, and who reports to whom—me to the company commander, the company commander to the battalion chief, the battalion chief to the regiment colonel, the regiment colonel to the army general. And the higher up you get, the farther from the ground—and the fighting. Yet they are the ones who have experience."

I didn't quite know what to say. "Did you think I wouldn't come?" I asked, gesturing toward the untidy mess.

For the first time, Sasha looked directly at me. His eyes were full of sadness and bewilderment. "I suppose I didn't. It was all well and good when we could meet in your garden. How did you get away?"

"As you can see, Varenka helped me." I gave him a little curtsy and swung my egg basket. He smiled, looking for an instant like the impish Sasha I had come to know. "But I have to be back before Mashka wakes, or I'll get in trouble."

Sasha finished putting on his uniform and adjusted his cap smartly on his head. "Do I look like I command a platoon?" he asked.

"I don't know. How many soldiers are in a platoon?"

"Only fifty. And have you seen them?" He jerked his head toward the tent flap.

"Those are your soldiers?" I began to see why Sasha was so upset. "Most of them look too young or too old, and I'd say the majority I passed had just yesterday been in the fields."

"I knew I could count on you to be astute." His words were like acid on metal.

"I don't deserve your anger. I had nothing to do with this!"

"No, but your imperial father had everything to do with it. How are we to fight the Germans? They have all modern equipment, big guns, and aircraft, and a standing army that's trained. Our 'army,' such as it is, consists of officer dandies and peasants, thanks to our ancient law that calls up the poor and serfs—so many thousand for each landowner, like heads of cattle. Most of the fellows out there have never worn a pair of stout boots before, and God knows if they can fire a gun with any accuracy. To make matters worse, I have only the vaguest idea what the plan is. All I know is that we're heading west. We don't go by train except at the very beginning. We march. All the way to Prussia, apparently.

"Do you know, I have heard that we don't even use code to communicate because no one can remember what it is. It's laughable!"

Was this true? What of the spirit of the Russian people, who were invincible—even by the great Napoleon? "Surely the generals . . . I mean, it all must be part of a plan. You just don't see the entire thing, so it seems absurd." Yet even as I said it, I felt it was untrue.

"Do you know anything?" Sasha asked.

I opened my mouth to speak, actually considering lying to Sasha just to make him feel better. But the words would not come out. Finally, I squeaked out a pathetic little "No."

Sasha sighed, then drew his shoulders back and put his chin up. "I suppose I should try to be happy that I have been promoted so unexpectedly. And I would be if I did not suspect that platoons like mine will be used as cannon fodder. Isn't that what a soldier does? Fight, and probably die?"

"You don't seem to be fighting very much!" I said, becoming irritated with his self-pity. "I would go to the front and lead a whole battalion, or even a corps, if I had to!"

"Have you ever seen a man killed by gunfire?"

"No. But it's a war. People get killed."

Something closed in Sasha's face when I said that. I wished I could have swallowed back the words. "You had better be going before you get in trouble," he said. I blushed to have my own cowardice thrown back in my face. And Sasha looked so vulnerable there, his uniform a little too big for him. What a photograph that would make. Yet if I had my camera with me, would I take it? I did not want to be reminded of Sasha in that weak state. How could he take charge of even ten men? I wondered. I wanted to run up to him and fling my arms around his neck, tell him that he should come with me, that my papa would make things all right and he wouldn't have to go to war. But even as I took a step toward him, he flinched.

"Take care, Alexander Mikhailovich," I said, feeling the tears close my throat. I turned around, not wanting to prolong our good-bye. Not wanting to ask him to write to me, especially since any letters he sent would be read by several pairs of eyes before they ever reached me.

"Wait!" he said. I stopped just before opening the tent flap. "Would you keep this safe for me?" He darted to the corner of the tent and picked up something wrapped in cloth. I could see by its shape that it was his balalaika. He held it out toward me.

"Won't you want it? To play to people and soothe them?"

"The less I have to carry the better. And besides, if something happens to me, I want you . . ." He didn't finish. I reached my hand out and grasped the instrument firmly by the neck. He moved his grip so that his hand covered mine, and it sent a charge through me. Our eyes met briefly, and I could tell that he felt it too.

I was too confused to continue looking at him, so I forced a smile and lowered my eyes. "Of course, Sasha." I pulled the instrument toward me. He let go of it and my hand. I still felt the warmth of his skin.

"Good," he said. "Good." Then he gave me a half-hearted salute. I left, looking even more like a peasant than when I arrived, with my wrapped-up balalaika slung over my shoulder.

I got back to the palace gardens just as the sun was rising. Varenka anxiously paced back and forth by the kitchen entrance. "I'd have never forgiven myself if something had happened to you, Princess!" she said.

We went inside and exchanged clothes hurriedly. I realized how selfish I had been in getting her to help me with my little excursion. She would have been severely punished—and not just by her mother with her switch and harsh tongue—if there had been some mishap.

Mashka was already taking her cold shower when I got to our room. I quickly hid the balalaika behind my dresses in the wardrobe, then sat at the dressing table and brushed my hair, trying to decide how to explain my early morning absence to my sister.

She came out wrapped in a large white towel. "Where have you been?"

"Up," I said, deciding the less I told her the better. "I couldn't sleep."

To my surprise, rather than quizzing me further, she said, "Neither could I. I lay awake for the longest time last night. I think of all the officers we know, the ones Olga and Tatiana have danced with and had tea with. And . . . you know who. Some will die."

I nodded. Mashka had had a flirtation with a soldier, but it was not serious. She had stitched him a shirt, though, to wear on dress parade. Somehow her romance was tamer than my friendship. I supposed that was because mine was secret.

"I've been thinking," she continued. "It may be impossible to make enough shirts to be useful, but we can help the soldiers by knitting socks and making bandages for the wounded."

"Yes, it would be good to actually do something, even so small." I couldn't help thinking that no amount of socks would improve the training of our army. And as for the wounded—I couldn't bear to think about them, not yet.

We had breakfast together in our dining room. It was the four of us with Zhilik and Trina. Mama and Alexei had breakfast in her room, and Papa never joined us anymore, spending all morning with his military maps and his generals. I had to find a way to talk to him at some point, to let him know that his great army might not be as strong as he thought. Yet even then I knew I would never dare speak to him about it. He would ask too many questions about how I knew. I, the youngest girl, the one no one took very seriously because I was always clowning around.

In any case, the opportunity never arose. Matters were already too far gone for anything he might have done to have made a difference. And as for me—how could I have thought any action of mine would have mattered?

# ❧ — CHAPTER 6 — ❧

We departed for the trip to Moscow a week later to ask God's blessing on the war and protection for our soldiers. Our train arrived on August 17, at a crowded and jubilant Moscow station. We made our way slowly in a file of carriages through the streets toward the Kremlin. All the bells of all the four hundred and fifty churches pealed out, but they were not loud enough to drown out the raucous cheers of the people who swarmed the streets, hung out of windows, and surged onto balconies—some even perched on low rooftops. I had never heard so many voices singing "God Save the Tsar," our national anthem. Mama's cheeks were pink with happiness. Olga and Tatiana tried hard to look very dignified. Alexei stood straight and tall, despite the fact that his ankle was hurting him, and Mashka and I grinned like fools. For a brief moment, it seemed that all the bad things I'd heard or that had been hinted at had evaporated with the morning mist.

At the Iberian Gate, Papa got out of the carriage and went into the chapel, as is the custom—or was at any rate—to kiss the icon of the Virgin of Iberia. When he returned, we proceeded through the gate into the Red Square. I remember the look on his face as if it had all happened just yesterday. It's a look I have seen many times since, but have never managed to capture in a photograph. He did not look proud or triumphant. He seemed overcome with sorrow and yet at the same time content, listening to the voices of his people glorifying his name. I wonder if he had some premonition of what was to come. Perhaps he was thinking of Alyosha, who weakened visibly throughout the day, and who awoke the next morning in such pain that he could not walk.

The next morning I went to see Alexei in his room. "Are you really unwell, Alyosha?" I asked. All our teasing and tormenting ceased when he had one of his attacks.

"It's my ankle. It hurts so terribly. I'm not as bad as I've been, but look." He lifted the covers and I saw his ankle, swollen and bruised, misshapen. I wanted to touch it and kiss it and try to make it better, but even the lightest touch was agony to him. "I don't want to miss the blessing. It's terribly important," he said.

When Alyosha was ill, his eyes looked much older than his years, as if all the pain he had suffered in his young life had lodged there. He was only eleven, yet he had had a lifetime of agony. "As long as you're not moaning or can't sit up, one of Papa's Cossacks can carry you. You won't miss it," I assured him, stroking a stray hair out of his eyes.

Mama came in, already dressed in her caftan with the heavy embroidery in gold thread and wearing her imperial crown. If it wasn't for the anxious expression in her eyes, she would have looked like an icon herself. "Baby, are you too ill to come?"

"No, Mama. I must go. Only I cannot walk."

"Perhaps you should stay here and rest."

"No, Mama, I am going. I am the tsarevich. I must be there."

I had shrunk away from Alyosha's bed while my mother was with him. When he was ill, she seemed not even to see me. This occasion was no different, until Papa came in.

"How's your little brother?" Papa asked me quietly.

"He's in pain, but he will come. He can't walk, though."

Papa nodded, then walked forward and took Mama's hand. "I'll send Nagorny in to help you dress in your uniform. You'll be carried in to the service."

"I'm sorry, Papa," Alyosha said, looking down.

"It can't be helped." Papa put his hand on Alyosha's head, then bent down and kissed him, his ornamental sword clanking against the iron bedframe. I could tell by his expression that he was unhappy about Alyosha's attack, not just because he was in pain, but because having to be carried into the very public blessing would show weakness. At times like these, I felt sorry for my brother rather than envying him all the attention and special treatment he got. What was it all worth if he couldn't even enjoy the smallest things in life, and if at any time he could be stricken and have to spend weeks in bed?

On our last day in Moscow we took a trip out to a famous, ancient monastery outside the city, fortified and containing thirteen churches within its walls.

"Mama says if there is time we'll visit the hermitage at Geth-semane," Tatiana said. She always seemed to have information from Mama that the rest of us didn't.

"Why is that so wonderful?" I asked, thinking that we'd have enough of visiting old churches and seeing long-bearded patriarchs by visiting the monastery and we'd have little need of any other religious touring.

"Don't you know? They have real hermits there who are virtually buried alive," Mashka said. "They live in holes in the ground and just get their food handed to them through a slit that's not even big enough for an arm to pass through.

"And when one of them dies—which they only know by the smell, because they don't always take the food that's given to them—they simply seal over the slit and leave them there."

I shivered. Who would choose such an existence? Aside from the question of bathing, I couldn't imagine ever wanting to be away from the sunlight and air. I had a terrible fear of being imprisoned. Even the low ceilings of the basement rooms in the Alexander Palace made me start to panic if I remained down there too long. Perhaps I was spoiled by having twenty-foot-high ceilings in most of the places we lived.

I wondered if Mashka knew that what she was telling me would give me nightmares. Perhaps she did, and told me on purpose. I think I brought such things on myself with my mischievous behavior, but I never did anything that would really upset one of my sisters—except for that snowball, of course, the one with the stone in it. But as I remember, Tatiana was being rather high and mighty at the time, and I never did anything as dangerous again. Oh, well, I used to throw things at my tutors and sabotage their satchels with live toads and such. But that didn't really hurt anyone.

Fortunately, there wasn't time for the visit to the hermits.

We were in Moscow for less than a week, and then we returned to Tsarskoe Selo. I was glad to get back to our familiar rooms. Of all the palaces we lived in, the Alexander Palace in Tsarskoe felt the most like home. Of course, Mama always made certain to have her photographs and mementos around her wherever she went, but Mashka and I—as if by mutual agreement, although we never actually discussed it—kept few belongings other than a favorite doll and some books. We made do with whatever existed in the different palaces rather than bring our possessions from place to place. I expect that would have surprised many people, who no doubt imagined us traveling around with trunks and trunks of toys and books. We did have some jewels, but they were in the charge of Mme Zanotti and worn only on state occasions, and hardly seemed to belong to us. And I must say that the playrooms in our wing of most of the palaces were stocked with just about anything we could want to amuse ourselves with—including an artificial hill for tobogganing in the Winter Palace that was even bigger than the slide in the Mountain Hall of the Alexander Palace. We often rode our bicycles around the rooms in the Alexander Palace, and it was the smallest of all our homes.

Because everything we packed for our trips was taken care of by the servants, and the household staff looked after our clothing and other belongings, it was extremely difficult to keep Sasha's balalaika hidden. I decided it would be safer to confess something about it to Mashka. I couldn't say that I purchased it myself, because we never had any money at all, and I wouldn't have known how to go about it or how much to give. It had to be a gift from someone, and I settled on it having come from one of the servants whom I had heard playing it in Peterhof. People did that sort of thing for us children sometimes, although less now that we were getting older. I still remembered the old man who had come from Siberia with his tame sable. We wanted to keep it, but it was only tame for him, and when he left it behind it ran around and knocked things on the floor. I thought it was terribly funny, but we gave the creature back to the old man.

"Why would you want such a thing as a plain old balalaika when we have pianos to play here? I simply do not understand," Mashka said after I told her and showed her the humble instrument.

"Just because it is a peasant instrument doesn't mean it isn't beautiful!"

"Yes, I know, and you play it very well. But that is such a plain one. Not like Alexei's."

"What matters is the sound, not the look." Sometimes Mashka exasperated me. She was not a snob, but every once in a while she spoke without thinking. I doubted she really had any idea of what was going on around us. "The point is, I wanted my own to play, but I want it to be a surprise to Papa and Mama. Alexei and I shall learn to play a duet. It will be something I can tease him with so he will get better when he is ill. So you mustn't tell anyone." It was the best I could think of at the moment.

"You're a strange creature," Mashka said. "But you know I won't say a word. If they find out, though, I won't lie."

That was all I needed. I wasn't sure why I felt the balalaika had to be a secret, except that if it was known I would then have to explain everything, and I didn't want to face the teasing—even if it was good-natured—from my sisters. I realized with some shame that they might think it a wonderful opportunity to get back at me for the tricks I had played on them and the cruel things I had said about their crushes and admirers. They wouldn't understand—or wouldn't believe—that Sasha was simply my friend. My sisters and I didn't really have friends except for each other, not counting the younger maids of honor, and they had court appointments that paid them to be nice to us. I wanted Sasha to be my friend alone, to like me for myself, not because he was a member of the court and it was his job.

Thoughts of the balalaika were driven out of my mind, however, by the bad news of the war. Papa came into Mama's room, where we were all knitting and reading quietly one late August evening. His face had gone beyond pale to gray.

"Samsonov was routed at Soldau. They say we won't know the extent of the casualties for some time."

Samsonov was one of the generals. I didn't know which armies he commanded, but my heart pounded against the walls of my chest. Moments passed in utter stillness, no one daring to breathe or break the silence. At last, Tatiana, the practical one, spoke. "What does this mean? Why did it happen?"

Papa dropped into a chair and passed his hand across his eyes as if he wanted to erase a vision of something horrible.

"He advanced too far too fast. But it was not his fault. We don't have the means of supply. We are not sufficiently mobilized."

I had been sitting with my mouth open, and when I tried to ask my question, I found that my tongue and throat were so dry I could hardly squeak out a word. Eventually I said, "Which army did he command?" wondering how much I could ask without giving away that I had any personal interest in the answers.

"The Second," Papa replied.

Sasha's platoon formed part of the Second army and he was in the Thirteen Corps.

"They say casualties were particularly heavy in the Two and Thirteen Corps."

For a moment I saw white spots before my eyes and the room began to darken. Since I had never fainted before, I didn't know that's what was happening. Tatiana jumped up and came to me, pushing my head down between my knees. Gradually my normal vision returned. "Are you all right, Anastasie, dear?" I heard Mama's voice at first from far away, but when I felt her cool hand on the back of my neck, I took a deep breath and sat up.

"Yes, I am fine. I don't know what came over me."

"It's a shock. To all of us." Papa stood and paced around the room. He was disturbed, I could see that. But in a way that had more to do with Germans being on his territory than about the thousands of men who had died. I think it was then that I realized how right Sasha was. Papa loved Russia, but he was separated from it by a cushion of something—his ministers and advisers perhaps. Russia was too big to fit into his mind, too big to fit into anyone's mind, like a very, very large number, or the distance of the nearest star besides the sun from the earth.

Mama, with her long experience of tending to Alexei night and day, immediately made the leap to what I imagined in my worst nightmares. "They will need nurses to tend to the wounded. Tomorrow we shall begin our training, Olga and Tatiana and I."

"What about us?" I asked. "What will Mashka and I do?" I pictured us sitting at home knitting socks night and day while everyone else was being really useful.

"You will visit the wounded and read to them."

And that was all the discussion we had about it.

## ☙ CHAPTER 7 ❧

Our first casualties started streaming into the hospitals in late August, changing our daily pattern of life as it had never before been changed. Every day I dreaded that I would come upon Sasha in one of the beds next to which I sat and read, hour by hour. Not that I did not wish him out of the battle and back near me. It was more complicated than that. I was afraid of how he might have been wounded. Afraid to see him maimed, changed forever.

"I want Tatiana to read to me," a young soldier on the point of death said as I opened a volume of Pushkin. I had heard that many times by then. The ones who were going to die especially wanted my sister Tatiana's beautiful face to be the last thing they saw on this earth. I usually answered, "Tatiana's assisting in an operation and cannot come. She will visit tomorrow." Then the soldier would turn his head away and close his eyes. I don't know whether they listened or just shut themselves off. The ones who moaned softly with pain that no one could relieve were the most difficult. I sometimes lost my place in the book, and then others around me who had been paying attention would protest, and I would have to go back and find where I had gone wrong.

It's not that I was ugly. Nor am I now. In fact, I have been told the opposite. It's just that Tatiana grew into such a beauty that she quite eclipsed the rest of us. Tall and willowy, with almond-shaped, gray green eyes and a perfect nose, a mouth with lips not too full but, as I once overheard one of the soldiers say, begging to be kissed. I am shorter and a little on the plump side compared to my sisters, and my hair persists in kinking into unruly curls. I'm just one of the grand duchesses, not usually singled out for any kind of comment. Even Mama, who makes an outward show of treating us all the same, scolds me for not being as graceful as Olga and Tatiana, or as sweet tempered as Mashka.

Mashka and I didn't have to nurse, only read and comfort the men, as Mama said. That was bad enough. Some of the men hardly looked wounded, the ones in the convalescent ward who had been mended quickly and were destined to return to the front. But we also saw men whose faces had been half blown away by shells. Many were missing limbs or had holes in their stomachs too big to simply sew up, waiting for surgeons with enough skill to patch them together. The first few days I was there, it was all I could do not to run off and vomit. The smell, if nothing else, would have overpowered me. Burned skin has a particularly horrid scent. And then there's the festering gangrene, more and more common as the hospitals—even the one in the Catherine Palace—ran out of supplies to keep wounds sanitary and as it took longer and longer for the wounded to be transported back from the front.

Yet how can I speak of the horrors I saw when I recall that my mother and Tatiana actually stood by while the wounds were dressed? Even Alexei once held a basin so that the pus from a wound could drain into it. Mama assisted in the operating theater as well, carrying amputated limbs and administering drops of anesthetic. When I remember her calm compassion, her ability to face the grimmest circumstances without flinching, I cannot imagine why people believe her capable of betraying Russia.

We nursed and read, and the war continued. As news came in, Papa was incensed at what was happening. "Those damned generals are more interested in their careers than in cooperating with each other!" he roared one night when we had all returned from our day in the hospital, exhausted and disheartened.

"What is wrong, Papa?" Olga asked, the only one who was likely to get an answer.

"Our telegraph lines do not go far enough to reach the First Army, which has pushed well into Prussia. And the generals fight over corps and contradict each other's orders like children fighting over lead soldiers. If they would only keep to the plan. And I expected so much more from Nicholasha." He was speaking of our uncle, Nicholas Nicholaevich. In all, with brothers and cousins and uncles, there were nineteen grand dukes in our family. Even I got them confused sometimes.

In those early days of the war, Papa would spend all day in his study with his advisers. Every day when we returned home for luncheon I could hear them talking and arguing. Once I saw inside briefly when a colonel threw open the door and stormed out. Papa's office was full of trestle tables covered with huge maps. I could see flags stuck into them at different places, and my father leaned over them and studied them intently, as if they might solve a great riddle if he looked long enough. But at the end of each day he locked his study and pocketed the key. None of us—not even Mama—were allowed in to see what he was doing.

The war had an odd effect on everyone in Russia. At the beginning, wherever we went we heard blessings called out, just as in Moscow only with not quite as many people. "The Tsar and Russia! Victory over the German foe!" echoed after us as our carriage or motorcar passed. I didn't recall hearing such jubilant, enthusiastic greetings since the time I was a very young child.

But as the war went on and people grew tired of the death and hardship, the reaction cooled. I assumed that what affected everyone else were the same feelings we were having: anxiety about the war and sadness at the terrible waste of life. I had no idea then that there could be any other cause for the unenthusiastic greetings we got when we went anywhere.

But still, despite the horrors I saw every day in the hospital, the war seemed far away and a little unreal to me. All these wounded soldiers were strangers. They did not exist in my life except as wounded or dying or recovering, and that was really everything I knew about them. I became quite good at telling who would live and who would not. It's something in the eyes, a distance from the here and now. One poor fellow breathed his last right in the middle of a conversation with me, as if he had only just paused to think of the right word to say. I sat by his lifeless body for a long time, hoping I was mistaken, until a nurse came and pulled me away.

I thought of Sasha in every spare hour I had. I had heard nothing from him—I didn't expect to. We didn't say anything about writing at our last meeting in the camp. His face haunted me, and I desperately wanted to see him smile again. Every day I wondered where he was, whether he was cold or had enough to eat. I had no way of asking without admitting to knowing him. There were some platoons kept in reserve, I heard. How I prayed that his was one of them!

I kept picturing him walking into the garden, wearing his smart Semyonovsky uniform and his impish smile, waiting to tease me and tell me how they had all gotten lost and missed the action, and now were sent back to Petrograd to form part of the palace guard again. Sometimes I managed to convince myself that my pleasant daydreams were true.

That is, until I discovered with horror that they were not.

On my way into the convalescent ward in the hospital in the Catherine Palace on a beautiful September morning, I passed the orderlies carrying newly arrived wounded soldiers on stretchers, as I did every day. This seemed like a particularly badly wounded lot. Their bandages were dirty and ragged, and so many of the wounds were gangrenous that even though I had accustomed myself somewhat to the smell, I nearly fainted from it.

I had an unconscious habit of scrutinizing each face I could see, thinking *thank God* each time I realized they were all strangers, not Sasha. But that day, one of the faces caught my attention in an odd way. The left side of it was completely covered with bandages. A dark brown spot of congealed blood made it look as though a child had painted a crude eye on the white linen. The other eye was exposed, but closed. Something in the shape of the nose and the color of the skin, a trace of light freckles and delicately flared nostrils, struck a chord in me. Just as the orderlies were about to wheel the gurney down the corridor that led to the operating theater, the unbandaged eye opened, and I knew in an instant it was Sasha.

My first instinct was to simply run after the gurney, but what if I was mistaken? What if I so longed to see Sasha that even a faint resemblance brought him to mind? Yet I knew I had to find out for certain. "Sister," I said to the nurse who was leading me away toward the ward where I was expected to go and read, "There is something I must do right away!"

She turned her weary eyes upon me as if to say, *I have no time for capricious grand duchesses.* "Yes, Anastasia Nicholaevna?"

"Please excuse me—my mother—" I couldn't formulate any other excuse to get away in the direction of the operating theater. I had lost all capacity to think of words, conscious only of the feeling of my heart dropping into my stomach.

She frowned, but I knew she would not deny me. I hurried

without running—I had been told that in the hospital only a hemorrhage was cause for running. Nonetheless, I walked fast enough to catch up with the orderlies just as they were pushing the gurney through the swinging doors—the swinging doors beyond which I was not allowed. The two men handed their cargo off to the nurses on the other side just before I reached them. I wanted to defy regulations and go in, but I had been told that to do so could endanger the lives of those undergoing surgery. The next best thing, I decided, would be to find out from the orderlies what they knew about the wounded soldier they'd just dropped off.

These orderlies were men I had become quite accustomed to seeing. They made an odd pair. One was small with a sharp chin and round eyes, a nose that was a little too long for his face, giving him the appearance of an oversized rodent. The other was as exaggeratedly large as the other was small, with a stomach that protruded so much that he had to lean forward slightly to push the gurneys and carry stretchers. I never heard them talk to each other. Once the wounded started streaming in almost everyone was too busy to utter a word that wasn't necessary. They had already started walking purposefully back to the admitting ward to take another soldier to treatment and I had to call to them three times to get them to stop.

"Excuse me!" I said, finally raising my voice. They turned and looked at me with the same expressions of astonished impatience on their faces, despite how completely different they looked. "That boy—soldier—you just brought in. What happened to him?" I asked, breathless.

They turned their heads toward each other at the same

moment and then looked back at me. The ratlike one spoke, surprising me with his rich, deep voice. "We don't know. They come in so fast, and we take them where we are told." He touched the hank of hair on his forehead as if doffing his hat to me, then the two of them turned to walk away again.

"Please!" I called out. "Who would know?"

"You might try downstairs at admitting." He gave me this information without turning around.

Of course that would be the right place. But would they know his name? Or whom, among the many hundreds that day alone, I was talking about?

I made my way against the tide of incoming wounded, some walking and weary, clutching arms or sides covered with dirty bandages, others, like the one I feared was Sasha, carried by on stretchers or rolled on gurneys and already looking past help. Still I pushed determinedly toward the doors where the overworked admitting nurses kept lists and checked off names.

I should have been ashamed for putting my needs above the others then, but I could think of nothing but my desperate desire to know: was it Sasha, and what had happened to him?

"Please, Sister," I said, trying to be as polite as I could, "I would like some information about one of the wounded soldiers."

Without looking around, she snapped, "Who sent you? Don't you see we barely have time to get them in?"

"It's important. He might be—"

"A sweetheart? A husband? A brother? They all are!"

At that she turned toward me, her hand raised as though

she would cuff me on the ear for my impertinence. I stood as tall as I could and stared her down. I admit, a little part of me enjoyed the look of horror that washed over her face when she saw me.

"Forgive . . . Your Imperial Highness . . ." While she was fumbling for words and turning bright pink, another nurse came over.

"She's no different from any of us. It's an accident of birth. She'll have to wait her turn." The second nurse was short and coarse, her hair bobbed beneath her cap. She looked young, but her eyes were old.

"You're right, of course, but I desperately need to know something."

The second nurse pushed the first back to work and planted herself in front of me. "Know what?"

"About a soldier they just carried upstairs. I think I know him. I want to know what happened to him."

"Hah! I doubt you can be acquainted with any of this lot! From the lower ranks mostly. No one who's likely to have penetrated into your sheltered world."

Now she was making me angry. "Is this part of what you call my sheltered world?" I gestured around the stinking, filthy mass of incoming wounded. "I come here every day to help. I'd nurse, but I'm too young, so I read to them."

"Yes, I know what you do."

She stood quite still for a moment, not taking her eyes off me.

"What is this soldier's name?" Without saying she would

help me, she turned toward the great ledger book where they wrote what names they could, based on information from the wounded themselves or those who came with them.

"His name is Sash—Alexander Mikhailovich Galliapin, in the Second Army, Thirteen Corps."

The nurse looked up and stifled a gasp when I said "Thirteen Corps." I thought I saw her hesitate when she turned back and traced the lines of names that had been written down just that morning. There were already five or six pages closely filled, and it was not yet ten. The nurses had pads of paper they jotted names and other information on as quickly as they could, to be transcribed neatly by a wizened little man sitting at a desk. "We have had may from Thirteen Corps this morning. But I see no one by that name."

"He—he probably couldn't speak. How do you write down the ones whose names you can't find out?" I touched her arm so that she could not dismiss me yet, although she flicked her eyes in the direction of the others and was clearly anxious to get back to her real work. But this would be my only opportunity to find out, and I had to grasp it.

"Here. Here is what we write. You can look at it, but I must return to my work."

She thrust the ledger into my hands. I opened it again, half dreading, half hoping. I saw that at the end of the long list of names were some ten or more that simply said "Unable to identify" and then listed a quick description of their wounds, followed by a triage determination: critical, surgery, or hopeless. I scanned down until I found one description of head wounds. Someone had initially written "hopeless," but that was crossed off and "surgery" was written above it.

I still knew little more than I did before. My pulse raced. I knew I should just wait until the soldier I believed was Sasha came out of surgery. But what if he died in there? Head wounds were very tricky, I had heard my mother say.

I forced myself to calm down and return to the convalescent ward where I was meant to be reading to the men. The sister gave me a frosty look as I entered. I went and sat by a young fellow who didn't seem to mind that it was I and not my sister Tatiana reading to him, and started on the tales of Gogol. I soon lost myself in them, and amused the men by using funny voices for the characters, making more than one of them smile, and redeeming myself somewhat for my tardy appearance that morning.

Late in the day, I decided I had to make one last attempt to see the young soldier who had gone into the operating theater with a head wound. I knew where the post-surgery ward was, although I wasn't supposed to enter it. I decided that I could use the excuse that I was looking for my mother, hoping all the time that she wouldn't be there. She did not know of Sasha's existence, or of my friendship with him, and I had no desire to explain it to her now.

The lights were lower in that ward, as if the cots contained not men who had just had limbs amputated or bullets and shrapnel pulled out of their bodies and vital organs, but babies newly born who needed sleep. I was lucky in finding it deserted for the moment, perhaps because the nurses were changing shifts. I scanned the cots, quickly eliminating all but one of them as possibly containing Sasha. That one held someone whose head was almost completely bandaged, with holes for his nose, mouth, and one eye. I was certain it was the soldier I had seen earlier, and crept through the ward until I was at his bedside. Even less of him was visible than when he originally came in. I thought at first I must have been mistaken, and sighed.

"Oh, Sasha," I whispered. "Where are you?"

So quietly that at first I thought it was nothing more than a breath, the soldier's lips moved. I put my ear to those lips, deciding that even if it wasn't Sasha, perhaps he would say his name and I might be able to tell the nurses so that they could inform his family where he was.

"Na . . . stya," he said.

"Sasha!" I nearly cried out, but stopped myself, and his name came out in a coarse whisper. "Sasha, I'm here," I continued. I didn't know whether to be overjoyed or devastated. What if he died? Many did after their surgery. "I'll come see you every day. Does it hurt very much? When you can, you must tell me what happened."

"What are you doing here?" The loud voice of the nurse made me jump backward.

"I—I can identify this soldier, Sister," I said.

"You are contaminating this ward. Leave at once!"

"Yes, of course," I said. I was so elated to have found Sasha that her rude dismissal didn't bother me in the slightest. I'd make sure they gave me access tomorrow so that I could come and visit, and I'd use what little influence I had to ensure that Sasha had the very best care.

Sasha was alive. Wounded—I didn't know how badly—but alive. My heart swelled with gratitude. When we knelt for our evening prayers, I actually meant all that I said for the first time in several years.

# CHAPTER 8

Sasha's convalescence took a long time. At first, he could only squeak out a few words. I learned that the doctors hadn't expected him to live at all—a piece of a shell had lodged in his left eye, and they feared that it might have caused irreparable brain damage. But luckily for Sasha—if you could call it luck—the jagged piece of metal that struck his face missed every important artery and nerve, except for his optic nerve. He is blind in that eye, and has worn a patch over it ever since he left the hospital.

Immediately after the surgery, he was grateful to see me.

"You remember me?" he asked.

"How could I not? You do realize you're the only friend I have."

He managed to look puzzled without being able to move the muscles in his face very much. "But everyone must want to be your friend."

"Oh," I said, "many of the daughters of the nobility want

to know us, but Mama won't allow us to become friendly with them. She says they have been brought up in decadence, without any responsibilities, and that they are not religious enough for us."

He made a sort of snort that I realized was a laugh. "I'm sure they have enough religion when called upon."

Already, even before they took the bandages off, I noticed that something had changed about Sasha. He had an edge that wasn't there before. I wanted to ask him about it, but I didn't know how, and I didn't want to upset him.

I had to continue reading to all the wounded soldiers, but I always made time in my day for Sasha. It was the only instance where I ever used my rank to achieve something. I wasn't really supposed to go anywhere except the convalescent wards, but I demanded they allow me in wherever Sasha was, even if he had just come out of another surgery. In all, he had three. None of them managed to repair his eye.

I wasn't certain how conscious Sasha was of the extent of his wound, until the day I came in and all but one bandage over his eye had been removed. He had several gashes on his face that had been stitched up, but only one appeared deep enough to leave a scar.

"You look quite well, considering everything," I said with a smile, attempting to adopt the teasing tone we once had with each other. But his face remained immobile. He looked at me with an expression I could not read. He was harder than I had ever seen him, and yet underneath, more vulnerable. Frightened, I thought.

"You may wish to laugh at me, but I assure you, I am not in the least amused to know that I have lost the use of my eye forever."

I didn't know what to say. I reached for his hand. He clenched it into a fist and pulled it away. I leafed through the book I had brought, pretending to be looking for the place we had left off the day before, but really I was trying to compose myself.

"Maybe we would be winning this war if your mother wasn't a German spy!" he burst out.

I couldn't answer that. It was the most preposterous thing I had ever heard. Mama loved Russia more than anyone. I stood and glared at Sasha, hoping he saw the anger I felt but couldn't express in that crowded ward. Then I turned and walked out.

I returned early to the Alexander Palace and found Olga lying on a sofa, still wearing her nurse's uniform, and staring blankly at the ceiling. Countess Hendrikova, the maid of honor we called Nastinka, came in a moment later stirring a bromide, a worried crease in her forehead.

"Olga, dearest?" I said, approaching my sister. She was twenty-one at the time. I thought of her as almost as much of an adult as my mother.

"She cannot answer you," Nastinka said. She sat beside Olga and tried to tip the bromide into her mouth. It dribbled out down her chin.

"What's wrong? Is she ill? Has she got a fever? Is she hurt?" Any of those events would be worrisome, in the midst of everything else. Even Alyosha had cooperated by being in one of his healthy phases. Yet Olga didn't look unwell. She looked . . . blank. Empty.

"Not exactly ill. Just overwrought."

Olga didn't seem to see or hear anything, but as I watched, great tears welled up in her eyes and rolled down her face. She didn't move a muscle to wipe them away. Nastinka blotted them with her handkerchief. "Nastya, be a dear and go and fetch Dr. Botkin, would you?" Nastinka was trying to appear calm, but I could hear panic on the edge of her voice. Something had happened, clearly, and Nastinka either wouldn't or couldn't tell me what.

I didn't have to be asked again. I ran to find a servant who could call one of the other ladies-in-waiting to telephone Dr. Botkin, who lived in the village. It seemed an eternity until he arrived. He came in immediately to see Olga, opening his medical bag as he walked so that his stethoscope was already out by the time he reached her side. Mother returned home a short while later and came directly to the parlor. "Nastinka, please take Nastya to the schoolroom to prepare for tea," she said, not looking at me.

I opened my mouth to protest. I wanted to know what was wrong with Olga. But one did not contradict Mama. She had a delicate heart and any unpleasantness made her short of breath. "No need to take me, I know my way," I told Nastinka. She cast an apologetic look at me as she closed the door after me.

❧

That night, Olga did not come to tea or supper. No one said anything in the parlor, although often it was Olga who read or played the piano, or played bezique with Papa. We were the usual circle: Mama, Anya, Nastinka, Isa, Lili Dehn, the elderly Count and Countess Benckendorff, and Prince Dolgorukov—marshal of the court and Papa's aide-de-camp. There were also one or two officers who were on leave and whom Anya had invited, thinking they would be company for Olga and Tatiana, but only Tatiana was there. The atmosphere was tense, and Mama went up to bed early, probably to check on Olga.

When Mashka and I were at last alone in our room, I asked her if she knew anything.

"Olga collapsed at the hospital. She just collapsed."

I didn't understand. "What would have made her do that?"

"Anya says she could not bear the sight of so many torn limbs and dreadful injuries. It happened right after she saw someone die following an amputation."

It made sense that Anya spoke to Mashka. She was Anya's favorite. Still, I was a little hurt that people not even in our family knew more than I did. "Will she be better?"

"Dr. Botkin says yes, although they've called a mentalist from Petrograd. She won't nurse again, though."

I pictured someone who looked like Grigory Rasputin, but with a watch that he would dangle in front of Olga's eyes to mesmerize her. "She looked so sad."

"The injuries are horrible to see. Who is that soldier you spend so much time with? The one with the bandage over his eye?"

I was startled for a moment that she would have noticed, then I realized that when I was with Sasha, I barely looked anywhere but at him. She could easily have come into the ward and seen us and I wouldn't have noticed. I had taken no pains to conceal my concern over him. "Oh, only someone I feel particularly sorry for. He will never be able to see with that eye again." I didn't think she was entirely convinced, but we were both tired, and turned out our lights to go to sleep.

I returned to the hospital the next day and didn't feel like going to see Sasha. Between his awful accusation and my worry over Olga, I was little in the mood to confront anything. I went directly to the convalescent ward, where I knew he wouldn't be, and began reading from the Bible to a young boy barely older than I was, who specially requested it.

I hadn't been there long when a nurse came to me with a folded note. "The officer in the ward upstairs asked me to give you this."

I thanked her and opened it.

> Can you forgive me? That was a horrible thing to say, and I don't really believe it. Please come and visit me when you can.
>
> S.

Of course, I finished the chapter and, resisting the boy's entreaty to read another, went directly to see Sasha. He smiled when I came in. I brought a chair over to his bed.

"You look sad," he said.

"Olga is not well."

"Has she caught a fever from the wounded soldiers?" he asked.

"No. Her illness is in her mind. She will not come back to nurse anymore."

He nodded. "And yet you come every day, with so much blood and carnage around. Why?"

"Because I must. Because it is my duty." I didn't want to tell him that I raced to the hospital mainly because I knew I would see him.

He reached his hand out to me. I couldn't help but remember how he had shrunk from my touch the day before, and I didn't take it. "I really am sorry, you know," he said. "But I'm not sorry too. You should know what people have been saying about your mother."

"Is there more?" I asked, curiosity erasing my annoyance.

"They say she's in league with Rasputin, who has cast a spell over her and tells her what ministers he wants the tsar to appoint."

"That is not true and you must know it!" I honestly didn't know whether to laugh or be angry. Grigory was a little odd, but Mama's belief in him had only to do with Alexei. She believed he had made him better when all the doctors had failed.

"Really? Then how do you explain Protopopov? He's incompetent, yet he stays. He's thick with Rasputin." Protopopov was the prime minister, I knew that much. But I really had no idea about anything else, only trusting that because Papa had appointed him, he was capable of doing his job.

The next day Sasha was in the same convalescent ward where I was supposed to be, and I didn't have to make excuses to be with him. He kept the bandage over his eye, but the stitches on his face had been taken out. He looked almost like his old self, except that the metal that struck him had dug a channel from his eye to the corner of his mouth, leaving a visible scar. I think it hurt him to talk for quite a while after the stitches were out. He never complained to me directly. I just noticed that after he had been speaking for a while his face iced over, like the Neva River in the wintertime.

But once our conversation about the war and politics had begun, it could do nothing else but continue. "Listen, Nastya," he said to me one day, "If you have any influence over your papa at all, you must convince him to use his reason. If he does not let the Duma have its constitutional monarchy, everything will be lost."

The Duma, the closest thing we had to an English Parliament, had been dissolved by the prime minister Stolypin when I was just a small child. Then Stolypin was assassinated at the opera, with my father, Olga, and Tatiana looking on. They came back and told us about it, and their description left a strong impression on me. It made me feel that somehow the Duma was a bad thing. I didn't know what to think when it was reconvened recently for the fourth time. I remembered my parents talking about it. My mother was completely against it. Papa said, "It will make no difference to let them have their petty squabbles in public. I am not bound to take any of their decisions as more than suggestion. How can intellectuals and merchants govern my Russia?"

As far as I was concerned, it was truly Papa's Russia. He was the divinely appointed tsar, the representative of our God on earth. He was responsible for everything that was good and safe. I found it very difficult to believe all that Sasha said. We spoke and argued, and he tried his best to convince me that Papa's stubbornness was driving the country into the ground and making a disaster inevitable. Disaster! How could the rightful ruler of all the Russias cause disaster?

"If he would only concede some power to the Duma, all might yet be well," Sasha would say, pleading with me and holding my hand—which I allowed him to do once I had truly accepted his apology. "If he does not, there will be revolution. Perhaps anarchy!"

I usually waited with my response, just to delay the moment when he would let go of my hand, but my answer was always the same. "There's nothing I can do. At home they barely notice me, let alone listen to me. I'm 'the youngest grand duchess' at best. Little better than useless, except to make others laugh."

But Sasha didn't laugh. Instead, he squeezed my hand.

## ❧ CHAPTER 9 ❧

By the time Sasha left the hospital in the early spring of 1915, much had changed. The war that had started badly began to go in our favor. The factories increased their production of munitions, and some of the generals my father had complained of were relieved of their command. I thought that success would bring everyone together, that the country would once again rally around the common cause of combating the German invaders, but the opposite seemed to occur.

We all felt it when we did our war work, whatever that consisted of. Olga recovered, but she never went back to nursing, instead helping to raise funds and organize supplies. Tatiana turned her energies toward finding ways to help the Polish refugees, in addition to nursing. Mama continued her nursing duties as much as she could, but her health began to decline under the strain, and she often had to stay home.

Once Sasha left the hospital, I found it more and more difficult to continue going there, knowing I would no longer see him. He still sent me messages through one of the orderlies, but we weren't able to meet until one day, a message said:

*I'm out in the back, behind the hospital laundry.*

Fortunately, there had been a lull in the fighting recently, and only one or two men occupied the beds in the ward where I was reading at the time. I told the nurse I had a headache and wanted to leave. I lied yet again to say the motorcar was coming for me, and that I was to wait for it outside.

Instead, I went to the ground floor and walked purposefully to the back where the laundry was done. A few people cast curious glances in my direction, but no one stopped me. It was now common to see a grand duchess or even the empress in different parts of the hospital.

At first, the vapor of boiling bleach made my eyes sting. It took a moment for the tears to clear from my eyes. Once they did, I peered through the dense mist and saw Sasha. He did not see me. He was gazing, rapt, at a stout laundress with her sleeves rolled up to her shoulders and her arms red from the hot water. With ease she plunged her arms up to her elbows into a milky vat and hauled out a lump of fabric that must have weighed fifty pounds with all the water it had absorbed. She slung it, hardly spilling a drop of soapy water, onto a washboard over another vat and began squeezing it out.

"Ahem!"

I jumped. In my turn I had become so fascinated watching the laundress that I had taken my attention away from Sasha, and he had crept around behind me and surprised me. For a moment, his unpatched eye danced with mischief. Then as if he remembered he had much to be bitter about, his hand flew to the patch over his bad eye and he frowned. The wound near his mouth had almost fully healed, the only evidence of it a fine, red scar that was not very noticeable when he smiled, but that became more visible when his mouth settled into any other expression.

"I miss seeing you every day," I said. "I'm glad you're here."

He smiled and patted my shoulder. I shrugged his hand off angrily before thinking about it. "What?" he said. "We aren't friends anymore now that I'm not helpless and in bed?"

"No, I didn't mean that, only . . ." I couldn't explain to him that I found his treatment of me annoying. It was as if he considered me a little child. I thought we had gone beyond that at least to being real friends, but here he was, looking down at me again.

"Don't be cross with me, Nastya. I have something important to say to you." He stood a little closer to me. I held my breath. What could he have to say? I was so young! Did he feel something for me? As I had begun to feel for him? I didn't dare hope. I remembered Mashka, sighing over her lieutenant, and all they ever did was bow to each other and smile.

"I'm going back to the front."

At first, what he said passed by my comprehension, it was so completely different from what I expected. When I recovered my composure, my first feeling was anger. "Why must you go?" I asked. "Can't wounded soldiers be allowed to rest awhile? We've hardly had any time together!"

"I have to do it, for my career. My family is not wealthy or educated. If I expect to have a future, to be able to support a family one day, I must excel now."

"But you're the one who says it will all be over! That the war is a foolish show. Why are you trying to impress someone who may not matter, if all happens as you say?"

He shrugged his left shoulder toward his patched eye as if to say, you have to ask? It was a new gesture, just started since he had recovered. It infuriated me. "Don't try to understand, Nastya. You can't have any idea what a normal person's life is like. You've been so protected you're more like a child than a young lady."

"What is that supposed to mean?" I was furious at him for calling me a child. I would soon enough be fourteen, and after all I had seen in the hospital I no longer felt young.

"Look at you in your nursery dress. They don't want to let you grow up. They think of you as their little girl. Can you imagine what they would say if they knew all the things I told you?"

I blushed. That way he had of referring to my parents and the court as "they." But he was right. I think Mama kept me in Olga and Tatiana's castoffs so she wouldn't feel old herself. Marie too was still in short skirts, but she didn't seem to mind. I, on the other hand, wanted to wear long skirts and heels, and fall in love.

Then Sasha did something that took me completely by surprise. He grasped me by both shoulders, looked straight into my eyes, said, "I may never see you again," and then kissed me hard right on the mouth. I couldn't say anything after that.

He gave me a peculiar little smile, the same smile he had when the slash on his cheek was still stitched and it hurt him to lift that corner of his mouth. He touched his cap in a cheeky salute, then turned and walked away. I watched him disappear into the fog of laundry steam we'd been standing in. It was a picture I wish I had been able to capture. He looked for all the world like a fallen hero ascending into Valhalla through the mist, just as in the epic poems we read in the schoolroom.

I was too numb to cry for him. So many went away and never came back. Both Olga and Tatiana had had news of young officers who had courted them falling in the field against the relentless German artillery. I thought my one friend had escaped that fate. Now, he was running toward it again with both arms open.

For the rest of the spring I went through the motions of getting up, dressing, going to the hospital wards, and attending state occasions once or twice. There was no question that year of taking a cruise on the yacht, or a vacation at Livadia in the Crimea. Instead we traveled wherever there were hospitals nearby, restlessly roving from Tsarskoe Selo to Peterhof to Petrograd, where much of the Winter Palace had been given over as hospital wards, and occasionally as far afield as Moscow. The war took up everyone's time. Until our other troubles started, that is.

Funny that I can look back now and think of the wartime as somehow better than what followed. It seems insensitive to be nostalgic about a time that condemned so many young men to pain and death. Yet because everyone at court was so consumed with the war, it enabled me to be more independent. I also learned much that I would never have known before. That knowledge—and Sasha's influence too—had begun to show me the world beyond the closed walls of the imperial court. It was a very troubled world.

For a while, we thought perhaps things were going better. In 1915 the army had had some successes against the Germans, and our casualties were not so heavy as they had been the year before. Papa said that the factories were producing munitions at a faster rate, and that transportation routes had been improved so that they could more easily get supplies to the army. "I don't want another fiasco like last August," he told Mama while we sat quietly and knitted socks and mufflers to help stock Mama's *sklady*, the warehouses that supplied linens and all other necessities to the troops at the front lines. "Thirty thousand brave Russians killed in a single battle. Tens of thousands taken prisoner. It tears at my heart to think of it."

Papa had taken to eating quickly, and when he came to join us for our late-night supper, he paced back and forth, never sitting quietly in his chair. This worried Mama, who was frailer than ever with her heart condition. I watched her big, hazel eyes follow him, sadness nearly spilling over their brims. The more agitated Papa became, the more pale and withdrawn was Mama. I never was able to understand how people could have circulated such horrible rumors about her. She was as kind as could be, although when Papa asked her opinion she gave it firmly. At times he even changed his mind about something because her argument was so convincing. That certainty of hers was comforting when I was younger. Yet I could see how it might be taken as blind stubbornness by someone who disagreed with her, and I assumed that was how she managed to disturb so many people despite her quiet place in the background.

And for several months, it seemed as if perhaps, as Sasha had predicted, the war would end quickly and everything would go back to the way it was before. In two years I would come of age. I wanted a ball and a diamond necklace—just as Olga and Tatiana had been given. But it was not to be.

During the summer, the news of worker unrest reached us. A telegram came for my father while we were eating our dinner one sultry August evening, a year after the first offensive of the war. A servant brought it on a tray and bent forward at the waist in the way servants have, his lips barely moving as he spoke so that only Papa could hear. Papa nodded and took the paper off the tray, snapping it open and smoothing it out on the table. Before he could read it, he put his glass to his eye. I watched his face change from its normal, rosy color to something that looked as stormy as a thundercloud.

"How dare they! Don't they understand we are in the midst of war? Don't they appreciate that I raised their wages? They are better off than they have ever been, ungrateful wretches!" He stormed out of the dining room. The footman barely had time to open the door for him.

Mama, who had hardly touched a morsel on her plate, was pale and shaking. "I shall go to my room. Come in later to read if you like," she said to us all, attempting a smile.

"Let me help you, Mama." Alexei stood—he had grown so tall, and been much less ill lately—and offered her his arm. That left me and my three sisters alone at the table. We sat in silence for a while. I don't know what the others were thinking, but I was wishing that Sasha had not gone back to the front, that I could send him a message to meet me and talk things over.

It was Tatiana who surprised us with information. "The workers are earning more, it is true. But the price of bread and flour and other necessities has gone up well beyond the increase in their wages. And supplies of food are scarce because of the war. Little wonder there have been riots in the streets."

I surveyed the untouched meat and vegetables on our plates. It would be enough, I knew Sasha would say, to feed a family for a week. If only there were a way to give our extra food to others. But that was foolish. Nothing changed at court. No matter how little we ate, the lavish table was always heavy with food.

And yet change was coming. Fast. Those riots felt like the beginning, but in my heart I knew things had been simmering below the lid of everyday life for a long time. I could see it in the servants' eyes. I could read it in the troubled look on my mother's face, in the angle of her head as she bent over her needlework. I could feel it in the biting cold of my morning shower, sense it in the confusion of my dreams. For a while longer I was able to pretend it didn't exist. But, a year later, that simply wasn't possible anymore.

# CHAPTER 10

The workers' revolt was short-lived, but the war continued and in the autumn of 1915 took a turn for the worse. We were forced to retreat, drawing the German army onto Russian soil.

"Sukhomlinov assured us at the beginning of the war that our supplies were adequate to the task of meeting this foe. For his miscalculation, he has been relieved of his post."

Papa paused to sip his evening tea, but we knew there was more to come than the expected news of the chief general's dismissal. He had that pensive air, and his eyes gazed off over our heads.

"He should have been convicted of treason," said Mama, although she leaned back on her chaise with her eyes closed, a cloth soaked with lavender water on her forehead.

"No. He was ignorant, not traitorous. My cousin could not bring himself to get rid of him, nor any of the others who have proven incompetent. And therefore I have come to an important decision."

He put down his cup and stepped away from the window

where he had been standing. Autumn was advancing, and there was a smell of decay on the breeze that came through the opening. Mama sat upright, taking the cloth from her forehead. We all waited for him to continue.

Before he did, he walked over to Alexei, who had a book in his lap that he wasn't actually reading. "I shall take the supreme command myself," Papa said.

"Oh, Nicky! Must you?" Mama's face turned a shade paler.

Papa placed his hand on Alexei's shoulder. "And since my son has been better lately, he shall come with me to Mogilev, and review the troops at my side."

Mama often got her way with Papa, but she also knew when it was futile to try. She lay back again, and simply murmured, "Very well. But if he is at all sick he shall return to me at once."

Papa walked over to Mama and kissed the top of her head.

That evening when Mashka and I retired, I took Sasha's balalaika out from the back of my wardrobe. So far, with all the time we spent at the hospitals and doing charity work, I had not been able to find a moment to play it. Something about that day and my father's decision made me feel like I needed to play it, that it would connect me to Sasha, make me feel less alone and bewildered.

Mashka sat up in her bed, writing a letter to one of our cousins in England. I unwrapped the balalaika, and very quietly touched the strings. I turned the pegs to tune it, and started to pick out a folk melody, pressing my fingers down on the frets, sliding them along to get the smooth, lyrical sound so character-istic of that simple instrument. The strings cut into my finger-tips, which had lost what few calluses they had had through lack of playing. I didn't mean to strike a mournful melody; it was simply what came to mind.

"Nastya, dear, must you?" Mashka said.

She was right. Such songs were too sad for right now. I put the balalaika away for another day.

Taking the little things and making them big. Expanding the significance of everyday moments to have something of the eter-nal in them—it's very Russian to do that. And yet, at court, it was the opposite. Mama always seemed to be trying to take the big and make it little. She chose the smallest palace in Tsarskoe Selo, the Alexander Palace, for our principal home. She always seemed to be attempting to be domestic, hiding away from the public, pretending we were a family just like any other. She almost succeeded.

After he took over command of the armies, Papa was away for great lengths of time, off near the front where the fighting went on unceasingly. I didn't really think his advisers would let him put himself in danger. Nonetheless, those were anxious times. Not having him at home made me feel very exposed, even though we didn't see him that much when he was there, except at tea and in the evening. He wasn't a formidable character. Not very tall, and slightly built. In some ways, Mama appeared more imperious than he did. He had been trained in battle, was a colonel by rank, but I doubt he had ever killed anyone, or come close himself to being killed. But somehow just having him near reassured me.

A significant detachment of the elite guards remained at Tsarskoe Selo even though Papa wasn't in residence. Yet I couldn't help feeling they were a bit less vigilant in Papa's absence. Especially because Alexei had gone with him. We girls were of no importance. Except my mother, who, as tsaritsa, was Papa's representative in all government matters when he was gone. Yes, she was important. The secret police and the servants rarely took their eyes off her when she was in a room. What did they expect? I wondered. What were they looking for?

Mama did her best to manage without Papa there, which meant she had to greet diplomats and receive members of the Duma. She wrote letters every day, some personal and some matters of business. The rest of us wrote letters to friends who were away. Most especially to Papa and Alexei. Mine were full of silly things I thought they would find amusing. They were childish, not because I felt like that much of a child, but because I understood that Papa wanted to think of me that way. It was my place in the family.

Mama's heart was weak, and the constant activity tired her. No one outside the family was allowed to know of her condition, and so when she canceled meetings or did not receive people, they thought her rude and remote. I heard them myself once. A countess had come to plead for a government position for her son, but had been turned away by the servants with no explanation. I knew Mama would write to her later and do what she could, but the damage was done. "She's above us. Probably spending all her time with the Germans, plotting the downfall of Russia!" I heard the lady say. I doubt she ever knew how wrong she was.

I did not repeat what I heard to anyone. It would have done no good. Mama believed that everything was going along for the best, and refused to believe reports of unrest or trouble. I doubt she could have managed if she had. Her main concern was that she had to neglect her charities when so much else fell upon her. Mashka and I tried our best to visit the hospitals since Mama couldn't, Tatiana carried on with her nursing and her refugees, and Olga helped with her charities. The time went quickly.

I suppose I shouldn't have been surprised that with so many pressures on her, and without Papa to talk things over with, Mama turned to Grigory for comfort and advice. He rarely came to the Alexander Palace, but although Anya spoke in a kind of code with my mother—as much to baffle the secret police as to keep their conversations from us—I knew that she was the constant link between Mama and Rasputin. She carried letters from Mama to the *starets*, the holy man, in his lodgings in Petrograd, and Mama received letters from him by the same courier—although not nearly as many as she wrote. It did not occur to me that there was anything wrong in this, since Rasputin had always been kind to us, and usually ended up making Alexei feel better too.

One blustery October afternoon, soon after we had all returned from our nursing and visiting, Anya came in to speak to Mama. They stole off to a corner of the room where I could not hear what they were saying, but I knew instantly by the joyous look on my mother's face that it had to do with Rasputin. I was not surprised, therefore, when his tall, gaunt figure entered the parlor. He took three steps toward Mama and bowed. A servile, old-fashioned bow that let his long, lank hair practically drag on the floor.

"Daughter," he said when he rose, and took her hands in his. They both closed their eyes and stood together for what seemed a long time, then he spoke again. "Courage. God has great deeds for you to accomplish. So long as the tsar is upon his throne, no harm can come to you and your family."

What he said sounded impressive enough, but when I thought about it later, it meant nothing, and might have been uttered by anyone.

"Won't you take tea with us?" Mama said. I was vexed. I always looked forward to tea as a time when we would be alone together. Even the suite—Lili, Isa, Nastinka, the maid of honor on duty, and the officers of the palace guard—normally did not join us. Isa and Lili were usually on errands visiting hospitals for Mama, and we had seen less of Anya recently, who was off doing secret things of which I knew little.

We sat in glum silence as Mama filled the cups from the samovar, all sorry that we could not chatter happily about the people we had seen that day as we normally did. Mama didn't say anything to us about it. Perhaps she interpreted our lack of courtesy as religious awe.

I could hardly taste the biscuits we ate, and only sipped at my tea. As soon as it was polite, I asked leave to get up from the table, and moved away to a window seat to continue my knitting.

"The little Anastasie has lost her healthy appetite!" said Rasputin. I blushed. He turned to Mama. "You know what that means, of course. It means she is in love."

Mama laughed. "Nastya? My friend, how could you imagine such a thing. She is a little child."

What Mama said made me even more cross than Rasputin's remark. But that wasn't the end of my embarrassment. "Come here, little child, as your mother calls you," Father Grigory said, "and as you once did when you were only so high." He held his hand at a distance of about three feet from the floor. I was not tall even then, and I hated being reminded of having been so little before. My mother nodded to me, indicating that I must do as he said.

I walked over to him, standing about an arm's length away. "Come, come, come!" he said, reaching his long arm out to grasp my hand. I was tempted to pull away, but I didn't dare, not with my mother watching me closely. I moved to just in front of his knees. He looked me up and down. "She has not the beauty of Olga and Tatiana, but she has fire. Oh yes, God will protect her. She is a survivor."

I thought after his pronouncement he would pat me on the head and let me go. I knew I was blushing violently. He had a way of making me feel like the child I believed I had left behind, and yet at the same time very conscious of the woman inside me. But then he did something much worse. He reached out with both his hands and cupped my almost nonexistent breasts in his long, clawlike hands. I gasped and turned to look at my mother. But she had glanced down at her sewing, and by the time she looked up, Rasputin had taken his hands away. Only Tatiana had seen what happened, and she gave me an almost imperceptible shake of the head. Even without her warning I was too dumbstruck to say anything, so I simply walked back to my knitting basket. I refused to look at Rasputin again that evening.

That was the last time I saw him. I later realized that Tatiana's signal probably meant that if I had said anything, Mama would have believed I was lying. In her mind and heart she could not accept that Rasputin was capable of any evil. As far as she was concerned, he had saved Alexei's life, and foretold everything that has happened since then. She has always believed that the fate of our family was bound up with his, and I suppose events have proven her right.

※

But all was not work and difficulty. I was thrilled when I discovered that Sasha came back from the front for a brief leave in Petrograd in November. We managed to meet for an hour when he was sent with a dispatch to Tsarskoe Selo.

"Your sister Tatiana could end up saving you all, you know," he said to me as we wandered through the winter garden, as far away from the windows as possible.

"Tatiana? Why?"

"Her Refugee Committee. It's the most well-run, effective effort in the entire government."

I smiled. Tatiana was awfully good at organizing things.

After a while she also decided that the hospital work was too depressing and wanted to concentrate on something with more possibility of a positive outcome. Mama had approved her idea, and that was all it took for her to put herself in charge of finding places for all the Polish and other refugees who were fleeing into Russia from the German and Austrian onslaught.

"There is much to admire about your sister," Sasha said, glancing sidelong at me.

"You mean, besides her committee?" He was testing me, and so I would test him in return. I would make him tell me that he thought her beautiful. I didn't mind when other people said it, but coming from him, I knew it would sting. Yet still I prodded him.

"People say she is beautiful and unpretentious."

"People?"

"Yes! I hear it from others often." He stopped and turned me toward him. "Are you jealous of Tatiana?"

I couldn't look at him. "No. Not jealous. I love her. I love all my family." I didn't know what to say.

"I don't know Tatiana," Sasha said. "But I cannot imagine that she has a truer heart and soul than you. And that's the most important thing." He kissed me on the forehead, like a brother, not on the lips as he had before. And I would be fifteen in a few months!

I should have been glad that Sasha still thought of me as a friend, and that he had kissed me again, but instead I had a disappointed pang in my stomach. I felt him drawing away, becoming completely engrossed in the war and in his new position of importance as an aide-de-camp to a colonel. "I sometimes play your balalaika," I said, clutching at the only thing I could think of that might remind him that we had a connection to each other.

"That's good. It likes to be played." He nudged me in a friendly way as we walked through the garden.

"How did you learn to play?" I asked him.

"By listening and watching," he said. "How else?"

"You didn't have music lessons?"

"Hah! In my house? A man must be a man, not a dandy." He put on a deep, authoritative voice.

"We have lessons for everything. Piano, dancing, English, French . . ."

"All very useful, no doubt, when you are someday married and can torment your own children with lessons in piano, dancing, English, French . . ."

I nudged him back, hard. He almost fell off balance. "Be careful! Would you put out my other eye?"

He was laughing, but I realized that I hadn't even thought about the patch and what he had looked like before. This new Sasha, who had fought and killed and stared his own death in the face, was now the only Sasha there was. I was a little sad, but also a little in awe. He was a man. My friend, my only true friend, was no longer a boy. "Will I see you again before you go away?" I asked.

"If I can find an excuse to come here. It's not easy, you know."

"If I were a real grand duchess I could order you," I said, putting my nose in the air.

"Grand duchesses can do many things, but they cannot give orders to soldiers," he said, and tweaked my nose.

"My brother once ordered a whole regiment of guards to march into the sea," I said.

He laughed. "Ah, but he is the tsarevich. And a boy." Sasha walked a little way out of the trees and looked left and right, to see that no one was watching, then came back. "I have to go. You've made me waste too much time already!"

He gave me a smile and a quick salute and strode off. I liked watching him from the back. He had a straight-shouldered, rhythmic walk. He had grown taller too. But he was so caught up in the war and his new position of responsibility that I was very much afraid he couldn't see beyond his own advancement and change to recognize mine. I so desperately wanted him to understand all the ways that I had grown too. I looked down at my outfit. My child's coat covered a mock sailor's uniform, not like anything one actually saw officers wear on board a ship, of course, but the kind beloved by mothers. No wonder he thought of me as little more than a child.

## ❧ CHAPTER 11 ❧

In December of 1915, more than a year after the start of the war and months after we had all been told it would end, tragic events began to pile up again. A dear friend of Mama's, one of her maids of honor, died after a short illness. I thought Mama's heart would break. Then if that wasn't enough, Papa returned home unexpectedly with Alexei, who had broken a blood vessel in his nose and was dangerously ill because of it.

Again, the doctors tried everything and failed to make a difference. And again Mama called in Rasputin, who prayed and touched Alyosha's face (so Mashka told me, since I refused to be in the same room with him). Alyosha began to recover after that, and the doctors could not account for why. But Mama was convinced it was the holy power of her trusted Grigory. No one could ever have persuaded her otherwise.

Always, after Alyosha had been ill and was recovering, we made a great fuss over him. The kitchen would prepare endless delicacies to tempt his appetite. "Let's go try Alyosha's food!" I said after Mashka's and my lessons one day, knowing that a little mischief would cheer him up more than anything. We went to his room just as the first footman arrived carrying trays with special morsels for him: sweets and sausages, noodle cakes and dumplings, caviar and blinis.

"Come, Alyosha!" I said. "Surely you can't eat this all by yourself. We've come to help you so that Dr. Botkin doesn't get angry and make you stay in bed for weeks."

I helped myself to a few of the little portions. "Leave some for me!" he cried. "I'm feeling much better now, no thanks to you."

"What? Didn't we visit you enough while you were sick?"

"You came and tormented me with all the things I couldn't do until I got better." But he smiled when he said it. It was a trick I had, once the very worst was over: I would tease him into a fighting frame of mind.

Mashka and I ate our fill of Alexei's treats, and I think because we were eating them, he ate more than he would have otherwise. I told him all the naughty things my puppy, Jimmy, was doing, that he'd left a mess right in the middle of the semicircular hall and one of the footman had stepped in it while I was running to get a shovel to pick it up. He laughed and laughed. We didn't leave until Zhilik came to get us for our afternoon lessons.

Mama too was very ill that winter. Her heart gave her such trouble that she had to use the elevator to go up and down from our floor to hers, and spent much of the day just lying on her chaise. But she and Alyosha both recovered by spring. The doctors decided that Alexei was well enough to return with Papa to Mogilev.

"Darling, must you take him away again? Remember what happened last time."

Mama's eyes followed Papa as he looked for books he wanted to take with him from the small library. Mashka and I had been enjoying some time quietly reading when they both came in.

"He must learn. And he has been better for quite a while. Gibbes will go with us so he can continue his lessons, and Nagorny, of course." He didn't look at her, just pulled out books, leafed through them and put them back.

"But if he becomes ill? What then?"

"Derevenko will be there too. He's an excellent physician. And the army hospital is well stocked with everything he could need."

Just as Mama threw herself into a chair and put her hand-kerchief to her eyes, Alyosha entered. He did look handsome, and so grown up in his uniform. He had told me that he loved being with Papa and the army, that it was good to get away from Mama's intense worry for a while. "I'm ready, Papa. Chemodurov and Nagorny have seen to everything, and the motorcar is waiting for us outside."

I couldn't help smiling over in my corner, hearing Alyosha trying to make his voice deep. He was nowhere near a beard yet, though—something I made sure to remind him of as often as I could.

"I shall be fine, Mama. Please don't worry." Alyosha took Mama's hand. She smiled. "And I promise to write home every day. I shall have to, to make sure Nastya doesn't drive everyone insane!" He cast me a sidelong glance. I balled up a piece of paper I was using as a bookmark, put it in my mouth, and spit it out at him. It struck him right in the forehead.

"Nastya! Is that any way to treat your brother when he is on the point of departing?" Mama asked, but Papa had turned away and I realized he was trying very hard not to laugh.

"No, Mama. Only I hope Alexei won't become too much like the soldiers, and curse and tell lewd stories." Now Mashka started laughing. Alyosha just drew himself up taller.

"For that, you shall get your letter last," he said. But I knew that I would be the first person he wrote to.

Papa, Alyosha, and Sasha, of course, had gone back to the war. The house was quiet and dull again. I contented myself with writing to Papa and Alyosha, and thinking of Sasha when I played his balalaika quietly at night after everyone had gone to their rooms. Mashka actually came to like it, and would often fall asleep to the sound.

This secret practicing was all I thought I would have to preserve me from the quiet drear of Petrograd, Peterhof, and Tsarskoe Selo. Tatiana had started her nursing duties again, and she and Olga went to Petrograd every other week for committee meetings and other charity work, leaving Mashka and me to knit, sew, and read to Mama. Occasionally Anya invited us all to her house in Tsarskoe Selo for a party. She also invited any officers she knew who were on leave, and sometimes we danced to the gramophone. Or rather, I should say I only danced if there were more officers than women, being the youngest and still in short skirts. I asked any of the ones who were from the Semyonovsky guards if they knew the colonel Sasha was with, hoping by that means to get some information about him without giving away our acquaintance.

Did Mama know I had a secret friend? I am not certain. I think it would have been quite easy for her to find out. I have gone back and forth thinking that she didn't care enough to ask, and that she understood my need for a friendship unconnected to the court and not influenced by court manners and traditions. I like to give her the benefit of the doubt, and believe that although she didn't often take the time to know my thoughts and feelings, she still recognized that I had them.

Whatever the case, the spring of 1916 was much happier than our previous two had been, and not only because I knew that Sasha, with his blind eye, would probably not be sent to the front lines to fight. We all—my mother, sisters, and I, and the suite—went away on an extended visit to the south, to see the hospitals and *sklady* there and make sure the soldiers and wounded on the Galician front had all that they needed. We were within a stone's throw of Livadia, but Mama would not let us go there because she said it was too self-indulgent to do so when the country was at war. I think it was mostly because she couldn't bear the thought of being there without Papa and Alexei, who spent much of their time at Mogilev.

Still, the warm weather was heavenly. The war seemed farther away around Sebastopol, even though the German fleet had entered the Black Sea, and we had to black out the windows on our train at night along with all the lights in the cities and towns, fearful as everyone was of possible air raids.

After that we went to Eupatoria, a very exotic seaside town that remained largely Mohammedan. I will never forget going to a service of thanksgiving at the mosque. We were invited specially, women not usually being permitted in the mosques. The chanting was beautiful, although I didn't understand it. We went to a synagogue too, and heard the psalms chanted in Hebrew. I wished I could have talked to these strange, different people more, but we were hurried from one place to another. So many people seemed to want to see us.

※

Perhaps the most extraordinary time was in the summer, though, when we took the imperial train to Mogilev to visit Papa and Alexei at the front. It wasn't really the front, in that there was no fighting nearby. But occasionally we could hear the distant guns, like thunder.

I remember the first time we actually heard them, in fact. We had pulled into the siding where our train would stay, as the train was the only suitable accommodation for our family in the vicinity. We sisters all dressed to go to the nearby villages, where we were told we could talk to the people and see if they needed anything. These villages were so small that most of them did not even have names. And there were several within a short walk, so we split up into our usual two pairs, accompanied by a few guards to keep us safe, so we could get to as many as we could.

"I can hear someone chopping wood in the distance," I said to Mashka, who was convinced that we had become lost in looking for the first village we were to visit. The guards who accompanied us simply followed, not offering much help. Perhaps they were secretly laughing at us.

"That's better than nothing, I suppose," she answered, cross with me again.

We continued toward the sound, and it did, in fact, turn out to be our village—more a hamlet, really. About a dozen thatch-roofed cottages surrounded a well. Each cottage had a chicken coop and manger behind it, sometimes inhabited by goats, sometimes by a cow. We approached a fellow chopping wood at the back of one of the cottages. He didn't hear us coming, and so I had to say, "*Zdravstvuytye!*" very loudly a few times before he looked up. When he did, he made the sign of the cross. I suppose he thought we were ghosts!

I stepped forward, being a little braver than Mashka about these things, and tried to explain who we were and why we were there. He said he knew the emperor was at Mogilev, but did not expect the grand duchesses to have braved the journey from Petrograd.

As we spoke, people began to filter out of the cottages and from the surrounding woods. By the time we had discovered that the fellow's name was Botichev and that he had a wife who was out at the market, five strong sons who were off fighting the war, and a daughter who stayed home to help, quite a crowd had gathered. There were several girls our age among them. At first everyone was quiet—in awe, I suppose. But then I turned to a girl who appeared to be the one all the others looked up to, and said, "You have on a very pretty dress. Did you make it?"

I stepped forward to where she stood, a little out of the center of the group.

"Yes," she answered, and smiled.

"I love to do needlework," I said. "Your embroidery is very fine."

Botichev said, "That is my daughter Anyushka. She will marry in the fall."

My mouth fell open. She was hardly older than we were! A vexed look crossed her features. "Perhaps you can show us around, tell us what you do here, and how the war has affected you," I said, trying to sound official, but really looking for a chance to talk in private with this girl who didn't look happy about getting married.

She and her friends took us around the tiny settlement and then led us to one of the cottages, the one where she lived.

"I would be honored if the grand duchesses would take tea with us," she said.

I turned and looked at the guards, who had stayed respectfully behind the crowd of girls. I said, "We would be delighted. Our friends will wait for us outside."

Before we could be stopped, I took Mashka's hand and stepped through the doorway into the simple dwelling. The girl brought two stools out and placed the samovar over the fire, measuring out something that might have been tea, but in these times of limited supplies might have been a substitute. Everyone else positioned themselves around on the floor, kneeling or sitting cross-legged.

That was when I heard what I thought was thunder. "The

sky looked clear when we came in," I said. "Do you expect rain?"

The girls suppressed giggles, and I suppose my naïveté must have seemed laughable to them. "It's the German guns," our hostess said. Everyone listened silently for a minute. "They are still far away, but no doubt we will have to flee like the others when they come too near."

"If you do, I will make sure you are taken care of," I said. I didn't really know if I could, but Mama always seemed to promise such things and make them happen, and I would tell her.

"If only you could convince my papa that it would not be right for me to marry Grigor Ippolytevich," Anyushka said, introducing the very subject I had hoped she would.

"Do you not love him?"

"Love? How can I love an old man from the next village! Papa only wants us to marry so he can have more land."

"Our parents wanted our sister Olga to marry someone from another country."

"But it must have been a prince!" said a little girl lisping through the gap between her front teeth.

"Yes, a prince."

"And she did not marry him? How could she refuse?" Anyushka asked, wonder in her eyes.

I shook my head. "Our mama and papa would never force us to marry if we did not want to."

"That's enough, Anyushka! The cows need milking." The voice startled me and I jumped involuntarily. I turned to see the girl's father standing in the doorway.

"But we have not served tea! It is impolite! And I milked the cows this morning," Anyushka pleaded.

I could see a cloud gathering in the man's face, and I feared for the safety of Anyushka if we stayed. "Do not trouble yourself. You have been most hospitable," I said. Mashka and I stood—Mashka had not said a word all this time, although she nudged me once or twice as if to warn me against something. Anyushka looked crestfallen.

"Wait!" she said, and went to a small coffer in the corner, below the one window. She opened it and removed a small piece of cloth. She held it out to me, and I saw that it was an elaborately embroidered handkerchief. "Please, take this."

I accepted it from her gratefully. The cloth was a little coarse, but the work was very fine. "Thank you, Anyushka. It's beautiful."

"You are welcome, Grand Duchess."

"Call me Nastya. Everyone does."

She blushed. "I couldn't."

"Then Anastasia Nicholaevna, if you must. Farewell."

As we left the cottage, I heard Anyushka call after us, "Farewell, Anastasia Nicholaevna. God go with you."

## ❧ CHAPTER 12 ❧

I think it was during our visits to Mogilev that I began to see why my mother might be distrusted by people who didn't know her. Her shyness in large crowds, which I had always noticed, didn't seem strange. But even in the comparatively small society of army headquarters, she was not capable of making easy conversation. I could see that many interpreted her behavior as arrogance. If she wanted to talk to someone at the luncheons my father gave at headquarters, she would send one of us into the crowd to bring that person back to her. I couldn't understand what she was afraid of. She was beautiful, kind, and the tsaritsa. Nonetheless, it was how she behaved, the entire time we were in Mogilev.

She wasn't really herself, the Mama I knew, unless she was in the privacy of her own home. It was a great relief to all of us to return to Tsarskoe Selo that autumn, after having been away for such a long time. We were going to celebrate Mashka's sixteenth birthday, her coming of age. It was sad that it had to be during wartime, I thought, although Papa and Alexei said they would come back for it.

One late October morning as I had just started rereading *David Copperfield*, longing for something to take me away from the reports of battles and wounded soldiers and incompetent generals, Mashka waltzed and twirled into the schoolroom, her face glowing.

"You'll never guess!" she said.

"Well, if I won't, you had better tell me."

She did another twirl. "I thought we were all finished with balls and state occasions because of the war, but Crown Prince Carol of Rumania is coming to visit, and I'm to go—it's my first state function, now that I'm of age! I shall have my diamond necklace! And a long gown, of course."

Prince Carol was the one who had been presented to Olga as a potential suitor. She refused him because she didn't want to leave Russia. I couldn't imagine why he was visiting again, but assumed it must have something to do with the war. I sighed. Now I was the only one of us left who was a little girl. At fifteen, I didn't really feel like it. I thought that Mashka seemed younger than I was in many ways. Maybe it was because she was still slightly plump, and had wide, innocent eyes. Marie's saucers, our cousins called them. But Marie's looks were deceptive: she was so strong, we always got her to lift heavy things. Once, when we were bored with our English lessons, she lifted Mr. Gibbes right off his feet.

Mashka was so excited about the ball that I couldn't help getting caught up in it myself. I would be allowed to watch her grand entrance from a balcony. Like a child. Accompanied by Trina. I almost declined, thinking I would pretend a headache, but for Mashka's sake I knew I would have to go through with it. I hoped no one noticed me there—the last, extraneous grand duchess, waiting to come of age so she could attend a ball. I remembered when Tatiana had her first ball, and Mashka and I stood on the balcony watching her enter. She was so beautiful. But I couldn't resist the temptation to make some mischief—I was only twelve, after all—and took great pleasure in dropping grains of rice on the coiffed and tiaraed heads below me. I always took care to step back from the railing when people looked up. It was all I could do to control my laughter. Mashka was beside herself with hysterics.

The day of the grand occasion, I helped Mashka prepare, assuring her that she was lovely in her pink gown and that she would outshine every young lady there with her beauty. I kissed her before she went away to be announced, and then made my way to my observation perch above everyone's heads.

It was the tradition for the grand duchess who had come of age to be the last to enter. All the guests down below— there were well over five hundred of them, which was not as many as the two or three thousand who had attended Olga's and Tatiana's debut balls—were turned toward the door, waiting for the master of ceremonies to announce Mashka's entrance. I held my breath, knowing how nervous Mashka was, hoping she would not faint on entering the ballroom.

Mama and Papa stood directly below me, greeting the guests—Princess This, Count That, General the Other— the titles tripped off the tongue so easily. I could hear Papa's rich voice making polite conversation and see my mother's hand shake as she held it out to be kissed. I had almost lost myself in a private reverie, imagining that I was about to make my grand entrance, and that Sasha was waiting to lead me out on the dance floor in a waltz, when I heard the master of ceremonies call out, "Her Imperial Highness, the Grand Duchess Marie Nicholaevna."

I prepared to applaud her entrance, but my hands flew to my mouth instead, when for some reason—Mashka said later it was the fault of her heels—she tripped, at first seeming to float through the air before landing sprawled out on the floor, her tiara rolling across the parquet toward a group of crusty dowagers with their lorgnettes to their eyes.

I gasped, tears springing to my eyes at the thought of Mashka's embarrassment. The entire company hardly breathed. Papa said, "What was that?" and someone next to him whispered in his ear. He looked up and saw an officer helping Mashka to her feet and handing her the wayward tiara. "Hah! Of course! Fat Marie."

I never thought of my father as unkind, but at that moment I realized how little his hopes and dreams were bound up in us, especially his younger daughters. It was only Alexei who mattered. We were simply the grand duchesses, with single adjectives to distinguish us from one another: Lively Olga. Beautiful Tatiana. Fat Marie. Mischievous Anastasie. We were doomed to be what he saw of us, nothing more.

Later that night, when she came in after the dinner and ball was over, Marie cried on my shoulder. I did my best to comfort her, assuring her that no one would remember. "Oh, Nastya!

You know that is the only thing they'll remember. I was mortified. I felt so silly and stupid and awkward."

"But you say you danced every dance!" I said. "Tell me about your partners."

She sniffed and shrugged, wiping her eyes on her lacy handkerchief. "Most of them danced with me because they felt obligated, I think."

"But not all of them?"

"No," she said, looking shyly down to where she traced the outline of a flower on the counterpane. "One of them danced with me three times."

"Who was it?" I asked, wanting to enjoy her night secondhand at least, even if I could not have been there myself.

"It was a young guard. In the Semyonovsky."

I froze. I had not seen Sasha there. With his eye patch, he was easy to spot. But he could have been in the back somewhere. I braced myself. "What was his name?"

"Count Boris Alexandrovich Volkonsky."

I let out my breath. It wasn't Sasha after all. That would have been unbearable. "What did you talk about?"

"Nothing much. But he asked if he might call on me."

"Oh, Mashka! How exciting! What did you say?" The idea of Mashka having a suitor was too strange and wonderful.

"I said I would ask Mama. And I did."

"Well?"

Mashka looked away again. "She said, 'perhaps when the war is over, or when I'm feeling better, or when the moon turns blue. . . .'" A note of bitterness crept into her voice. I took her hand.

"It doesn't seem fair."

"No. But she's right. What right have I to happiness when so many are suffering?"

I couldn't answer her. I too felt the gathering threat around us. I thought then that it was just the war, just the enemy outside Russia that pressed so on my heart. I would soon enough learn otherwise.

Soon enough turned out to be little more than a month later, when we traveled to Novgorod that December. The reception we got was not just lukewarm, it verged on being openly hostile. I didn't really know why just then. But I could see by the expression in Isa's eyes that everyone except Mama noticed. No one made an effort to talk to her at the tea we were given, which suited Mama because she was so shy. There were no happy crowds waiting to greet us—again, my mother was not disappointed about that since crowds always make her nervous. Toward the end of our visit to the ancient city of churches, we went to call on a *staritsa*, an elderly mystic, over one hundred years old. On seeing my mother she said, "Here is the martyr Empress Alexandra." Her words sent a chill down my spine. Mama and my sisters didn't seem to hear her, though, and I never brought it up.

When we returned to Tsarskoe Selo, things really became strange. It started with well-meaning letters to Mama. I was on hand to witness her response to one in particular that arrived while her guard was down because she was worried about Alexei, who had fallen ill again. A servant brought in an envelope on a salver late one afternoon while we were all gathered with her for tea. She must have been too exhausted to consider whether she should accept it, and opened it without thinking in front of us all.

I watched her face pale and the blood drain from her lips as she read it, a lengthy letter scribbled on scraps of paper. Before reaching the end of it, she let the sheets fall from her fingers to the floor and covered her mouth. Tatiana was at her side in an instant, followed by Olga and Mashka. I went too, but my goal was to pick up the letter—my sisters were doing a good enough job comforting our mother, who in any case would rather be tended by them than by me. I quickly took in what I could before having to return the letter to Mama.

> . . . As one who has remained faithful to the Imperial Crown, I felt it my duty to inform Your Imperial Majesty of the deep resentment and anger against you that is prevalent throughout society and among the people. You are reviled not only for your haughtiness and lack of concern for the state of the government, but for your evil influence over the tsar's decisions, caused largely by your infatuation with the charlatan, Rasputin, whose partisanship for Protopopov is well known . . .

The letter continued in this vein, accusing my mother— or rather, telling her she had been accused by others—of the most disgusting and debasing crimes. My initial reaction was anger. Mama had not a wicked bone in her body, and had always tried to serve her family and Russia. And yet, I couldn't help remembering what Sasha had told me of the way her actions and behavior had been misinterpreted by those who didn't know her. It was unfair, but sadly understandable.

The secret police discovered who had written the letter, and I heard later that the lady was sent away from court to her country estates. But there were other letters and even more dreadful insinuations. While it might have been easy to disregard one or two bitter attacks, they became so numerous that eventually members of our own family came to plead with Mama and Papa to pay more attention to what the people thought, and take measures to act differently.

We hadn't seen our Grandmama, the dowager empress, since the beginning of the war. She was a great favorite with us and with all of Russia. She was able to do everything Mama was not. She was charming and sociable, and knew just what to say to everyone so that they would not gossip about her or get the wrong idea. I don't think she ever really liked Mama. I believe every time she came to visit she criticized her in some way or other.

In any case, things had reached such a terrible state that Grandmama swept in one day unannounced and stormed into Papa's study. She was always lecturing him about something, but usually she took him on long walks or was discreet and quiet so that we would not hear. Not this time, though. She didn't even close the door to Papa's study before she tore into him in a way that only his mother would have dared. I, of course, stood near enough to hear but far enough away so as not to be noticed.

"How can you remain so blind, Nicky!"

"Blind to what exactly, Mama?" Papa's voice was always a little pinched when he had to respond to Grandmama's criticism.

"Oh, honestly! Can you not see that Alexandra is ruining you? Everyone at court hates her. They think she has you wrapped around her finger, and that all the decisions you make are at her behest."

"Sunny? No one would credit such a vile rumor!"

Grandmama began to pace up and down. I could hear her petticoats swish. "But they already do! Can you not see it? You must give in to some of the demands of the Duma, show that you are willing to compromise, or all will be lost."

"Mother!" Papa's voice sounded shocked. "I cannot believe that you of all people would suggest that I should yield to the radical elements and relinquish my power into the hands of . . ."—he struggled to find the words—"petty revolutionaries. Bolsheviks. Anarchists!"

"The Duma, my son, is your last chance for survival. You will not have this choice next time."

"Thank you, Mother. I have always known I could count on your support."

I had gradually crept closer so I wouldn't miss a word. I didn't expect their interview to end so quickly, but obviously Grandmama decided she could make no more headway with Papa, and strode toward the door. I hid around a corner as quickly as I could so that she would not see me as she flounced out of Papa's study.

Despite their disagreement, we all had dinner together that night. From Grandmama's expression and lively conversation no one would ever have known the real reason for her visit. Only Papa gave any hint that there had been the slightest unpleasantness. He seemed remote from us, and even if I hadn't heard their conversation, it was easy enough to guess from long experience that he had received a stinging lecture from her.

Grandmama wasn't the only one who tried to talk Papa into granting some of the Duma's requests. The British ambassador, Sir George Buchanan, visited Papa one day. He had always been a good friend to Mama and Papa, and they liked him well enough to invite him to family occasions once in a while. We all liked him too. He was funny and enjoyed playing tricks on us. He also always let us win when we played draughts or cards—a sure way to recommend himself to us.

But that day when he arrived and was shown to Papa's study, he didn't stay very long. That was quite unusual. Normally he would have been asked to tea at least. What's more, he left without even greeting Mama. I couldn't imagine what had happened.

After supper, it all became clear.

"I had a visit from Sir George today," Papa said, putting his napkin on the table and pushing his chair back a little—a sign to the waiters to clear the dishes. "I regret to say that, to my complete surprise, he is no longer loyal. He admitted to me quite brazenly that he treats with our enemies!"

"Surely he has not been conspiring with the Germans!" Mama said, her hand clutching the diamond pendant at her throat.

"Not our enemies abroad," Papa said, "our enemies at home. He admitted as much to me. He has had discussions with the most radical factions of the Duma. How can I trust him anymore?"

A gossiping, ambitious society hostess might well exaggerate and be untrustworthy. But Sir George? I exchanged a look with Mashka. We liked Sir George. I could not believe that he would deliberately mislead Papa or work against our family.

After that, he never came to visit us again. I was sorry. It felt like a door closing.

❧

I think of that winter with such a mixture of feelings. All around us confusing and terrible things were happening. But within me, in my body, I was finally outgrowing my childishness. I began to develop a womanly shape, although the clothes I still wore hid it. It was almost as if Grigory's hands themselves had been prophetic, reaching not for what had been there at the time, but for what he somehow knew was soon to blossom.

Papa was away at the front, and in one of the letters he wrote to Mama, he gave permission for us to bathe in his special bathing tub. This was an enormous treat, because his tub was more like an indoor pool, set in a room like a Turkish bath. Olga and Tatiana each had a turn, then Mashka and I took ours together—there was more than enough room.

We didn't often share baths, so we hadn't seen each other naked for a long time. I had become accustomed to my own new body, but somehow had preserved a memory of Mashka as a little girl with smooth skin and tiny pink nipples on her flat chest. When we removed our robes to get into the water, we each stopped for a moment and stared. I could see by her eyes that she was just as startled at me as I was at her. She had developed round hips that reminded me of some of the paintings in our palaces by Rubens and other masters. She was still a little plump, but in a completely different way than she had been as a child.

"Look at you, Nastya!" Mashka said. "When did you become such a woman?"

"You just didn't notice because I'm still wearing children's clothing." I couldn't help smiling. I knew my breasts were nicely rounded and I was just developing actual hips. I didn't quite have Mashka's curves, but that didn't matter.

Of course, once we dipped ourselves in the warm, scented water of Papa's pool, we were just like fish, diving beneath the surface and turning somersaults underwater, seeing each other and holding our breath until we had to push off the tiled bottom and break through to the air again. How we laughed! We all wrote to Papa to thank him for allowing us such a treat. For me, it was worth everything to have at least one member of my family recognize that I had changed. I was no longer a little girl.

Mashka must have said something to Mama, because the very next morning Mme Zanotti came to our bedroom followed by a maid, and began emptying my wardrobe of all my clothes. "You're to have these old ones of Olga's for now," she said, laying out a few skirts, blouses, and sweaters. "A new dress and a new skirt are to be made for you."

She took my measurements as I stood barefoot on the cold floor of the room, and as quickly as she had come in, she was gone again. I smiled at Mashka. A maid helped me wind my hair into a knot and put it up, instead of letting it hang down below my waist. When we met the others for breakfast in our dining room, they all pretended this new way of dressing was entirely normal. I couldn't help casting my eye around us all sitting there, looking like young women together.

But that was one brief pause in the looming crisis. And as I had always expected in my heart—I'm not entirely certain why—it came by means of Rasputin. I said I never saw him again after that time he visited. And I didn't. But we certainly heard of him in the most distressing way.

We had all been protected from knowing the true depth of feeling against Rasputin among not only the public, but also among the members of the government and the nobility. This tide of bad feeling had reached a fever pitch—and although I was wary of Rasputin, I had no idea to what lengths people might go to end his supposed influence over Mama and Papa.

I found out the details much later from Sasha.

Soon after Christmas, Prince Yusupov, one of the highest-ranking nobles, and Grand Duke Dmitri Pavlovich, one of my father's own cousins, were joined by a man called Purishkevich, who was a member of the Duma. Together they lured Rasputin to the prince's house, saying there would be a party. Grigory believed them and as was apparently his usual practice, drank a great deal. He did not know that they had poisoned his wine. Unfortunately, the poison they used had an antidote: alcohol. Rasputin still lived. When they realized their first plan did not work, they shot him several times, and then threw him in a hole in the Neva, which was frozen over. His body surfaced several days later. Apparently even the many shots fired at him failed to kill him, as he was frozen in an attitude as if trying to make the sign of the cross.

Anya was the one who brought us the news initially, on a day when Mama was receiving ladies and hearing their requests for help with their charities. I don't know how Mama continued on, but she did not allow herself to grieve until we were behind closed doors, just the family and Anya.

"It is all hopeless now! My poor boy! Only our friend could cure him!" Mama wailed and wept on Anya's shoulder. We all tried to comfort her, but she would not be consoled. "You know, he told me that when he went, that would be the end of us as well. And I believe him! All is lost. No one else can intervene with God for our safety."

Tatiana brought Mama a cup of tea. Mama all at once pushed herself away from Anya and grasped her shoulders. "My dear Anninka! You are not safe. If they have murdered Rasputin and they think you were his agent, they will try to murder you!"

"Hush, Alex," Anya said. "What would they want with a poor crippled woman like me?"

"Humor me, Anya," Mama said. "You must move into the palace, for your safety. There have been threats, you know, against all of us."

I could not help myself and gasped. I had not heard before of any such threats. Mashka covered up my gasp with a cough.

"The murderers must be punished! They must be put to death!" I had never heard Mama sound so fierce. But she believed completely that only Grigory could keep Alexei healthy. And now he was gone.

I felt curiously revolted by the whole idea of his death, and yet also free, as if some vague shadow over our life had been removed. Although I had never experienced Grigory's faith in the way my mother had, I had to admit that there was something of the sorcerer about him, that he could do nothing and somehow Alyosha would get better. This was enough to cloud any feeling I had that his death was good. What, indeed, would we do now when Alexei hurt himself or had an attack?

In the end, the murderers were only banished, not executed. Mama was very angry, but Papa refused to sentence such high-ranking nobles to death. With Papa's blessing, Mama had Rasputin's body brought to be buried near the chapel at the Alexander Palace. She and Anya went often to his grave to pray.

That may have been one of Papa's last true decisions as tsar. Perhaps there were numerous smaller matters he had to attend to, and for a while he was still the commander-in-chief of the armies. But no other gesture remains so fixed in my mind. Mama was right. It was the turning point.

January changed the year to 1917. The year of my coming-of-age. In other times, it would have been joyful. But 1917 became a year I thought would never end. It began with terrible shortages of food in the cities. The railway lines and all available transport had been concentrated on the war effort, and Prime Minister Protopopov had mismanaged the food distribution terribly, or so Papa said. But Russia was enormous, and to the people nearly starving in the streets of Petrograd and Moscow, a far-off war with Germany seemed a much less pressing concern than filling their bellies. We too limited our own rations, and gave what relief we could—which wasn't a great deal. The Americans had entered the war, yet in the end we didn't get very much news of them. We had troubles at home that eclipsed all other matters. Troubles very near to home indeed.

# CHAPTER 13

*I have to see you. It's important—for your safety and that of your family. Meet me by the oak tree at noon.*

He didn't sign the note that came to my hands from a scullery maid's, who had been given it by an undergardener, who had probably received it from someone else. He didn't sign it, but I knew it was from Sasha. My heart leaped at first. I hadn't seen him for nearly a year. And that year had been one in which I had changed so much. I knew some of the guards had come back, the reserves, to help with the unrest in the streets. Perhaps he had come back to stay for good.

After I got over my initial joy that I would see him, I thought about what the note actually said. What could he know that would have to do with our safety? And why was our safety suddenly such a concern?

In the tense, preoccupied atmosphere of the Alexander

Palace, where nothing was quite the same since Rasputin's murder, it was not difficult for me to get away at the appointed time. As always, because I was the youngest grand duchess no one paid much attention to me. The secret police kept their unceasing vigil primarily on Mama, even following her to the chapel for prayers. I knew because we children had made a game of figuring out which of the servants or visitors were from the Okhrana. It had been Alyosha's idea, that game, when he was convalescing after one of his attacks and couldn't get up and play. We would all report to him what and who we saw and construct our little counterespionage. I got rather good at spotting the Okhrana, which made me think they weren't very good at their job.

This childish game also helped me avoid being seen by the secret police, and I think was partly responsible for my ability to keep my secret about Sasha. To give myself a reason to walk in the garden on a cold, dreary day, I pretended that I was look-ing for a place to build a snowman that Alyosha would be able to see from his playroom windows—which happened to be on the opposite side of the palace from Mama and Papa's suite of rooms.

As I left the palace and walked out of the courtyard itself, I told myself not to run like a schoolgirl. If I wanted Sasha to view me differently, he would have to see that I could walk in a dignified and purposeful manner.

I saw him before he saw me. I paused, just to look at him for a moment. He appeared taller, and his face was set in a serious expression that made him look as though he had seen many terrible things in his life—which I knew he had. But somehow being with him erased all that for me. I wanted to cry looking at him then. Only the merest hint of the boy with the balalaika remained inside his crisp, clean uniform and erect stance. I lifted my chin and walked forward, putting a smile on my face. "Sasha," I said, "So good to see you."

He turned toward me, at first with a look of complete blankness and then his eye widened in surprise, and a smile spread over his features. There was the Sasha I knew! "Nastya! Or should I say Anastasia Nicholaevna?" He bowed gallantly. I couldn't help laughing.

"Still Nastya, I assure you!"

I stopped about an arm's length in front of him. He removed his cap, and I put out my hand to shake his. He took it, but instead of shaking it, he turned it over and kissed the patch of skin just above my glove. "I'm sorry, but I can't get over . . ."

Sasha was at a loss for words! I was so pleased. I knew I had changed, but of course it was a gradual change to me.

"Did anyone see you coming? Did you tell anyone?" Sasha asked, shaking himself out of his momentary stupor.

"No, of course not," I said. He still held my hand. "I'm delighted to see you, and glad that you are safe," I said, "which I would never have known for all that you bothered to write to me!" I jerked my hand away in pretended pique, but really, the contact with him began to make me feel a little nervous, uncertain of myself.

He immediately reached out and took both my hands in his, gripping them so hard that the ring I wore on the middle finger of my right hand dug into me. I ignored the pain.

"Nastya, there is no time to play games. I have made some

new friends, friends who are not of one mind with the tsar." I noticed then that his face was leaner, sharper. And I realized that in seeing him again, I hardly noticed the patch over his eye. It had simply become one of his features, as much a part of him as his nose or his hair.

I was so caught up in taking in all the ways that Sasha had changed that I realized I hadn't comprehended what he had said. "Are you saying that you are a traitor?" I asked, wondering who these people he'd been talking to were.

"No! No. Everyone who disagrees with the way your father is running this country is not a traitor. I'm no Bolshevik. But I am close enough to others like them to see what is coming."

The fear in his eyes made me more attentive. He had something important to say.

"Your father will be asked to abdicate in favor of the tsarevich."

"Abdicate?" The word simply didn't exist in our vocabulary. Could Papa ever give up his empire? It was unthinkable! "He will never agree! He will never let Russia go."

"It is the only way to avoid civil war. And that would be a disaster for the war against Germany. All would truly be lost." Sasha lowered his voice to an intense whisper and pulled me closer to him so that I could hear.

I forced myself to think about what Sasha said, not the nearness of him, or the smell of his freshly laundered uniform. If Papa were really faced with such a choice, what would he decide? I felt that he would say no. But what then? Perhaps Sasha had got it wrong.

"If he agrees, the tsarevich will be a constitutional monarch, with a regent who is sympathetic to the reformists' cause. If he doesn't agree, the Bolsheviks will strike. There will be anarchy. The only choice is the Duma if we are to preserve Russia as we know and love her."

This was a great deal for me to take in, but it made a certain sense out of the mass of conflicting information we had gotten in bits and pieces over the last months. Perhaps Sir George had talked to my papa about this, and that was why he had been so angry. All those notes and threats against my mother—were they also related to the difficulties that had such a dire solution? "What can I do?" I asked. "Papa pays no attention to me. He wouldn't expect me to know anything."

"Of course you can do nothing. You must simply promise me to be prepared. If your papa does not do exactly as they ask him, matters could take a turn greatly for the worse. And then you must allow me to try to save you."

I couldn't help smiling. What would Sasha need to save me from? "I assure you, there are guards enough to protect us here!"

"Guards that are loyal?"

"Of course!" I responded, angry that he should even question them. Many of the guards had known us since our infancy. We sometimes played with their children. We gave them presents at Christmas and Easter, and acknowledged their name days.

"Well, nonetheless, whatever happens I shall do my best to be nearby, whatever games I must play to do it."

"What could happen? Papa will do what's best, I'm sure."

Sasha looked at me with such sadness. "You're almost a woman now." He looked me up and down. "And yet, still such a little girl."

I blushed and looked at the ground. He let go of both my hands and took one only, in a companionable, brotherly way. "Do you still have my balalaika?" he asked.

"Of course I do! Did you think I would give it away?"

He smiled. "No. I hope you still play it." He began to lead me toward the main path in the garden that would take me back to the palace, and him to his barracks. I felt inexpressibly sad, as if something important had gone unsaid, and we would never again have a chance to say it.

I tried to dispel that sadness and take the familiar, teasing tone I always used with him. "I do. I've become quite good, in fact," I said, smiling. "I wouldn't be surprised if I'm better than you now."

But instead of pinching me or responding with a challenge, as he might have done once, he became serious again and stopped me, just before we would step on the broad avenue where everyone would be able to see us. "I'll tell you what. If you are in real danger and you need me, send a note through one of the servants to the barracks, saying only that you want to return the instrument you borrowed, and I'll know."

"Would I have to give it back then?" I asked, looking up at him impishly.

"Promise me," he answered, taking both my hands in his again, looking as if he wished to say something more. But instead, he just said, "Adieu," and turned away. I watched him until he turned a corner, then went back in to do some more knitting.

⚘

Papa returned to Tsarskoe Selo after the New Year. He looked thin, tired, and ill. It was too much for him to try to command the armies and deal with the troubles in Petrograd and Moscow. We tried to divert him as much as we could. At least his presence cheered Mama up and took many burdens off her shoulders. Ministers constantly streamed into his study, leaving him alone hardly at all. But in the evening Papa still came to take tea with us.

Anya—who had obeyed my mother's request and moved into the Alexander Palace—did her best to lighten everyone's hearts, and I began to alter my opinion of her a little. She included me in all her diversions, making me think that her previous neglect had possibly not been purposeful, just absent-minded. After all, it was Anya who gave me Jimmy, my King Charles spaniel—even if he did make a mess everywhere, and I had to clean it up. Anya was sensitive, just not very intelligent.

Nonetheless, without Anya there, we would have been much duller. She had musical evenings in her apartments to which we were all invited, along with Lili Dehn, Nastinka, and some officers from the *Standart*, Papa's yacht. We all tried to act as though everything was as it had always been. She invited a Rumanian band that entertained us with its multiple balalaikas, but every song they performed was so sad, reminding us of a Russia that seemed very far away just then. I couldn't help thinking of our holidays in the Crimea, how carefree they seemed, how happy the Tartars were and what amusements we had. Something told me those days were gone forever. I'm not much one for crying, but even I felt an unaccustomed tug at my throat while the musicians played. As for Mama and Papa, they grew sadder and sadder by the moment.

After that, Anya invited livelier musicians to play, or organized evenings of bezique or faro. At the times when Papa was there, we felt like a family again.

But even with all our effort, we could not ignore the constant rumblings of disquiet outside the palace. Olga asked Papa about his command of the armies one evening, and we all expected him to say that he would soon be returning to Mogilev with Alyosha. But instead he said, "I have been advised . . . I believe . . . that it is more important for me to stay here at Tsarskoe Selo than return to the front. Much is happening with the government, and we have better men in command now. It's vital that we have the unflagging support of all Russians in order to vanquish our foreign foes."

We took him at his word, and expected that he would be with us for a long time. Mama was visibly relieved, and even regained some of her strength to go and visit the hospitals. But one afternoon after dinner Papa came into Mama's boudoir, where I sat reading while Isa was taking instructions from Mama about the *sklady* on the southern front.

Papa looked annoyed and a little confused. "They insist I depart immediately for Mogilev!" he exclaimed, waving a telegram. He paced back and forth, talking all the while. "I cannot understand what is suddenly so urgent that I must leave matters here in a dangerous—"

"Hush, Nicky!" my mother said, glancing in my direction. I had looked up, but I immediately pretended to pay the most rapt attention to the book whose pages I had only been skimming before.

"Nonetheless, it is a bad time. But I suppose I must go."

Mama sighed and reached out her hand to him. "Aren't you the tsar, darling? Can't you give the orders?"

He frowned. "I'm not obeying orders. I'm responding to the situation, which is clear."

Mama stood and approached Papa. "Don't stay away a moment longer than you have to," she said, drawing him to her. He kissed the top of her head.

I often thought of that moment in the coming weeks.

# CHAPTER 14

While Papa was gone to headquarters, Mama did something I had not known her to do in a very long time. Because of her shyness and her frequent illnesses, Mama only attended state functions when she had to. But something must have spurred her to push herself. She held two diplomatic receptions, one after the other on two days in early March. She invited all the foreign ambassadors and their assistants. Although I was not yet officially of age, I was allowed to go with my three sisters, I think because Mama needed the support of her entire family. I don't remember very much specifically about those occasions except that they weren't like balls, and there were no young officers waiting to ask a grand duchess to dance. So other than stand by and smile, enjoying the feeling of the long gown that Mashka had worn to her debut, and that only had to be taken in a little so that I could wear it, I kept my eyes trained on Mama.

She was calmer than I had seen her for a long time. She had something to say to each of the guests, and I could read the surprise on everyone's faces when she turned out not to be a haughty schemer but a gentle, interested lady. It was just like occasions I remembered watching from afar when I was little: the master of ceremonies, servants in satin livery with gold lace, and runners wearing feathered caps. I imagine the diplomats, who weren't all from countries as wealthy as Russia, must have been very impressed.

We heard about the strikes in Petrograd, of course, but all of us—Mama included—thought they would be resolved as soon as the government was able to get more food into the people's hands. Protopopov had come several times to the palace to assure Mama that this was so.

Then, in our own private world, disaster struck.

My sisters and Alyosha and I were playing a game in his playroom, which consisted of trying to shoot each other with very realistic toy pistols.

"Bang! I think I killed you, Alyosha," I said. My brother stopped and was about to pretend to fall down, when his face became very pale. All of us stopped what we were doing at once.

"Are you unwell?" Tatiana asked as we rushed over to him as a group.

"I don't feel good," he said. He was almost white. I immediately thought he was having one of his attacks.

"Do you have pain anywhere?" I asked, getting ready to fetch Nagorny from the next room, where we had banished him during our game.

"All over. I can't stand up."

He slid to the floor.

"Nagorny!" I screamed and within an instant the sailor was with us.

"He's burning up with fever!" he said.

"I'll fetch Mama," Tatiana said.

"Olga, we should get Dr. Botkin." I hadn't realized how quiet Olga was until I noticed that she was sitting in a chair and looking very pale herself.

"I feel rather peculiar," she said. I went over and felt her forehead. It was very hot.

"I think you're sick too. Come, I'll help you to your room."

"I'm just too tired to walk," she said.

"You can't stay here. Come."

Nagorny had already carried Alyosha away, and Olga leaned on my shoulder so I could support her to her room. Dr. Botkin came and visited both of them, and what he said surprised us all.

"Alexei is not having one of his attacks." The doctor paused to sip his tea while Mama, Tatiana, Isa, Nastinka, and I waited for him to continue. "It's measles. And it will make its way through all the susceptible very quickly. I suggest you make an infirmary so that when they succumb, the others can be tended easily alongside their family."

I didn't know whether to laugh or cry. Mama looked relieved at first, then switched into her nursing mode. Within another day or two, Tatiana and Anya were also sick. That left only Mashka and I who had not had measles, and the other members of the suite, who had. We did what we could to help

Mama, knowing that at some point we'd be occupying the remaining two beds in the infirmary.

During a brief respite, Mama and I were sitting in her boudoir with Isa, reading letters. Nastinka, who would normally have been there too, had gone away to tend to a sick relative.

"Isa," Mama said, as she rested on a couch with a moist cloth on her forehead, "I must not ignore my friends at this time. It is vital that I help my husband at least insofar as I can. Please, telephone Mme Sazonova and ask her to come to lunch at the palace today."

The baroness nodded and sat at the telephone table, waiting for the exchange to put her through to the wife of one of our chief generals. I wasn't really paying attention at first, but something in the expression on Isa's face caused both Mama and I to sit up and watch her end of the conversation.

"I see. No! It cannot be . . . Truly? I—we had no idea. Yes, yes, of course I'll tell the empress. Immediately."

She replaced the phone in its cradle and held on to the mouthpiece for a while, as if trying to draw some strength from it. I always liked Isa. She was intelligent and kind, and devoted to Mama. But she also treated her court appointment as what it was—a job. She was always businesslike and practical, and one knew that if she said something, it wasn't idle gossip or exaggerated to make an effect.

When she turned her wide, frightened eyes upon us, I felt a chill deep inside. "She says she cannot come."

"What are you saying, Isa? What has happened?" Mama stood now and walked over to her.

"She says that it would be impossible for her to reach the station. The—the Preobrazhensky Guards have mutinied. As have the Pavlovsky and the Volinsky regiments. Last night. They're shooting outside with machine guns."

Mama was silent for a moment. Then, in a calm voice, she said, "Fetch Colonel Grooten to me. Perhaps it is not so bad as it sounds."

Isa left to do as Mama said. I sat holding my breath, hoping she would forget I was there so that I might hear what the colonel had to say. She sat at the desk and scribbled a note. Within minutes, the colonel and Isa had returned.

"Tell me. Spare nothing. I need to know."

Colonel Grooten had always been a strong, kind man. But I could see that he was nervous talking to Mama then. "What precisely do you know, Your Majesty?" he asked, listening closely while Mama told him what Mme Sazonova had said on the telephone.

When she finished, she asked, "Is it true? How can this be and I not know of it?" Mama seemed more angry than frightened.

"I wanted to tell you, only—" He stopped himself, as if he didn't want to get someone else in trouble. "All I can say is that yes, indeed, it is true. We have been aware of the troubles for some time, and keeping a close watch on developments. Only certain of the regiments have mutinied. The palace guard and the Semyonovsky are still utterly loyal. There is nothing to be concerned about. The emperor has already sent troops to help the police restore order."

What he said seemed to reassure my mother. Perhaps, with

her children and dearest friend so ill, she wanted to believe whatever good she could. But I could see that the colonel was hiding something. "Please send this telegram to the tsar," Mama said to Isa. I breathed a sigh of relief, expecting that within a few hours as usual, a telegram would come from Papa explaining everything and telling us that all would be well.

But no telegram arrived. Our dinner that night was quiet and tense. At every little sound, Mama expected the arrival of a message. Yet nothing came, and eventually we all went to bed.

Mama returned to her nursing the next day, but I had a strange ache in my head. I thought at first it was only my anxious worry about what was going on in Petrograd, and the horrifying thought that the guard regiments had mutinied. But by that evening, to my annoyance, I had become ill with the measles too. While so many dramatic events occurred over the next week, I was only dimly aware of them. My fever rose and fell, the sores came and went. Mashka remained well for a few days longer before she too was stricken, and so she witnessed much that she was able to tell me later.

What I do remember clearly, though, was Mama coming into our sickroom to tell us that the guards were practicing maneuvers, and we mustn't be frightened if we heard gunshots. It seemed odd to me that they would do such a thing at night, but in the half-light of my sickness, the odd felt almost normal.

I later discovered that Mama told us this after Isa had given her the distressing news: now the Composites themselves had mutinied and were on their way to the palace to seize her and Alexei.

Mashka was with Mama the whole time. I didn't hear about what had happened until the day after, when Mashka came to my bedside and whispered to me, "Count Apraxin and Count Benckendorff have come to stay at the palace and help us. Mama sent for them and requested that they ensure that the palace guard be instructed not to fire on the mutineers. She did not want any blood shed on her account.

"Mama took me down to the basement to meet with the guards as they came in to warm themselves in groups. I was afraid, but Mama didn't seem to be.

"We went from room to room, talking to all the guards, Mama telling them that she knew they would be loyal to her, but that they mustn't fire on the mutineers. There was to be no shooting. All would be well if only they did not shoot.

"After that, we went outside. It was dark. The only light was from the snow, and all I could see was the metal on the guards' rifles in the courtyard, all twelve hundred of them. It was quite a sight, Nastya! There they were, in battle order, the first row kneeling with their rifles aimed, the others standing behind them. They were so still, they looked like Alexei's lead soldiers."

"Where were all the servants during this?" I asked.

"They vanished. One moment they were here, the next—gone. Mama's staff remains, though, of course. But they cannot do everything."

"But the attack. We're here, so it must not have happened." I was confused. I could understand what she was saying, but I was just ill enough not to be able to put it all together.

"I don't know what stopped it. No one fired a single shot."

"And so?" I asked.

"We have heard that Papa is on his way back to us at last. His train was held up, though, and Mama is so anxious I fear she will make herself very ill. She telephoned Uncle Paul, who is supposed to be in charge of the defense of Petrograd. I heard them talking. Mama yelled at him, called him incompetent for leaving no better than factory worker reservists available to counter what is clearly becoming a revolution."

I think the word "revolution" was the last thing I heard her say before sinking into something between sleep and semi-consciousness. All I know is that it seemed as if no time at all passed before she came back.

"Has Papa returned?" I asked, dredging up from my memory something she had said last time we spoke.

"No."

I couldn't understand it. "Why not?" I asked.

"They keep promising he will come and then there are delays. But you'll never guess what happened today," she said, taking a quick look around to make sure Olga and Tatiana were asleep. "A deputation came, with a paper for Mama to sign. It was a manifesto, granting a constitution. Mama was furious. She said, 'Me? You want me to sign this? On what authority?' 'You are the tsaritsa,' Uncle Paul said. And she answered, 'But I have no authority! I am not the tsar. If I sign this, I will be doing precisely what they accuse me of, and that I have not done.' And she has refused to sign."

"Mashka," I said, having only vaguely comprehended her news, "You must do something for me."

"You know I'll do anything, darling," she said, taking the cloth off my brow and soaking it in fresh, cool water.

I pulled myself as upright as I could and gripped her arm. "You must get a message to the Semyonovsky barracks. It's for Alexander Mickhailovich Galliapin. Write that I want to return his balalaika." I lay back, exhausted from the effort.

"I don't know, Nastya! In these times, it seems rather silly."

"I can't explain." My mind was becoming foggy again after such a long stretch of concentration. I just hoped she would see that I meant it and do as I asked.

❧

The next day brought even more changes. I heard the band and the drums outside, and begged Mashka to tell me what was happening.

"The Garde Equipage has been recalled to Petrograd."

"The colors are leaving the palace?" I asked, not really able to believe it. The standards of the guard regiments that flew wherever we were in residence were to go away. It was to be as if we were not there anymore.

"Has Papa returned yet?"

"No. Not yet."

"Where is he?" I felt the tears start in my eyes. It was the illness. Normally I never cried. I had begun to feel a bit better but was still very weak. "How are Olga and Tatiana doing?" I asked.

"They are still not well. Tatiana has abscesses in her ears, and Olga has developed pericarditis."

Why was God doing this to us? Weren't there enough troubles without all this sickness in our family? "At least you are well," I said. Mashka smiled, but not with her usual cheerfulness.

No time seemed to pass before the next day, when Mashka joined us in the sickroom. Her fever was so high she was delirious. Lili Dehn took over her place as mother's nurse-helper, and I then had to persuade her to tell me what was going on.

"There's nothing any of us can do now, especially when we're sick," Lili said.

"But I must know!" I cried. "I can't bear it."

She sighed deeply, pulling a chair up to my bedside. "Your father was intercepted at Pskov, where a delegation met with him. They told him that the only way to avoid civil war was to abdicate in favor of the tsarevich."

"He did not do it!" I exclaimed. Sasha's words echoed in my mind. But Lili's downcast eyes told me otherwise.

"Not exactly everything they asked. He refused to give the tsarevich to them, saying that at least they might grant him his family."

"So . . . Papa is . . ."

"No longer the tsar."

"Then who is?" I could not imagine Russia without a tsar. It was inconceivable.

"He gave the crown to the Grand Duke Michael."

That could have been much worse, I remember thinking. Things would change, but the empire would survive. The Romanov dynasty. Yet Lili still did not look happy.

"What? What more is there to tell me?"

"We have just been told that your uncle has refused to reign. There will be no tsar, only a provisional government until something can be decided."

I closed my eyes against the news. I could not fathom what it would mean. It was too much to take in at once. When I am well, I thought, I shall think about it then.

By the time Papa was able to come home after many delays, I was strong enough to get out of bed. It felt very odd the first time I dressed and walked—feeling rather wobbly—to my mother's boudoir. It didn't take very long, though, to see that much had changed.

The first thing I noticed was the difference in the palace guard. Soldiers from the First, Second, Third, and Fourth Rifles came to replace the Composites, who simply didn't exist anymore. The new guards were very different from the ones we used to have, some more than others. Their uniforms were sloppy, they slouched at their posts, and they didn't really seem to have any officers, although Zhilik told me that the officers were supposed to have been elected by the men. No one showed Papa much respect, and we were likely to come upon soldiers wandering the halls at any time.

At first, I was more bewildered than anything else. It was as if I had fallen ill in one world and awakened in another, where everything was upside down.

"Where did all the servants go?" I asked Tatiana one morning as we sewed in Mama's boudoir, with Alexei looking at a large photograph album.

"Most of them ran away when they heard the news of Papa's abdication, and that the soldiers had mutinied." We spoke in hushed tones; I mouthed the words so Tatiana would understand me despite the fact that she was nearly deaf in one ear because of the abscesses they had to drain. So long as we were quiet and secretive about it, it seemed as if we could keep everything at bay. Saying the words out loud would make the changes all too real.

"Why are there so many soldiers around the palace?"

"Mama was arrested."

I gasped. "Arrested? Why?" It seemed so odd to have her calmly sitting as she was when the Provisional Government had basically accused her of being a criminal.

"They say she is a traitor, that she conspired with Grigory against Russia."

"It is time for your lessons, Anastasie," my mother said, interrupting our muted conversation before I had time to comprehend what Tatiana told me.

"Must I yet?" I asked. "Can't I have a few days just to rest?"

"Come, Anastasie. We can do some drawing today." Trina had risen on Mama's cue and held out her hand to me as she had when I was ten. I knew she meant to be kind, but I felt quite angry about being dismissed to the schoolroom. Doubtless Mama wanted me to go away so she could talk to Tatiana about things she thought I was too young to hear. But I didn't want to make a scene, so I went with Trina—without taking her hand. As soon as we reached the schoolroom I took out my drawing pad and pencils and sketched a soldier I could see from the window, who was asleep at his post.

After a long silence I asked Trina, "Who is left here? Please tell me. I know what's going on."

"Do you indeed?" Trina said, not really asking a question.

"Yes. I do. I know Papa had to abdicate, and Mama has been arrested. Now I'd be grateful if you would stop treating me like a baby and tell me the rest." I laid down my pad and pencil, crossed my arms over my chest, and put my feet up on another chair.

Trina looked quite uncomfortable, but she did as I asked. "There is your family of course," she began. "And M. Gilliard, although they won't let Mr. Gibbes in because he was at the Catherine Palace in his apartments when the arrest was made, and since then they've been strictly controlling who may come and go. So Alexei's lessons have been somewhat curtailed. Baroness Buxhoeveden, Lili Dehn, Countess Hendrikova, Count Fredericks, Count Benckendorff, Count Apraxin . . ." She stopped to think for a moment. "And oh yes, Prince Dolgorukov has come to stay with your papa. And Anna Demidova is still here to take care of your mama, along with Dr. Botkin and Dr. Derevenko, and the maid Madeleine Zanotti. Then there are the officers . . ." She held up her fingers, counting off the members of the household, who were once too numerous to list in that way. ". . . General Voyeikov and Colonel Grooten, and the valets—Chemodurov, Volkov, Sedner. There are enough cooks and footmen to do for us, as well as the barber, butler, and wine steward. The faithful servants have remained."

And I knew that Anya was in the sickroom, having gotten measles herself and still suffering from them terribly.

As I continued to gaze out the window, I saw Papa and Prince Dolgorukov walking in the garden. Papa looked small next to the tall, thin prince with his clipped mustache. The prince had a way of loping elegantly, like a wolfhound. Papa took about one and a half steps to every one of the prince's, yet somehow he managed to look more regal and remain unhurried. They were followed by a motley group of half a dozen soldiers who kept right behind them whichever way they turned. How could Papa stand it? I thought. He loved to take his exercise outdoors. Now he had to wait for the soldiers to accompany him.

I felt very alone while Mashka was still sick. I went to sit by her and read to her, but she was often delirious with fever. At those times, I would tell her all my secrets, as one would do with a favorite doll, feeling the relief of getting them off my chest, and the security of knowing they would go no further. I told her about Sasha, and how worried I was about him, that he had kissed me once, although sometimes I thought he still considered me a child. I wished I could have seen Sasha then, for things to go back to the way they had been. But I realized that would never happen.

In fact, the more we tried to pretend everything was normal, the stranger it all became. One morning I went into Mama's sitting room to find her kneeling by the fire, her correspondence scattered around her in piles. Isa was trying to help her sort it out. Mama was never very organized, but I had never seen a mess like that.

"What are you doing?" I asked.

"Paul—Count Benckendorff—has advised me to burn all my letters. He says they could be used against me if I am taken away. But I shall only burn the most personal ones. The others I intend to preserve so that my loyalty to Russia and your father's loyalty might be proven by what we wrote to each other while we were tsar and tsaritsa." Every once in a while Mama said or did something that reminded me she had officially been arrested and was a prisoner here in her own home. I tried not to think about the possibility that she might actually be taken away to be tried or imprisoned. It was inconceivable.

Mama stopped what she was doing and looked around. I thought perhaps she would cry. But instead she just sat silently, very pale, her hands shaking a little. "Be a darling, Nastya, and bring Tatiana to me. You can take her place with Marie and Olga."

It hurt me to be sent away, but I knew that Mama got more comfort from Tatiana's practical presence than from any of the rest of us—not counting Alyosha, of course, who was with Zhilik having his lessons.

I went as Mama asked to the sickroom. It was rather restful in its way. Wherever else they went in the palace, the soldiers never entered the darkened room where the measles sufferers lay.

On my way back to our floor, I saw through a window my father and Prince Dolgorukov setting out on their habitual walk through the park. They were flanked by eight soldiers with their rifles, bayonets fixed. Papa looked so harmless and vulnerable there, wearing a plain coat and a fur hat. They began to take their usual route, but then another soldier came running up and stopped them. I could not hear what was said, but they were turned back, and came trudging dejectedly toward the palace. I gathered they were no longer being allowed the run of the garden. Our garden. It was unbearable.

There was still quite a lot of snow on the ground, and with few servants to care for the grounds anymore, it lay in drifts all around, except on the paths worn by the soldiers, and Papa's daily walks. But what I saw next surprised and saddened me. Papa said something to one of his usual guards, who turned and spoke with the others around him. After some conferring, they apparently agreed on something, and one of them went off in the direction of the stables. A few minutes later he returned bearing two snow shovels. My father and Prince Dolgorukov reached out for them, and to my complete astonishment, began with great energy to shovel the snow from the courtyard area into large mounds.

There was my father, bending his back like the meanest peasant, and yet he looked contented doing it. I moved on, continuing to the sickroom to deliver my message to Tatiana.

🌿

Something about our situation brought the peasant songs of Russia into my head at the oddest moments. Perhaps it was because I no longer felt as if we were royalty living in a palace, but that the walls that separated us from the rest of the world had been torn down. I so wanted to bring out Sasha's balalaika—half glad that Mashka had never conveyed my message to him, for what could he have done anyway?—but I was afraid that it would be taken away from me by the guards, who were suspicious of anything unusual. Once I accidentally created a great furor by sewing next to a window in the evening, and covering and uncovering a red-shaded lamp as I reached for my scissors. The guards burst in with their pistols out in search of the person who was sending a "secret message" out the window. They were a little embarrassed, to be fair, when they discovered what had actually happened. But that didn't stop them.

One morning I heard Joy's excited yapping outside the schoolroom door, and an instant later Alyosha came bounding into our schoolroom and said, "Let's play at being spies. I've got some clever guns in my playroom, and we can wear cloaks and sneak around trying to evade the soldiers."

Except for lesson times, it was very tedious reading and knitting and sewing all day. I knew I was too old for Alexei's silly games, but he so enjoyed them, and it would be fun to try to beat the awful soldiers at their own game. "All right," I said. I put down my book and ran with Alyosha to his playroom, which was bigger than ours, even though there was only one of him and four of us. But it didn't matter, because we all played in both rooms at different times.

As we approached, Joy started growling and baring her teeth. Alyosha opened the door and stopped so suddenly I nearly crashed into him. He grabbed Joy up into his arms to stop her from running in. "What are you doing in my playroom!"

About half a dozen soldiers were methodically going through

all the toy cupboards and chests, turning out their contents onto the floor. They had made a pile of toy guns and other weapons. "We have orders to confiscate all weapons or weapon-like items in the palace," said one whose cheeks flamed red as he said it.

"Weapons!" I cried. "These are toys! What use is there in taking them away?"

A soldier whose uniform was dirty and face unshaven stepped forward slowly, tossing aside Alyosha's favorite stuffed dog as he did so. At that gesture, Joy struggled free of Alyosha's arms and flew at the man, her teeth bared. I knew Joy was in danger if she attacked any of our guards, so I ran forward and took hold of her collar, pulling her back as she struggled to lunge for the soldier.

"I insist you leave this instant," Alyosha said. He could put on quite a commanding voice when he chose to.

The soldier that Joy had almost attacked glowered at Alyosha. "We don't take orders from your papa anymore, and we won't take orders from you. Men, complete the search."

We stood there, helpless, and watched them remove the most harmless of toys, anything with moving parts, including a train that Alyosha especially loved to play with. They threw them all into sacks and gathered in front of us. We were blocking the door.

"You have more toys than a whole city of children," the surly guard said. "There's still plenty for you to amuse yourself with."

He marched forward, forcing us to step out of the way so

they could all pass. Neither Alyosha nor I had the spirits to play after that.

&

The day after Alyosha's toys were taken, we received a visit from Alexander Fyodorovich Kerensky, who Tatiana told me was the minister of justice in the Provisional Government. The guards made a great fuss about the fact that he was coming, and those of us who were not ill had to wait for him in the small parlor the suite had made out of the rooms they were allotted within the palace.

Kerensky entered at exactly the time we were told he would arrive, followed by several guards. He was not a tall man, but stood very straight. His face was sallow and there were bags under his eyes, as if he had not slept for a considerable amount of time. He spoke fast—sounding almost angry—and yet seemed nervous. Papa greeted him with respect that was almost cordial. Mama remained haughty. Kerensky held out his hand to her to shake, but I knew she did not want to touch him. Papa looked at her and she slowly extended her hand in return. She barely let him grasp it before she withdrew it again. Tatiana, Alyosha, and I stood quietly by, listening to every word.

"This is the new commander of the palace, Colonel Korovichenko," Kerensky said. Papa saluted the man who stepped forward, but everyone ignored him. "His men will take a tour of the rooms, and see that the regulations are being obeyed," Kerensky continued. He snapped his fingers, and four more soldiers with rifles and bayonets entered.

At first I didn't recognize Sasha. He wore the uniform not of the Semyonovsky Guards, but of a common soldier. His face was unshaven, and his expression was hard. If it hadn't been for the patch over his eye, I might not have known it was him. I found myself staring at him, until I realized that it would be a mistake to let on that we knew each other at all. With a great effort, I looked away, willing my face not to turn bright red and my heart to slow its pumping.

"Make sure there are no weapons or counterrevolutionary propaganda in the palace," Kerensky told them. They turned to leave, but not before I caught the quickest glint of an expression in Sasha's eyes. He acknowledged me. That was something. But what was he doing here?

"Are you all right, Nastya? Perhaps you should still be in bed," Tatiana whispered, taking my hand. "You're trembling!"

I shook my head. "I'm all right," I whispered back. I shuddered to think of these men searching Mashka's and my room, finding the hidden balalaika and making Sasha take it away.

We heard their heavy boots on the parquet hallways as they marched off. Kerensky turned to my parents. "The ex-tsaritsa is under investigation for anti-Russian activities." I saw my father stiffen and his face turn red. Mama just became paler and paler. "I am instructed to remove all correspondence from your possession. If you will accompany the colonel."

Papa went with Colonel Korovichenko and the two remaining guards to his study. I soon saw soldiers passing the doorway of the parlor with boxes and boxes of papers. I knew that some of them were family photographs and letters Papa had received from us on those rare occasions when we were not together—something that had happened only when he was commander of the armies.

While Papa was gone, Kerensky spoke directly to Mama. "I thought you would be pleased to learn that I have abolished the death penalty." A quiver went through Mama's frame, as if his saying that had some direct bearing upon her. "I hear from the soldiers that Mme Vyrubova is still here in the palace. She is a traitor to Russia."

"Anya is no such thing!" Mama said. She would not raise her voice in her own defense, but let someone she loved be accused and she sprang at the accuser like a lioness.

"That is for the court to decide. We are going to arrest her."

"We are all under arrest here, as I understand, M. Kerensky." Mama's voice was even but tense.

"She must go before the court. I have orders to remove her from the palace."

"But she is very ill! She is still in her sickbed."

"Does a doctor attend her?"

"Yes, Dr. Botkin. Our physician."

"Have him brought here," Kerensky commanded. It was jarring to hear someone order my mother to do anything.

With no servants to ring for, Mama looked at Tatiana and nodded. Without a word Tatiana lifted her chin and walked out of the door. It took only a few moments for her to return with Dr. Botkin, whose eyes were round and frightened.

"I understand you have Mme Vyrubova in your care," Kerensky said, without making any introductions.

"Yes, she is recovering from a dangerous case of the measles."

"You say recovering. Is she, in your opinion, able to be moved without peril to her health?"

I wanted to say something so that Dr. Botkin would know that Kerensky wanted to move Anya to imprison her, not to protect her, but I could say nothing. I listened helplessly as he answered, "Yes, I believe she is well enough to move, provided she does not have to exert herself too much."

"Thank you, Doctor." Kerensky inclined his head to him, showing more respect for a working man than for us, who until a few short weeks before had been the family to whom he was required to pledge his loyalty.

Mama did not cry out, but in a quiet, desperate whisper, said, "No. Not Anya. She would not hurt a fly. She is my dearest friend." The tears I had not seen her shed through all the dangers she had faced now coursed down her cheeks. Tatiana went to her and took her hand. Mama sank onto a chair, no longer able to support herself. Dr. Botkin rushed over to her as well.

"Madame! What do you mean? Are you unwell?"

She looked into his eyes. "You couldn't have known."

Kerensky cleared his throat and said, "Anna Vyrubova is being confined in a place of safety prior to being put on trial for crimes against Russia."

At that moment the soldiers who had accompanied Kerensky, including Sasha, came back, having removed all my father's correspondence and papers from his study. I discovered later that they had removed everything Mama hadn't already burned from her boudoir as well. But that seemed somehow much less important than the gradual tightening of bonds, the diminishing of our circle, that began then.

I could no longer prevent myself from looking imploringly in Sasha's direction. He gave me the merest glance, but in it was something beyond what I saw in the other soldiers' eyes, which was only hatred combined with curiosity. And as Kerensky took leave of us and prepared to arrest Anya, I noticed Sasha hang back a little. He casually put his hand in his pocket—something that would have been impossible in the days of the old army, when strict discipline was the rule—and placed his hand on a table by the door as he left. I saw the scrap of paper he deposited there, and waited until the doctor and Tatiana had taken Mama away to her room before rushing over and picking it up, hiding it quickly in my own pocket.

## ❧ CHAPTER 16 ❧

"Let me help you," I said to Anya, who stood looking forlornly at an open valise, two stern-faced soldiers waiting by the door. "You will need some clothes." I quickly found underthings and a few simple dresses, guessing that she would not need very much. She gathered up her tooth powder and brush and a bottle of eau de cologne, a few icons, and a cross. The valise was not very heavy, but Anya was still so weak from her illness that she had to walk with her crutches. "I'll carry it for you," I said, lifting the case.

"I must take my leave of the empress," she said to the soldiers.

"Our orders are to remove you immediately," said one, whose beard was straggly and greasy with that morning's breakfast. He was not one of the men who had come in with Kerensky.

"Not without saying good-bye to my dearest..." She could not continue.

"Please," I entreated, "what harm can it do?"

They turned to one another and spoke quietly. One of them walked away. The other said nothing, leaving us to guess what was happening, but I assumed his compatriot had gone to ask someone's permission to allow the "dangerous" Anna Vyrubova to see the tsaritsa one more time.

A few short minutes later, the guard returned with two more soldiers, again men I had not previously seen. I began to understand that the palace swarmed with them.

"You are to come with us."

"To see the tsaritsa?" Anya asked, her voice shaking with fear and emotion.

They did not answer. I started to follow.

"Not you. Just her."

"But her bag! She cannot manage it alone."

"I'll take it," said the youngest of the guards, and as I handed it to him I saw one of the others give him a black look.

I watched Anya hobble off, trying to keep up with her captors, barely able to support herself after her illness. But the most horrifying moment of all was when one of the other guards took Anya's case out of the young soldier's hands and left it sitting in the corridor. So, I thought, they're saying she will not need any personal effects at all. She was really going to prison.

I have no idea how Anya and Mama said their good-byes, especially in front of those cold and angry men. All I knew then was that this act of taking a few people away to prisons of which we knew only horrible tales materially changed our entire mood. It was not lightened when we discovered that Lili Dehn was arrested as well, although we heard later that they only kept her for twenty-four hours. Anya, though, was locked up for months in the Peter and Paul Fortress, an ancient, airless prison on an island in the Neva. I could not imagine what she must have suffered.

❧

In all the distress and commotion, I didn't have a chance to look at the note Sasha had left for me until just before I went to bed. I was in my room alone, since Mashka was still being nursed in the sickroom. I hardly dared to open the scrap of paper, afraid that it would tell me that we would no longer be able to see each other, even in secret. I took a deep breath and steeled myself for yet more disheartening news.

I had to follow the men and join
the Provisional Government's forces.
It was the only safe thing, the
only way I have a chance of being
able to save you. Meet me in the
cellar just after dawn tomorrow
if you can, by the back stair that
leads to the kitchen.

That's all it said. So at least I knew Sasha wasn't completely against us. But I had no idea what he could possibly do to help us—"to save you," he said. Did he mean just me, or my whole family? Did we need saving? Were things really so dire? And in any case, how would Sasha be able to make any difference? We were watched constantly if we weren't in our private apartments, and sometimes even then. I didn't hold out much hope that a meeting near the kitchen would go undetected.

I hardly closed my eyes that night, even though I hadn't completely recovered my strength yet. I didn't want to sleep too long and miss what might be my only opportunity to find out what had happened with Sasha, and whether he knew something that could make sense of what was happening.

As soon as I saw the faintest lightening of the sky, I slipped out from between the covers and put on a dark skirt and sweater, opened my door as noiselessly as I could, and crept down to the stairs that led to kitchens. Our movements within the palace were not technically restricted. It was only that there were few rooms where we weren't likely to be disturbed by soldiers who considered themselves to have more right to our home than we had. If someone discovered me, I might claim to be going in search of a glass of milk.

It was still dark. No one had turned on the lights yet. In earlier times, there would already be a bustle of activity as the kitchens prepared the breakfast for the suite and any guests who were staying. But now we generally had only bread and tea in the morning, the cooks not being allowed to fire up the ovens before noon.

At first I saw no one. It hadn't occurred to me that Sasha would not be there, that something might have prevented him from keeping his appointment with me. But just as I was about to give up and return to my room, he emerged from the shadows.

I didn't know what to say to him at first, how to greet him.

What if he had actually turned against us and this meeting was a trick? He had mentioned the Bolsheviks the last time we met. Could he have joined them? I resisted the impulse to run to him and embrace him as I would have done in earlier times. Our last meeting had been strange and awkward compared to when we were younger.

"Nastya! What's wrong? It's me!" Sasha spoke quietly but urgently, and walked right up to me and pulled me to him. His uniform didn't have the fresh smell it always used to, even when I had gone to see him in his camp. I could see it was dirty, quite frayed at the sleeves. But I buried my face in his shoulder anyhow, and did something so unlike me. I started to cry. "Oh, now this isn't the little grand duchess I used to know." Sasha reached into his pocket, pulled out a handkerchief and dabbed at my face with it.

"I know, I'm sorry," I said. I took his hankie and blew my nose in it.

"Besides, we don't have much time. I have to go on guard duty soon."

"You mean you're staying here?" I could hardly believe it.

"I managed to get the posting. You mustn't think I've turned against you. It was either this or go to prison myself. I figured I might be able to help if I at least appeared to be on their side." I was no longer wrapped in Sasha's arms, but he still held on to my hand as if he didn't want to let go of it.

"How can you help? We're entirely in their power here. Mama and Papa have said they might be willing to go away, possibly to England, which they both love. But nothing's been settled. And I won't go without them."

"You have more friends than you realize. It's just dangerous for them to be very public about it. You will all eventually have to be moved, and with your help, something might be arranged."

"With my help? Why mine?"

"Because no one will be expecting you, the youngest girl, to do anything. They are not watching you as they are your parents or your brother."

"I still don't see how it will be possible." I struggled to tamp down the surge of hope I felt just then, that our situation truly was temporary, as Mama tried to convince us when her spirits were not too depressed. "Might they take Papa back as tsar?"

"He would have to be a very different sort of tsar."

I realized when Sasha said it that I had no concept of what sort of a tsar Papa was. He met ministers, made decisions, appeared at public ceremonies. But when he was with us, he was just Papa. He did not speak of politics unless something directly affected us—which hadn't been often until recently. We got most of our news through the maids of honor or the servants. And now, with no one friendly coming or going, we had little idea of what was actually happening in the outside world.

"Tell me what you need me to do."

"Trust me, first of all. And try not to draw attention to yourself just for now."

"Do you have a plan? Truly?" Before the war and the revolution, it would never have occurred to me to question Sasha's loyalty or judgment. But now I didn't know what to think. I would have said the servants were fond of us as well, yet most of them vanished at the first sign of trouble. Even one of Alexei's faithful attendants, the sailor Derevenko—a servant who shared a name with Alexei's doctor, but nothing else—took pleasure now in ordering him about and abusing him verbally. Fortunately, Nagorny was still there to protect him.

"It's too early to say for certain. But do you remember the way we got out of the park that morning, a few years ago?"

"I think so, but I never went through that gate again."

"I can't look for it. I need you to see if it is there and unlocked." He bent down a little, so that his face was level with mine. "If you think you have the courage, you could steal out at night sometime and try to find it. Do you think you could do that?"

I could tell he was serious, that he wasn't lying to me. Even in his different role, I felt I could trust him. Yet how could I get out at night? They locked the doors tight. "I don't know. I don't even know if I could leave the palace. But, Sasha, really, why do we have to think of running away? Count Benckendorff says the Duma may let us live as private citizens. Wouldn't that be wonderful? Just to be able to come and go like other people?"

I searched Sasha's face for something, some response. Although he seemed the same as ever in many ways, even to the persistence of a few freckles on his nose that made him appear much younger than his twenty years, something was different. Perhaps it was not being able to look into both his eyes that gave me some misgivings. I knew, although I had never seen it, that the patch hid a horrible scar where his left eye had been. Yet I had the sense that he could see differently now, that he might be hiding some dark secret too terrible to reveal to me. His visible expression was trustworthy. But what about the one that was hidden?

The sound of a door opening in another part of the cellar made me jump.

"The guards come and go through the cellar. Come with me." He led me down a twisting corridor to the far end of one wing of the house, the one, I guessed, with my grandmother's empty rooms above it. He pointed to a low door at the end of the hallway. "That door is not often used. They won't notice if I leave it unlocked," Sasha whispered. "What do you say? Your futures may depend on it."

"I'll try," I whispered. He kissed me quickly on both cheeks, more like a brother than like the man whose kiss a year ago had left me breathless, then ushered me quickly back to the stairs that led up to our wing. I couldn't help feeling a little disappointed as I skittered noiselessly back to my room.

I was preoccupied all day with what Sasha had said. How was I to leave my bed in the middle of the night without anyone noticing? I was not even allowed out for exercise yet because I was still convalescing.

I assumed Sasha was assigned duty in the grounds outside

of the palace, because I did not see him for the remainder of that day, which passed more quietly, if also more sadly, after the terrible events of the day before. We ate our meals and said our prayers, Alexei had his lessons with Zhilik, and after dinner we played a six-handed game of bezique, while Tatiana read aloud. Dr. Botkin came to report that Mashka was getting much better, but that it might be necessary to shave her head because of a skin disorder that had developed as a complication.

"Poor Marie!" said Mama.

"She'll look just like an egg, but without all the jewels!" Alyosha said, referring to the beautiful eggs M. Fabergé made for Mama at the holidays.

Tatiana and I looked at each other, and I think in that moment we both had the same idea. But we didn't say anything about it then. Like so many things in those early days of captivity, we all had a feeling that the bad events would come to an end and the world would somehow right itself.

I went to bed, realizing that possibly in a few short days I would no longer have my room to myself. I was glad—Mashka and I had shared a room all my life, and I missed her being there—but if I was to see if I could get out of the palace and find that hidden gate, I would have to do it soon.

Despite my wish to get my task over with as quickly as possible, my early morning and disturbed night's sleep made me so tired that I could hardly keep my eyes open. I lay awake as long as I could, mentally going over the plan of the gardens: the ponds, still frozen but not safe enough to walk on; the route past the great Catherine palace, which I assumed was still partly a hospital caring for wounded soldiers; the ways out of the park and into the town, all with locked gates no doubt guarded by a soldier with a rifle. We had gone in the direction of Alexandrovsky Village. I remembered that at least. But it had been summer, and now it was barely spring. Would I recognize the place, and at night too?

# ❧ CHAPTER 17 ❧

The next few nights proved equally impossible. Mama hardly slept, although she was always tired, and sometimes our games of bezique would go on until past midnight. I did take care to look out of the windows, though, and try to see how the guard was set. I noticed that it was changed at around eleven at night, and during the day at seven in the morning and three in the afternoon. That meant that the guard probably changed at around three in the morning too, because I noticed that the same guards I saw at night were not on duty when I looked out before seven. So I would have to do my exploring between eleven at night and three in the morning.

Planning for my nocturnal expedition took my mind off the annoying reality of life. Each day, some new privation or restriction was imposed upon us. First our running water was cut off, then our electricity. We did everything by candlelight in the evening, and had to have water brought in from the ponds and heated in the kitchens to wash. We dared not complain. The investigation into Mama's supposed criminal activities was still going on in Petrograd, and we were all afraid that if we did not cooperate and keep ourselves quietly out of the way, she or one of the others would be hauled off to prison, perhaps to the same horrid place Anya had been taken to.

Where our evenings after supper used to be spent only with the family, the lack of comfort and the uncertain circumstances made Mama open the gathering to everyone who remained: all the remaining maids of honor, Prince, Dolgorukov, Count Benckendorff, General Tatischev, Colonel Grooten, Zhilik, and Trina. We sat in the flickering candlelight, some trying to read, others sewing, and always a game of bezique.

One night, I was simply too restless to sit at the table and play cards. It may have been the dancing shadows cast by the candles that made the room seem to shift and breathe around us. Whatever it was, I went instead to the piano and read through some waltzes quietly, letting Tatiana take a turn at the card game. She didn't like it very much because she always lost, but I knew Mama wanted her to play. She seemed to crave the company of my older sister. They were very alike in both looks and temperament. Tatiana always knew what Mama wanted, as if they were connected in some way no one else could see.

I paused to look for another volume of music—something light and cheerful, like Mendelssohn or Schubert—when Papa spoke.

"So, Marie will be able to leave the sickroom tomorrow, now that her skin is healing."

"I'm so glad!" I said. But at the same time I was also troubled. I would have my beloved sister back with me, yet I had not succeeded at all in locating the gate. If I did not do it tonight, I might never be able to.

Fortunately, our evening broke up early for a change. Mama won the game decidedly—which she was always determined to do—and Papa declared that they would retire at eleven o'clock, after drinking a cup of tea.

I waited in my room until all the little sounds of floors creaking and doors closing had died down. With no running water flowing to the sinks in the bathrooms, we all brushed our teeth and sponged ourselves down in our rooms using a basin and pitcher, and so the process of getting to bed was considerably shorter than it had once been. It was not long before I was confident that, troubled dreams or not, everyone else in the palace was asleep.

I had taken care to undress just in case Trina came in to say good night, and so when I rose I first had to put on my darkest clothing and quietest shoes. The weather had turned warm, melting most of the snow, but also transforming the grounds into a sea of mud that I knew from experience could suck my shoes off. I tied them tightly to avoid accidentally losing them if I stepped in a puddle.

I didn't dare take a candle, but a full moon cast enough pale light through the windows so that I could find my way through the house. I knew my way well, until I got to the cellar. I realized that I had been so absorbed in speaking with Sasha, in reacquainting myself with his expressions, and in feeling relieved that he was near, that I hadn't paid attention to where he had led me. I thought it would be easy; all four floors of the palace had the same general layout. But the cellar rooms had been carved up differently and had only tiny windows high up to let in any light. They were smaller and oddly shaped, with hallways that took unexpected twists and turns. I had a general sense that I needed to turn left, but I was soon faced with a choice that I didn't know how to make. The corridor split, one side going toward what I thought would be the back of the building, the other going toward the front.

I stood very still and listened closely. I thought when I turned my head toward the back route that I could discern distant voices. The other way, I heard nothing. Whether it was the right way or not, I would have to risk the route that took me away from the voices. Turning back unsuccessfully would be better than encountering off-duty guards who might have been at the vodka.

Once I'd made my decision, I moved quickly. I didn't have very much time. After a few twists and turns, I just made out the door I was looking for in front of me. Someone wanted me to succeed, I thought, and made the sign of the cross and promised that I would pray when this night's adventure was safely over.

Now the moon was both my ally and my enemy. It showed me the way clearly, but it would also expose me to anyone who happened to be looking in the direction I was walking. It would be quite difficult, I thought, to stick to the shadows enough to avoid detection. I hoped the guards who were at their posts had relaxed their vigilance enough to be dozing. There hadn't been any recent attempts by angry mobs or unruly soldiers to breach the iron palings and invade the palace grounds, and none of us had ever risked punishment by breaking the rules of our imprisonment.

Of course, that was my greatest fear: that my actions—if discovered—could cause the situation to become harder for Mama and Papa, Alexei, Olga, Tatiana, and Mashka. But I could not simply sit and wait, not when Sasha had given me a glimmer of hope. Every day things seemed to be getting worse, not better. And Sasha was right: no one paid much attention to me. I was the only one in the household who had a chance of making something like this work.

I stayed close to the walls of the palace, making sure I didn't put a foot out of the dark swath created by their shadow. I knew I would soon enough have to cut across open ground to get to the forest, which would lead me to where I thought I remembered the door. After that, I would either have to pass close to the arsenal or go via the stable for invalid horses. I thought of cutting directly through the woods and staying off the paths, but the snow melt had created puddles and muddy patches that would be impossible to see. In any case, the trees had not all leafed out, and the trunks would provide little camouflage. I could as easily keep to the side of a path and not be seen.

Checking first to make sure no sentries were making their rounds, I ran quickly over the footbridge between the two nearest ponds and then skirted around the white tower, heading down the path that led toward the elephant house and avoiding the arsenal, which no doubt would be heavily guarded at whatever time of day or night. I saw no evidence of soldiers once I was in the midst of the woods, and thought for a moment that they had become careless and no longer bothered to patrol the grounds at night.

My destination was several hundred yards to the left of the Alexander Gate, which led into the village itself, and so I turned down another path toward the thick yew hedges that hid some of the iron railings of the park.

I had so far seen no one and was beginning to have a false sense of security, imagining that the guards were either convinced no one would try to escape and didn't bother to keep watch overnight, or had simply melted into the darkness. But soon enough I discovered that they hadn't been quite so obliging. I heard the unmistakable tramp of approaching feet. I scampered off the path, stepping right into a muddy patch, and hid behind a box hedge. It was one of the few times in my life when I was grateful that I was not very tall.

I held my breath as the soldiers drew closer to where I hid, and I could hear the sounds of effort and muttered curses. "Easy, comrades," said one of them, "We don't want to wake up Colonel and Mrs. Romanov and family!"

I couldn't get used to hearing Mama and Papa referred to that way. It wasn't just the disrespect; it was the angry tone of their voices. I peeked out to see what the soldiers were doing together out in the park in the middle of the night, instead of stationed at their sentry posts.

There were eight of them: six shouldering some kind of long, wooden box, one at the front, and one at the rear. The two who were not carrying looked nervously around them as they walked. At first I couldn't imagine what load they were bearing through the woods with such suppressed excitement and urgency. Surely it was not some weapon to use against us. They had little need of more than rifles and bayonets to keep us in check.

When they finally drew level with me, I shivered. It became clear in the light of the full moon that they carried a plain wooden coffin, with a gilded and jeweled cross on its lid that glimmered intermittently with the rhythm of their steps.

"Let's take that bauble off before we do the deed," whispered one of them.

"No pilfering! We need it as proof," responded the one who appeared to be the leader.

Whose coffin could they be carrying, and of what did they need proof? I had to see for myself, and so, once I was certain they were beyond where they could see me crouched close to the ground, I darted toward them, moving from bush to bush, occasionally hiding behind the stump of a fallen tree.

After they had gone about another half mile or so, they left the path and turned into the forest. From my hiding place I could see them quite clearly. Just as clear to me from that vantage point was exactly whose coffin they had stolen. I didn't want to believe it, though. It was Rasputin's. However wrongheaded and strange he was, no one—not even someone accused of the most heinous crimes—deserved to be disturbed after death.

The soldiers were so intent upon their deed that I think I could have stood up quite brazenly and approached them and no one would have noticed. But I did not want to be foolish, and so remained cautiously hidden from their sight.

"They say he still rules the family from the grave, that the grand duchesses were all his mistresses in the flesh and that before their captivity, they would come out and dance naked around his grave."

"Ho-ho! That must have been a sight!"

A lascivious chuckle broke out through the ranks.

"Enough!" said the leader. "This seems a pointless exercise. The man is dead. There is no afterlife, no spirit."

I crossed myself quickly and saw two or three of the soldiers do the same. In the eerie light I half expected Grigory's bones to rise up and smite the desecrators of his grave. But no such thing happened. Instead, they placed the coffin on top of a pile of firewood. The leader took a screwdriver and unfastened the gilt cross from the lid. Then another man struck a match, and before long the wood beneath the coffin blazed high, casting so bright a light that I had to slink back further to avoid detection.

A wave of nausea overcame me, although I was not quite certain why. Rasputin's soul had long flown that rotting body, and a greater power than I knew where it went. But there was something so thoroughly evil about the gesture, here, in the grounds of the palace where the people who believed in him most still lived. No, I would not tell Mama and Papa. If they found out from someone else, so be it. The longer they remained in ignorance of such a vile crime, the better.

The flames illuminated a large area of the park through which I had planned to walk to reach the hidden gate. It would lead out not far from the imperial railway depot, I realized. Not that I thought for a moment we would be able to board one of our trains and steam away to Finland. All our automobiles had been confiscated for the use of the Provisional Government, as had the drivers. Probably the trains were similarly employed.

But if we could leave the park undetected, Russia was a vast land. There were hundreds of thousands of hectares where someone might not recognize the former tsar and tsaritsa, the heir, and four grand duchesses.

I sighed. There was the biggest obstacle. We would not be parted from one another. But singly or in small groups we might stand a chance for escape, if it ever came to that.

I shook myself free of these morbid thoughts, and concentrated on accomplishing the task Sasha had set me. I eventually reached the yew hedge, remembering how frightened I had been that early morning when I'd gone to meet Sasha, and how little danger I had actually been in.

I plunged through the hedge, scratching myself a little in the process. At first, I found only the high, close iron palings that terminated in sharp points. I was grieved to see that the points had been made even more forbidding by the addition of a thick coil of barbed wire. No one could scale such a barrier. I remember that it had once seemed a secure, protective enclosure, there to keep our private world safe and inviolate. But now, I saw that we had unwittingly created our own prison. Or if not we, the tsars from centuries past.

The moon had passed its highest point and started its descent toward the west. The night had become frosty, and I was chilled through. Only the hardiest spring flowers would survive early April, the snowdrops and winter anemones. How I used to love seeing their brave beauty blanket the woods for a few weeks, before the weather was warm enough to allow the crocuses, narcissi, and tulips to grow. Even in the moonlight, I could see little patches where tiny flowers had bravely taken root around piles of snow and sticky mud. The world went on, just as it always had, despite what had happened to us. How peaceful, I thought. How simple.

And then I couldn't help comparing the natural world to the actions of human beings, who are supposed to be better than the beasts and the flowers. It was those human beings who had thrown poor, lame Anya into prison. Who had made a terrible war, with millions of young men killed and so many lands and homes laid waste. Who dug up the bones of a holy man and burned them for no good reason.

I continued along behind the hedge, looking for the gate that I knew had to be there. Just as my hands were becoming numb with cold, I found it.

As soon as I saw it, I knew we would never be able to leave through it. Not only was it chained shut, a sentry sat just inside the yew hedge, snoring in the cold.

I had come so close to being discovered that my heart pounded. I would have to retrace my steps as quietly as I could. As I went, I stepped on a pile of leaves that just happened to be covering a hedgehog's burrow. The little thing shot out from under my feet and dashed to the open ground, where he rolled himself into a spiny ball.

"Eh? What's that!"

The soldier was instantly on his feet, his rifle aimed at the still-rolling hedgehog. I held my breath, not daring to move, feeling just slightly off balance and desperate to take one more step and be secure. He walked out slowly toward the poor creature as it came to a stop, got within a few yards of it, put his rifle to his shoulder, and took aim.

"Hah! Ahhaha! Ahahahaha!" It was the guard. He obviously recognized the hedgehog for what it was and was having a good laugh at himself. While he continued, sinking to the ground in helpless guffaws, I took my opportunity to creep back between the yew hedge and the iron palings, hoping he would have resumed his snooze by the time I had to make the dash through the woods and back to the palace.

## ❧ CHAPTER 18 ❧

I had no more mishaps on my way back, letting myself in silently through the same door to the cellar and removing my shoes so that I would not leave muddy tracks all through the building. When I reached my room, I quickly took off my clothes and hid my dirty shoes far back in my wardrobe, hoping that the few maids who remained with us would be too occupied with other matters to find them. It was not yet three in the morning. I knew I must try to get some sleep. But instead I mentally composed the note I would give to Sasha asking him to meet me so that I could tell him what I'd done. I then spent another restless hour figuring out how I would get it to him.

I eventually fell asleep, but I was exhausted for the entire next day and not thinking clearly enough to come up with any sort of plan. In the afternoon, Mashka left the sickroom and came down to Mama's boudoir.

"How are you feeling?" I asked her.

"Really, all well," she answered, although her voice was still hoarse.

"Are you cold? Shall we put more wood on the fire?" She was wrapped in shawls and wore a scarf close around her head.

"No, I am warm enough."

Tatiana nudged me with her foot. I didn't know why, but it was a signal not to pursue the subject, and so I didn't.

All through tea we hardly spoke. Finally at the end, Zhilik came in and said, "The guards have given the family leave to go outside in the mornings. Now that the weather is becoming warmer, I told them it was necessary for the full recovery of the children that they be allowed to exercise in the fresh air."

"You are too good, Pierre," Mama said. And I was so glad that we would be able to go outside for a long stretch of time that I didn't even mind him calling us all children.

Only when we went to bed that night did I discover why Tatiana had not wanted me to question Mashka closely about her health: Mashka removed her scarf to reveal a completely bald head. I laughed before I could stop myself, and saw the tears start in her eyes. "Oh, Mashka, dear, it will grow in."

"But I am so ugly!"

"We have only slovenly guards to impress here," I said, but I couldn't help feeling sorry for her. Then I remembered the look Tatiana and I had exchanged when we heard of the possibility that Mashka would have to have her head shaved. "Don't worry. All will be well. You'll see," I said before turning out my bedside light.

The next morning, I jumped up before Mashka was awake and ran to Olga and Tatiana's room. After a brief conference, we all decided what we would do and sent for Trina, who we could always persuade to do whatever we wanted. In short order we accomplished our goal and I returned to my room to dress.

We were allowed out as promised, and Zhilik organized us into a small working party to clear the ice from the sluices that fed the ponds. I did not mind the work—none of us did. It felt good to exercise and do something besides sit indoors. The sun shone, and the smell of spring was in the air. Mashka tired quickly and sat down to watch. We waited, excited, for our papa to come by on his daily walk and admire our work.

When he finally arrived with the prince, Olga called to him. "Father! Come and see what we have done!" We all looked at each other and put down the sticks we'd been using, and, at a signal from Tatiana, took off our scarves.

The look on Papa's face was priceless. His eyes went wide, then his mouth spread into a helpless grin. I had not seen him look so happy since before the war. Mashka shrieked with delight. There we all were, our heads as bald as ostrich eggs. "Didn't you know, it's all the rage in Petrograd," I said, imitating a society lady and pointing my nose up in the air. My sisters fell about laughing, and Papa too, so hard that tears rolled down his cheeks. Even the dour prince and dear Zhilik were laughing.

"Wait! My camera!" Papa jogged back to the palace, a guard on his heels. He returned and took a photograph of all four of us in a row. We still have that picture. It was one of the few they allowed us to take with us to Yekaterinburg.

But soon after that day something happened that clearly

reminded us of the danger that surrounded us all the time. We were outside, and as it was a particularly fine day, Papa, who loved all physical exercise, decided he would ride his bicycle around the part of the garden we were permitted to be in. I looked up from our work clearing the pond sluices to watch him go by, so proud and noble. It made my heart ache.

Then, as he went past one of the guards—one of the surly Soviet ones—the fellow stuck his bayonet between the spokes of the bicycle wheels. I shrieked, and my sisters all looked up. I watched the bicycle flip up into the air, but somehow Papa was standing to the side. He must have reacted quickly, and it was fortunate he took such care to be athletic and healthy or he might have suffered a terrible accident.

Papa simply stared at the guard, turned, and walked back to the house. The other guard that had been detailed to follow him was shaking with laughter. They were worse than children, was all I could think. Papa never rode his bicycle again after that.

❦

It was perhaps the Easter season of 1917 that truly signaled to everyone in the household the extent of the ill feelings toward our family, the old ways, and anyone associated with them. During Easter week, we all went to church twice a day in preparation for receiving the sacrament on Easter Sunday. My mother and father's devotion to religion was sincere and unflinching. But this didn't stop our guards from being suspicious of us.

They hated religion so much that throughout every church service, a soldier stood behind the altar and watched the priest carefully, as though he might use the implements of faith to make a bomb. But that was just a small annoyance. One afternoon, on the day that we would all go to confession, Isa strode angrily into the parlor where we all sat doing our needlework or reading.

"They tried their utmost to commit the foulest disrespect, but I won the day!" she declared, still quivering with anger.

"What is it, Isa, dear?" said Nastinka, who patted the place next to her on the sofa.

But Isa continued to pace back and forth. "I went to the chapel for confession. A soldier followed me in. I waited. He stood there, looking stupid. Finally I said, 'Young man, kindly leave so that I may make my confession to the priest in private.'

"And do you know, he planted himself more firmly in front of me and refused!"

"How insolent!" Nastinka said, rising and going to take Isa's hand and lead her over to sit.

"That was not the end of it, though. I realized that the fellow had gone there with the intention of listening to the tsar and tsaritsa's confessions, to see if there was anything he could use against them. I was determined that he would not remain in the chapel. 'No order has been given for you to listen to private confessions,' I said to him. 'Even condemned criminals have the right to their time alone with a priest. I demand you call your superior, who must telephone Kerensky concerning this matter.'"

"What happened then?"

Having told the most upsetting part of her story, Isa

finally sat with Nastinka on the sofa. "He got all in a sweat and went charging off to fetch his commander, who came right away. I explained my point, and the superior officer agreed with me. No call to Kerensky was necessary."

Nastinka took Isa's hand. "You did a very brave thing for their majesties. I'm certain they will be grateful for it."

Alyosha had been listening closely to all she said, and rose to look out the window. "Show me which of the guards it was, Isa," he commanded.

She went to the window and looked. "I don't see the one, and I'm not sure I'd be able to recognize him from this distance."

"Well, when you know who he is, tell me. Because I will kill him."

Tatiana and I both looked up at once. Alyosha had a stern look on his face, hard and set, as if instead of the sickly ex-tsarevich he was an enthroned ruler with armies to command. Perhaps he would have made a different sort of tsar, as Sasha had said would be necessary. Or perhaps he wouldn't. In any case, the matter was forgotten, and no soldiers followed us into confession.

The interference with our Easter observances continued nonetheless. On Maundy Thursday, the local Soviet decided that they would have the burial ceremonies for citizens killed in the revolution on that day as well. At first, we were told they would bury them beneath the windows of the palace, but there wasn't room, so they had to find another place, still within the palace grounds.

We all dressed for church and prepared to go to the morning service. As we were walking to St. Sophia, the small cathedral in the park, we saw an astonishing sight. Thousands of work-men and ordinary people had entered through the gate from the village of Tsarskoe, carrying red banners. In front of them marched a brass band and a cortege of pallbearers carrying dozens of red-painted coffins.

At first they walked silently. Then, upon seeing us, the leader of the brass band raised his baton and led his musicians in a very loud, out-of-tune rendition of "La Marseillaise."

"Just continue walking, darlings," Mama said, her face a picture of religious devotion. She had Alyosha by the hand, or by the look on his face I might have suspected he would go over and break the band conductor's baton.

We went on to the church, but the massive funeral was taking place not far away, in the midst of a broad avenue of trees that led right to the front of the palace. The speeches of the local Soviet drowned out even the words of the priest in the church. The familiar prayers mingled with increasingly angry, loud cheers, saying, "Down with the imperialist mur-derers! Death to the old regime!"

It was very hard to concentrate on the service. I saw Colonel Kobylinsky, the new commander of the palace guard who had come to aid Korovichenko, and Colonel Grooten exchange looks of alarm. The service was about to end, and we had to walk back to the palace. We would have our usual guards around us, but even with their weapons they would be no match for an angry mob of thousands.

As if in protest at the confusion of ceremonies taking place that day, the sky all at once grew as dark as night, and the wind began to blow so hard the shutters banged. The priest stopped chanting and crossed himself. We all stood in silence and listened.

At first the noise of the crowd continued. But after a few tree branches cracked off and thudded to the ground, we heard a general panic and the sound of people running away. Soon there was no music, and no more speeches. The priest crossed himself again and gave the benediction.

Fortunately, we had all worn fur coats over to the church, as the day was unseasonably cold for April. That hardly prepared us, though, when we emerged from our worship into a blizzard. We hurried home to the one parlor that was warm enough in the sudden chill. Everyone was invited to stay to tea.

"I don't know what might have happened if the snow hadn't come so swiftly," Colonel Kobylinsky said. "The mob in the park was very angry."

"Amen," Mama said, and sipped her tea.

As the weather continued to warm and the last bits of ice and snow vanished, we got permission from Korovichenko to plant a kitchen garden. We all spent hours digging the soil and planting seeds. People from the surrounding villages would come and stare at us working like peasants on our own little plot of land. I thought how the old gardener—heaven knew where he had gone—would have been horrified to see his flower beds turned over and given up to cabbages, potatoes, peas, and beets.

One day, just as the green shoots started to poke through the soil, I looked up from my weeding to see Sasha coming over to the detachment of soldiers watching us. He spoke to one who had just rolled and lit a cigarette, which dangled insolently from his lips. The fellow frowned but did not remove his cigarette, only hoisted his rifle carelessly over his shoulder and sauntered off. Sasha took his place. I tried not to watch him, but I could see that despite whatever he'd been doing to try to blend in with the revolutionaries, he had not lost his military bearing. He couldn't quite slouch as lazily as the others. He held his head too upright; he was too accustomed to standing at attention to achieve that careless look the others wore. And the black patch over his eye gave him an air of authority that I thought some of the men grudgingly respected. I was proud of him, and I longed to run to him and lean my head on his shoulder again—my head with its short fuzz of hair that was growing in tight curls. I wondered what he might have become in the old world, whether he would have risen to be a captain and then a colonel, perhaps even high enough in rank to—

"You there! You're missing all the weeds! You'd starve if you had to do for yourself on a farm." It was one of the other guards, who pointed to the beginning of the row I had just gone down, weeding distractedly. He was right. I had left many behind. Another of them said, "She's mooning over her sweetheart. She doesn't care about cabbages!"

This struck all the men as terribly funny. I felt myself blush.

"She's embarrassed! But I don't see why. Her sweetheart's dead."

Without thinking I looked directly at Sasha to reassure myself that he was still there. I caught him staring at me sadly before he turned and pretended to laugh with the others. Of course they meant Rasputin. It made me sick to think they could joke about someone whose body they had exhumed and desecrated. Mama found out, as I knew she would, the day after it happened. She just looked gray and tired, as though no one could tell her anything that would shock her ever again.

I returned to my weeding, but I was distracted. Why was Sasha here? Did he have a message for me? Had he found a way for us to meet again? It was too much to hope for.

I had to wait until it was time for us to go back inside to find out anything. The guards positioned themselves to escort us to the palace. Sasha stood so that he was near me. I still hadn't told anyone in the household that I knew him. I just was not certain enough that I could really trust him yet.

"Keep moving!" said a gruff voice, very close to my ear. I turned and glared, only to see that it was Sasha. I was so shocked I stopped. "I said, keep moving!" he repeated, this time shoving me a little.

"Don't touch my sister!" Alyosha cried out, and Zhilik hastened up to take my arm.

"It's all right," I said. "No harm done."

"I shall speak to the tsaritsa about this," whispered Zhilik to me. "He shall be removed from the guard!"

"I don't trust that fellow with the patch over his eye," Alyosha said, taking my hand. "I've seen the way he looks at you."

I doubted Mama could have any influence over who was guarding us now, and I had felt Sasha use the instant of contact with me to put something in my pocket. The last thing I wanted was for Sasha to go away, and so I said, "It's all right, Alyosha.

He's just guarding us. And please don't make any trouble, Zhilik. I'm fine, and it's not worth it." I glanced at Zhilik, hoping my look could convey that I was serious. "Please!"

He nodded. I hoped the incident was forgotten by the time we sat in the small parlor for tea.

## ❧ CHAPTER 19 ❧

Later that night, while Mashka was having a cold bath before going to bed, I unfolded the scrap of paper Sasha had put in my pocket.

We have to meet. There's something important I must tell you—it concerns your entire family. Come to the cellar again at about a quarter past midnight. I'll meet you in the same place.

It was nearly midnight already. Mashka was still weak, and usually fell asleep quickly. I hoped that night would prove no exception.

I was already in bed with my nightgown on over my clothes when Mashka returned. She lay down, but did not turn off the light. Instead, she rolled onto her side and propped herself up on her elbow. "I think you're hiding something from me," she said.

My heart stopped beating for an instant. "What do you mean?"

"It's something about that guard, the one who shoved you today. I feel as though I've seen him before."

I had to think quickly. How much did I dare tell her? It was torture keeping everything a secret, yet the more she knew the more it would endanger her—and risk even more people finding out. I wanted this secret to be my burden and no one else's. "Perhaps he was a guard at the palace before everyone ended up mutinying."

"Don't evade me, Nastya. You're not good at lying. I want to know."

I paused. I couldn't think what to say. And then, perhaps because at that moment the burden became just too heavy, I found I could no longer keep my silence. "His name is Sasha."

"How do you know his name? Where did you meet him? He's not from a good family, I imagine."

"What is a good family now?" I asked. "He was my friend before and he is still."

"Your friend?" Mashka asked. "Why don't you introduce him to us?"

"It would be dangerous. For him," I answered. "He used to be in the Semyonovsky. I met him in the garden. I have his balalaika. You remember, I asked you to send him a message when I was sick."

Mashka was silent for a while, staring into my eyes until I

had to look away. "You're blushing, Nastya. You like this soldier, don't you?"

"Yes!" I cried. "Is that a crime?" I could barely stand to hold in my feelings anymore. All the sorry hopelessness of my situation—of our situation—burst over me in a wave. All through my illness, through our dear friends being arrested and our own captivity I had been in too much of a daze to think about what it really meant. And the hope Sasha had given me, that perhaps there would be a way out, teased me into not feeling so desperate and alone. But now, a crack opened in my heart. I felt the pain in my throat, pain I had not felt since I was a little girl and wept bitterly when Alyosha was sick and no one could make him better. I buried my face in my pillow and let the sobs rack me until I could only take shuddering gasps of breath.

When I looked up, Mashka was sitting on the edge of my bed, stroking my short curls. "You have your clothes on under your nightgown. You'd better tell me what you're intending to do."

I sat up quickly. "I'm not running away! No! I would never leave the rest of you. That would be like dying."

Mashka took a deep breath and let it out in a relieved sigh. "Thank God. I was sure you were planning to go off with your handsome guard, your Sasha, and we'd never see you again." A few tears dripped down her cheeks. She cried easily ever since her measles.

"No. Not that. But I have to meet him tonight. You won't tell the others? It's important. He's trying to help us."

Mashka looked away for a moment, doubtless trying to decide what was right to do. "All right. I won't say a word. But if it looks as if you are being put in danger by this . . . young man, then I will break my promise."

I kissed her. She felt thin. There were still deep circles under her eyes. "Go to bed."

"Wake me when you return," she said, closing her eyes as she slipped between the sheets. She was deeply asleep within minutes.

❧

I heard the bells in the Tsarskoe village church strike midnight, and then waited for the last chime to die away. Mashka's knowing made it easier to get out of bed and leave the room at least.

I practically flew down the now-familiar route to the cellar, my ears pricked up, listening for any sound that could mean discovery. But the palace was quiet.

This time, Sasha was already there when I came in. Without thinking about it, I ran to him and flung my arms around his neck. He wrapped his around me too and buried his nose in my short hair. I could feel his heart pounding, and felt as though my own matched his, beat for beat. Perhaps, I thought, if we stayed like this long enough, we would merge into one person.

But it seemed only an instant we were so close. Sasha took hold of my shoulders and held me away from him. "I had to see you, to make sure you were all right."

"Yes, yes, of course I am. Oh, Sasha, I'm so glad you are

here." I threw myself at him again, and this time he pressed his whole body against me and moved his cheek on my fuzzy head. I felt his hands exploring my back, feeling the bumps of my spine and tracing it up to my neck and down as far as it went. I gasped. He took hold of my face between his two hands.

"Do you even know that you've become beautiful?" he asked. "You've grown so pretty. Prettier than any of your sisters."

Prettier than my sisters? Even Tatiana? I felt a glow creep up from my stomach and make my heart beat faster. I never thought I was pretty. I shook my head to make sure I wasn't imagining anything. I wanted him to repeat what he said, but at the same time I didn't want him to speak. I saw his face coming toward mine. I lifted my chin, wondering, knowing what would happen next. When his lips touched mine I wasn't surprised, and yet the feeling was so unexpected I couldn't breathe. Then I felt his tongue dart between my lips more and more insistently, forcing my teeth apart until our mouths were greedily joined.

I don't know how long that kiss lasted. While we explored each other's mouths, I was no longer a captive in a strange, topsy-turvy palace, surrounded by invalid and convalescing people and guards who looked as if they wished we would simply vanish and let them get on with their real business. And Sasha—why had I not realized before then who he might become to me? True, he was the only young man I ever really became friends with besides my brother. But how did it happen that we were suddenly so connected? Connected to the point that I couldn't imagine being close to anyone else. Sasha taught me so much. He gave me a glimpse of life outside our enchanted world that I never would have had, and that I believe helped me understand more than anyone in my family what was going on all around us. Somewhere in the timeless space that existed before my father's abdication, before the change in our status, he had become my secret life.

The kiss ended at last. We started to speak, no more than two inches between our faces so that every now and again we could interrupt the words with a gentle touch of the lips. I had a deep, pleasurable feeling. I felt light-headed, barely attending to what he said.

"There is a plan to move you," he said.

"Move me where?"

He kissed me before saying, "Not just you, your family, you goose! To Moscow. To the Kremlin."

"Will you be with us?"

He sighed. "I don't know. I have to be very careful how I ask. No one must guess how I feel about you. About your family, the tsar."

"How do you feel about me?" I asked. I think I knew it was a dangerous question. Tatiana and Olga had gossiped enough about their beaux in the regiments for me to know that a girl should act aloof, keep a young man guessing, if she wanted to retain his interest. But this was different. This wasn't flirting and dancing. This was real.

"Oh, Nastya! Times are so uncertain. The provisional government is now being shaken, and it seems that the Bolsheviks might seize control. Now all the powerful people are radical socialists, not just moderate reformers, and they take a very hard line about the monarchy."

I pulled away from him. Was it possible that he didn't realize what had happened with us? The actions of his body contradicted his words. He tightened his grip on me. "You didn't answer me," I said. I had to know, whatever it cost me.

He shook his head. "What good would it do for us to say we're in love? I think I've been in love with you ever since you were too young to know what that meant. When the revolution came, when I realized that the army was turning against the tsar, my only thought was of you. I thought of joining the monarchists, so that I might fight to restore your father to his throne, but I could see that way was doomed."

I heard only scraps of what he said after the words "we're in love." It wasn't those three words that I had dreamed of in my girlish fantasies, *ya tyebya lyublyu,* I love you, but close enough. Close enough in a time of such turmoil. I stopped his mouth with a kiss. At first he resisted, then he kissed me back, harder and more passionately than before. I let his hands rove where they wanted to, over the curve of my bottom, around to cup my small breasts. I could barely breathe.

He spoke the next words into my ear, sending a pleasurable tickle down into my belly. "Nastya, I need to tell you. The English won't have you anymore. The only way left is to escape in secret, perhaps to Finland or Switzerland."

I was lost in the feeling of his words, so that it took a little while for me to understand their meaning. He had told me something important. Vital. "They won't let us go at all? What are they planning to do with us?" The jolt back to reality made my head spin.

"I don't know. If they move you to Moscow, it will be more difficult for you to get to Finland."

The border of Finland was only about seventy miles from Tsarskoe. Moscow was hundreds of miles to the southeast. I remember thinking that Finland seemed like part of Russia, and yet different, far away. "I did as you said. I found the hidden gate. It was locked and guarded."

"I know." For a few minutes we did not speak. He knew? Why did he have me do something so dangerous then? I heard a mouse gnawing on something in a corner of the cellar, and somewhere a wooden board cracked as it settled. It was May, but the nights were still chilly. "I shouldn't have asked you to go. I just didn't know whether I would have a chance myself, and that the explorations of a child would be more understandable than if I started nosing around."

"So you think I am a child?"

He wrapped his arms around me again. "No. Not a child. But not quite a woman." We embraced again, but this time he did not let his hands wander over my body. I felt rather than heard him sigh.

"I'm old enough to know what love is, truly," I whispered.

"Are you? Love is suffering."

"My brother suffers, and I love him."

"It's not the same. If times were different, I would never have done what I did this evening. I would never have dared speak to you so frankly."

"So it's the speaking that worries you! Not this..." I kissed him.

He laughed. "That most of all, of course."

"So you wouldn't have fallen in love with me if we weren't in such trouble?"

"I believe I would have. But I never would have approached you."

"Why not?"

"You need to ask, Grand Duchess?" He tweaked my nose.

Yes, of course. He would not likely have ever been introduced to us in society. He wasn't from a high-enough-ranking family. I briefly wondered if Olga or Tatiana had ever been kissed the way Sasha kissed me. I doubted it. And I knew Mashka had not, because she would have told me.

"So, maybe I'm glad that Papa isn't the tsar anymore." As soon as I said the words I felt ashamed. How could my moments of pleasure in any way make up for what had happened? Yet in some way, they did. "When will I see you again? Tomorrow?" I asked. I couldn't bear the thought of time going by before I could feel myself surrounded by the protective warmth of Sasha's body.

"It's too dangerous. We can't meet every night."

"Why is every night more dangerous than meeting just one night?" I asked.

"Because." He paused. "Because I can't answer for what might happen."

It was a vague response, but in my heart I knew what he meant. Things were uncertain. If we were discovered, it could be disaster for Sasha—or not. If we weren't discovered, I knew enough about desire to understand how close we were to crossing a boundary between love and something more physical. Part of me didn't care. But part of me was frightened by the thought. I felt as if I was standing on the edge of a precipice, where stepping off would lead to the wonderful sensation of flying, but also the possibility of destruction.

"You'd better go," Sasha said, even as he held me tighter.

"I wish I didn't have to," I said.

"I'm here, remember, even when we don't see each other."

I nodded. That knowledge had reassured me in the months since Sasha had become one of our guards. But now it was not enough. "I'll be sixteen next month," I said, not sure what I meant to imply.

"I know," Sasha said, and kissed me again. "I don't think anything will happen before then," he added, leaving me unsure of whether he meant between us, or with the probability of moving my family.

I backed away from him until the darkness engulfed him, then I turned and ran silently back to my room. There was no hope of sleep for me that night. When I dozed, I dreamed of feeling alternately warm and protected, and exposed and alone. It used to be my family that gave me a feeling of calm and safety, in the certainty of our affection for each other. But all of that had changed. While we comforted each other, suddenly that very association was now where the danger lay. We were all huge in my dream, too big to hide anywhere. No matter where we went, people could see us and they mocked us, throwing rotten vegetables and stinking rags at us. Only when I saw Sasha, and he reached up to touch me, did I become small again and enter the world of normal people. As soon as I let go of him, I would expand once more into that monumental, unwanted being—a Grand Duchess of Russia.

# ❧ CHAPTER 20 ❧

I found it very hard to hide my feelings the next day. Fortunately, it was one of those May days that brings a promise of summer, so everyone's spirits were lifted by the weather. We spent hours working in our garden while Papa chopped wood. I didn't see Sasha the whole day, but it took little effort for me to imagine his kisses and conjure up the warmth of him.

One day stretched into a week, though, and Sasha did not show himself. I assumed he must have been put on night-guard duty. Perhaps that was how he had managed to meet me that time. I wondered why I didn't hear from him and began to worry that something had happened.

Things went on as they had in our altered existence. Alexei was feeling better, but Mama seemed to get worse. Just walking from one room to another tired her, and Papa often pushed her around himself in her wheelchair.

The days lengthened, both in the hours of sunlight, and in the difficulty of making them pass. Endless games of bezique entertained us in the evening, and we read and sang. We put on a little play for what was left of the suite. That gave us something to do and diverted the adults for a few hours.

For a while we were able to play the piano and had access to all the musical instruments, and I was happy to lose myself in the music. But then came an order that the pianos were to be taken away, as well as most of Alexei's remaining toys. It was an unnecessary and cruel maneuver. I wondered what would happen next.

The trial in Petrograd against Mama ended, and they found nothing with which to accuse her of treason. But that made no difference in what people still said about her and her associations with Rasputin. Every once in a while Korovichenko, who had remained as the palace commander for a time, brought us newspapers—usually weeks old—and there we would read the most awful things about us. And the guards would get hold of pamphlets with vile cartoons in them, and these also somehow came to our notice.

"My brother tells me he wrote a letter to the editor trying to set him straight about these horrible lies," Papa said one evening after supper. "But the editor would not print it. It seems that everyone is afraid of appearing to be a monarchist and being sent to prison as a traitor to the Provisional Government—or more specifically now, the Soviet."

Somehow, those lies upset me more than anything else, even more than being held captive. We were so helpless against them, and people all over Russia, who used to love and revere Papa, were being made to think he was a devil, and the rest of us little better than evil spirits who feasted on the flesh of infants. I didn't know how they could believe it of us. I could tell from the way the townspeople stared at us through the fences when we went outside that they did indeed accept what they were told as true. At least, I thought, they would find no evidence to support such lies in our actions. We wore simple clothing and worked in our garden. We were just like them. And yet completely different.

Sasha and I met twice more in the cellar during the month of May. But then I did not see him for the first two weeks of June. I began to worry that he had been sent somewhere else, because I didn't even see him from a distance around the grounds or the palace. My ecstatic feelings melted away, eventually transforming into almost unbearable, crushing disappointment. I started to imagine that the worst had happened: he'd been killed in some freak accident, and I would have no way of knowing because no one would think to tell me. Or worse, he had fallen in love with someone else, and the two of them were laughing about my naive, trusting affection, plotting ways to hurt me. I was in a misery of doubt and uncertainty.

All that ended, though, and I went back to feeling as if I had been lifted up to the sky again when I found a note from Sasha on my dressing table one evening. I could not imagine how it got there, because the guards were not supposed to enter our private apartments, especially our bedrooms—unless they accompanied Kerensky on one of his visits, and Kerensky had not been in Tsarskoe for over a week. Maybe, I thought, someone else in the palace knew about Sasha and me. But how could that be? Mashka would never have breathed a word, and she would have told me if Sasha had given her a note. She had no reason not to.

However it got there, his note said he wanted to see me that night. I will always remember the date. June 17, 1917, the day before my sixteenth birthday. I was happy to have a meeting with Sasha to look forward to, but also afraid. What if he had changed again? What if he did not welcome me and embrace me as he had? Perhaps he now thought he had made a mistake, or that it was too dangerous for him to admit feeling anything for me. Or he had met someone else. But immediately after I suggested it to myself, I knew it to be untrue. We had known each other too long for him to change toward me completely. And I hadn't changed at all. I felt warm all over just thinking of him.

"I'm going out after midnight tonight," I told Mashka. I left her an opportunity to say that she had delivered the letter. But she only said, "Be careful. They seem to watch us more closely since Damadianz became palace commander."

It was true. Korovichenko, the previous commander, had become quite decent, and we thought things were improving. Then one day the previous week Kerensky had informed us that Korovichenko had been transferred elsewhere, and that Damadianz, the former deputy commander, would take over. Damadianz enjoyed exercising his authority over us. Every day he reduced our privileges further. We were no longer allowed to work in our garden, and it had become sadly overgrown. Papa could hardly go outdoors at all, and if he did, he had to stay close to the residence. We had less food at every meal, and I sometimes went to bed with my stomach still growling. There was no more hot water for our baths—the servants were not permitted to use fuel to heat it, which is what they had done before, carrying buckets up to our bathrooms ever since the running water had been turned off. The rooms we were allowed to ourselves were reduced—although thankfully we children still had the same bedrooms and our schoolrooms, all on our own floor.

Damadianz also made several more of the servants leave, saying there were too many duplicated jobs. That meant we really had to do everything for ourselves. I didn't mind—we had actually been doing chores all our lives anyway. Only Alexei never had to clean his own room. Besides, it gave us more to occupy ourselves with. I enjoyed sweeping the floors and dusting all the little objects in Mama's boudoir. I especially liked dusting the photographs of our family that lined one wall of her room, and crowded each other on the mantelpiece. I had taken many of them myself. They made me remember how simple life had been then, when we were all still in short skirts. What pranks I used to play! There was one photograph of me and all the crew and servants on the *Standart* wearing roller skates. It had been my idea. And then there were all the plays we put on in the little theater in the Winter Palace, or in the makeshift theaters we created wherever we spent more than a few weeks of our lives. The Winter Palace was best for that, though. We had a real theater with lights and curtains and a dressing room. The attics were full of ancient clothing, and we used them to dress up in for our productions, great heavy brocade dresses with hoops from the reign of Alexander I.

In another photograph, we were all piled on one toboggan.

That was the beginning of OTMA—we four girls' initials—which we still called ourselves, as if we were one unit, one entity that could never be broken apart.

Yes, life had been simple. But it was unvarying. Now it was complicated and strange, more interesting in a way. Not in a good way, except for one. I had the deep thrill of my feelings for Sasha, which allowed me to stop longing for earlier times. On that day, knowing I would meet him at night, I wandered around in a fog—walking into rooms and forgetting why I was there, stopping in the middle of a sentence and getting distracted, staring out of a window at nothing at all, until Mashka poked me in the ribs. It was the first time I actually regretted having shaved my head for Mashka's sake, and I wished that I could take a long, warm, fragrant bath so that my skin would smell like spring flowers.

How wonderful it would be, I thought, to be a simple peasant girl who planned to meet her lover. I would be able to ask my sisters—at least one of them would have to be younger so she could look up to me—to help me choose what to wear, and arrange my hair so that it would look its best. Perhaps one of them would lend me a locket to draw my beloved's eyes to my neck, or a bracelet to set off my pretty hands.

Well, my hands were hardly pretty now. They were rough and dry from working outdoors and in. And there was the matter of my hair—it would be dark, I told myself. Perhaps Sasha too preferred the darkness. I could understand that he might want to hide his disfigurement. The patch gave him a certain distinction, but even I had been nervous to ask him to reveal the scar behind it. If we were ever to get married . . .

I began to allow myself a fantasy then, which I have continued to elaborate on through the months of our captivity. In it, my family was at last permitted to live like all other Russians, in freedom, on a farm somewhere in the Crimea perhaps, which would be best for Alexei's and my mother's health. Sasha would come and present himself to my father as my suitor, and we would spend a proper amount of time attending parties and going out with friends. We would have a real romance. I would experience my first kiss all over again, and then, perhaps on my seventeenth birthday, Sasha would ask me to marry him. The fantasy went on to include a small wedding in a village church and a cottage of our own not far from my parents. Sasha was a soldier, and his income would sustain us. Perhaps I would become a nurse and work in a local hospital.

Then I imagined us retiring at night. Sasha would take the patch off his eye, and I would kiss and caress the ugly scar, and we would make love until we both fell asleep, exhausted. Of course, I had no real understanding of what it was to make love, how it felt. My sisters and I sometimes talked about what it would be like. If Olga and Tatiana had ever experienced it, they never said. I imagined it little more than an extension of the kissing and embracing we had done the last time we met. All I knew was that it would make us closer, and I wanted to be so close to Sasha that there would be no distance between us.

At the appointed time I made my way down to the cellar floor. I had become very adept at getting there without making a single sound. The other times we had met, Sasha was always waiting for me at the bottom of the stairs, and would reach for me and take me by the waist, swing me gently around before putting me softly down on the floor. Except once, when he held me tight with my feet off the floor, and we kissed like that. I felt weightless and out of control.

So when I didn't see Sasha waiting for me, I felt ice go through my veins. What if something had prevented him from coming? What if the other guards knew, or this had been a trick? How would I explain what I was doing there if someone else discovered me? I was on the point of scampering back up the stairs and running to my room when someone came up behind me, grabbed me around my waist, and covered my mouth before I could cry out. I struggled.

"Shh! It's me! Come with me."

I was so frightened that at first I didn't believe it was Sasha, not until he lightly kissed the edge of my ear as he drew me back into a space that was even darker than the hallway. He closed a door behind us, struck a match, and lit a candle. We were in some kind of pantry.

"It's not very luxurious, but I think we'll at least have some privacy here. Everything they used to store here was used up weeks ago."

My heart was still thumping. "You scared me so much, Sasha!"

"I'm sorry, but I didn't want you to make a noise," he said.

"I wouldn't have." To be honest, I was a little cross with him. First I had suffered sadness thinking he wasn't coming, and then I was certain someone else discovered me and I was overcome with dread. I was a little short with him when I spoke. "What did you have to tell me?"

He took off his jacket and spread it on the floor, then grasped my hand as he sat, pulling me down next to him. "Don't be cross. I'm sorry it was surprising."

I still wasn't ready to forgive him. "Your note said you wanted to see me."

"Yes," he said, taking my chin and turning my face this way and that, letting his eyes take in every feature until I felt almost embarrassed. "I said I wanted to see you." He moved the candle closer.

So it was true. He had not forgotten me. He still liked me. He still loved me. He brought his face closer to mine until we were almost touching. I couldn't stand it and closed the distance between us with a kiss, which he returned.

When we stopped, he outlined my face with the tip of his finger, following its progress with his eyes. I felt him examine every detail, as if he were taking a long-exposure photograph to look at later when we weren't together.

I closed my eyes and felt his finger measure the length of my neck and continue down to the bone in the center of my chest. I opened my eyes when I felt him start to unfasten the top button of my blouse.

"Is it all right?" he whispered.

"I don't know," I answered. He stopped. "No, it's all right." I didn't want him to stop. I was a little afraid of continuing, but I was more afraid of losing him.

I closed my eyes again, as if not looking would lessen the

wickedness of it, or at least I wouldn't have to see his eyes when he saw my breasts. He was very slow, very gentle. By the time his hands cupped my small breasts, I was trembling, wanting him to go on and on.

"I want you," he said.

I opened my eyes to receive another kiss. This time I felt the rough serge of his uniform against my skin. "I . . . I want you too. I suppose I've always wanted you. Do you think I'm still too young?"

Sasha gently pushed me away from him. Everything was so new, I wondered what he was going to do. I watched, fascinated, as he made a great show of taking out a pocket watch and peering at it. "Young? According to Russian law and custom, you are now an adult."

He was right. It was after midnight. It was my birthday. Sixteen. The tears came to my eyes so suddenly that I couldn't stop them.

"What's wrong?" Sasha asked.

"Oh, it's just that I didn't imagine this on my birthday. Olga and Tatiana and Marie had celebrations and received pearl and diamond necklaces. They went to a ball and danced all night." I laughed through my tears. "It all seems rather foolish now." Sasha gave me his handkerchief and I dried my eyes. His expression was tender, but amused. "I suppose there will never be any balls ever again," I said. "Russia seems like such a different place. I don't know why I'm crying. I don't cry in front of anyone else."

Sasha didn't say anything more. He just gently laid me down beside him on the brick floor of the pantry. I didn't notice how hard and uncomfortable it was. All I felt was Sasha, touching me, kissing me. He was showing me, tenderly and adoringly, that he loved me. I, Anastasie, was loved by a man, a man I loved so much that I wanted to give myself to him completely. I wanted to be two people at once: the creature who had nothing but feelings and who was discovering her body in a way she never knew was possible, and my old self, standing aside and watching this love scene—so perfect, and yet real. But that feeling lasted only a moment. Soon I was lost in the sensations that welled up through my body in waves so powerful they made me forget who I was. I let all consciousness go and took that step off a high cliff, trusting that Sasha would keep me safe. Trusting that he cared enough for me to protect me against anything.

# CHAPTER 21

The following weeks were full of contradictions. Life became harder for us, but Sasha and I grew closer.

The lovely, graceful walls of the palace were covered with disgusting insults to our family painted in crude, black strokes. I could barely stand to look at the palace when we were allowed to go out, which was hardly ever now. And the process of getting this privilege was increasingly irksome.

First, Papa would announce that the palace commander had given us permission to take our daily exercise. Then we would all put on our outdoor shoes and clothing—not coats now, because it had become quite mild—and Mama's maid would help her prepare to go out in her wheelchair.

Next we would assemble in the semicircular hall that led to the courtyard, where we would then stand silently and wait. The doors were heavily locked. Chains and bolts that had never been there before, when the only reason for a lock was for our protection, were now draped and knotted around the great handles—to keep us in. The key would often mysteriously go missing, and our wait would extend to upward of half an hour, until we were all tired of standing still. But we didn't dare murmur a word. Mama refused to look at the officers, and Papa was always courteous, thanking them when finally the doors were unlocked.

Then the guards would stand behind us with their rifles leveled and bayonets fixed and herd us out the door as a group, as if we were the most dangerous of criminals.

Always waiting outside were clusters of slovenly soldiers.

"Hey! Look at the pair of tits on the oldest one!" "The little one has a good, round ass." "Who does Comrade Romanova think she is, lazy cow! Let her get up and walk, like the rest of us!"

And so it would go until the officers chased them away. This took longer and longer as time went on, and I began to dread setting foot outside, even on the most beautiful days.

But two or three times a week, Sasha managed it so that we could meet. Our hours together felt like dipping my limbs in a crystal clear lake and letting the water soothe away my agony. Sasha always told me I was beautiful, always asked after my sisters and Alexei, and hoped things weren't too bad for Mama and Papa.

"She really is very ill, you know," I said to him one night as we lay together on the floor of the pantry. My blouse was open, and Sasha traced the outline of my breasts with the tip of his little finger.

"You are not, though," he said, rolling over to kiss me. I pushed him away.

"I'm serious. It's her heart. She has been ill for years. That's why she kept so much to herself. That, and Alexei's condition, of course."

"Can nothing cure him?"

"You know it cannot. The only thing that made him improve, or at least appeared to, were the prayers of Rasputin."

I felt Sasha stiffen next to me. "Do you believe that?"

"Of course not! But prayers are very powerful."

"The Bolsheviks plan to abolish religion and take over all the monasteries if they seize power."

Now it was my turn to be shocked. "How do you know this?"

Sasha answered without looking me in the eye. "Oh, one hears things. The men talk."

It disquieted me that Sasha evaded my answer. "Besides," I said, "even the tribunal did not find anything they could convict Mama of."

"Your Mme Vyrubova is having a difficult time of it at Peter and Paul," he said, absently stroking my arm.

I buttoned my blouse. I didn't like it when our conversations turned to such things. I couldn't bear to think of Anya, poor crippled thing, without enough guile or wit to be dangerous to anyone, put in a prison that was more like a dungeon, or so the servants said. "And where do you get your information about Anya—who is not *my* Mme Vyrubova, by the way, but only Mama's friend who has always been kind to us."

"You see, the trouble is that so much went on that you had no idea about. Even your papa, who should have known better, trusted others whom he shouldn't have."

"What use is all this talk? Where will it lead?" I stood, brushing the dirt off my skirt and smoothing my hair, which had now grown to a gently curling two inches all over.

"You need to know, to understand. I think they will move you soon. The Bolsheviks tried to take over in Petrograd and nearly succeeded. They were put down, but the way I see it, they will eventually prevail. And the Bolsheviks are more of a danger to all of you than the Soviet. Kerensky is coming to see your parents tomorrow. There's a fellow named Lenin who is gathering followers like fresh flypaper. He would very much like all of you to be far away. Kerensky's not so bad. He'll put you somewhere out of harm's way, where you might be forgotten."

His words sounded like farewell. I tried to read his expression. "You'll go with us, won't you?"

"I don't know. It's possible, but I have no say in the matter."

I guess our ability to meet and avoid discovery had made us more and more careless of speaking quietly and moving around without making a sound. At that instant, before we had time to react, the door to our private sanctuary flew open and standing in the doorway was a guard I recognized. He was one of those who always stood around when we went outside and ogled us and called rude things after us.

"So this is how you perform your guard duty, Galliapin!" The soldier's voice was slurred, and his eyes were red rimmed and watery. "I see it's the little beauty for you, eh? Comrades should share with one another. No private property, says Comrade Lenin." He lurched forward and grabbed for me. I was so stunned that I didn't move fast enough and he caught hold of my arm and dragged me down to the floor. I scraped my cheek on a wooden shelf on the way and could feel the blood trickle down my neck.

The next few moments were a confusion of limbs in army brown. Sasha fell upon the guard and pummeled him with his fists. The other fellow was not in complete control of his movements, having obviously had a skinful of vodka, but he was bigger than Sasha. And he had enough of his wits about him to grab for the patch over Sasha's eye. Sasha cried out.

I don't know exactly what came over me, but I flew out of my corner and took hold of the attacker's neck, pulling with all my might. This surprised him and he turned away from Sasha briefly, giving Sasha just enough time to stand. The drunken guard raised his fist, aiming to bring it down in the middle of my face. I braced myself for the blow, closing my eyes and praying.

But the blow never came. I heard a stifled gurgle and opened my eyes. Sasha stood frozen in horror over the limp body of the guard, his dagger in his hand. I watched a drop of blood collect on the blade and fall onto the guard's head. The man had a fixed expression of surprise on his face, and I saw the thin line where Sasha had slit his throat. Blood pulsed from his neck and over the floor, staining my skirt and blouse. I fought back a feeling of revulsion, remembering that I had seen much worse in the hospital three years before.

"Sasha! What have you done? What shall we do?"

"I . . . I . . ." It was clear Sasha was having trouble tearing himself away from the spectacle. I heard footsteps in a distant part of the cellar.

"You must get out of here! You must get away!" I whispered, more concerned for him at that moment than myself.

"Yes. Yes." He wiped his knife on the dead guard's tunic and sheathed it in his belt. I saw that he had managed not to be badly stained with the blood. I, however, would have some explaining to do. The entire front of my blouse and much of my skirt bore a deep crimson stain. I had brought my cloak, though, to shield me as I crept through the palace, thinking perhaps that if someone saw me from a distance he might assume I was a whore making a living among the bored soldiers. We had seen them coming and going at all times of the day and night. I stood.

Sasha faced me across the barrier of the body. "I'm sorry. This shouldn't have happened." A tear traced a path down his cheek. He reached for my hand and pressed it hard to his lips. An instant later, he was gone. I wrapped myself in my cloak and ran as fast as I could to the safety of my bedroom, hearing behind me shouts of surprise and anger when some soldiers came upon the murdered man.

# ⚜ CHAPTER 22 ⚜

Mashka was sound asleep when I returned. I quickly removed my skirt and blouse and, deciding I would never get the stains out, I stuffed them in the stove in the corner of our room. We still lit it on chilly mornings, and I piled in kindling and one or two stouter logs, rolled up some paper, and struck a match. The cotton and wool of the clothes stank abominably, but they caught. I washed myself as best I could with the small basin of cold water and nub of black soap. Try as I might, I couldn't get the smell of the soldier's vile breath and fresh blood out of my nostrils. I slipped into bed and piled the blankets on, but I shivered violently, unable to feel warm despite the blaze in the stove.

"What's that smell?" Mashka's groggy voice stirred me.

"Just the stove," I answered, hoping she wouldn't hear my teeth chattering.

"What time is it?"

"Not yet dawn. Go back to sleep."

She sat up suddenly, slipped her feet out of bed, and ran to me. "Are you ill?" She placed her hand on my forehead.

"No, no," I said. Then I burst into tears.

"What is it? What has happened?" She put her arms around me and rocked me like a baby. "Is it Sasha? Did you quarrel?"

She had unwittingly given me the perfect explanation for my state. I just nodded, not trusting myself to speak.

"There now. You knew it could not last. Is he to go away?"

I nodded again, and pressed my streaming eyes into her neck. She smelled clean and wholesome. No one was more innocent than Mashka. I could never tell her what really happened. Although soon enough news of the murder would fly through the palace and even she might be a little suspicious.

That was the first time I understood that what had happened could have bad consequences for us. They might suspect a monarchist, a counterrevolutionary, of having committed this crime. They would question us, perhaps imprison our few friends left who were sympathetic to us. There was Princess Paley, who lived in Tsarskoe and had not been allowed to visit us, and whose occasional messages we received only after they had been well scrutinized by the guards. Or the elderly Count Benckendorff or Count Fredericks, marshals of the court, who refused to give up their friendship even when my father's own cousins had turned their backs on him.

How could I keep such a secret?

Mashka crawled in next to me in my narrow cot, and the warmth of her body eventually soothed me to sleep. By the time we awoke it was well after dawn, and the fire in the stove had burned down.

"I'll put on another log," Mashka whispered, bravely being the first one to place her feet on the cold floor.

"Oh!" I cried out. "Let me do it." I jumped up and tried to get to the stove before Mashka had a chance to see any evidence of what I had burned there the night before. But I was too late.

"What is this?" she asked, holding a scrap of wool twill in her fingers, its edges singed, but enough stitching still visible on it to identify it as my skirt.

"It's complicated," I murmured, and then I didn't know what else to say.

Mashka cocked her head to the side and examined my face. "You know you can't keep anything from me. How did you scratch your face? What happened?"

"Oh, it's nothing. Not important. I had a long nail and scratched myself in my sleep."

Mashka looked as though she didn't believe me. "But there is something, isn't there."

I wanted so to tell her, yet I knew it would be a terrible mistake. "Please don't ask me to say. I really can't. It wouldn't be . . ." I couldn't think how to put her off without hurting her feelings.

"You don't have to. I understand. I know more of the ways of men than you imagine."

"Thank you," I breathed. She thought it had only to do with Sasha's and my love. Perhaps she imagined that I had lost my virginity that night, and that I was upset over Sasha and felt so soiled that I had to burn my clothes.

"You must pray for mercy. Pray for Sasha. Will you see him again?"

I shook my head. "No. He has gone. It was for the best."

She put her arms around me. I felt wretched letting her believe the lie. I was afraid that once she heard the news of the murder, she might figure out that there was more to my story than she thought. But for now, I had bought some time to compose myself before facing the rest of the family.

⁂

When we joined Mama in the parlor after breakfast, we found Alyosha and Papa there, as well as the rest of the suite, along with four armed guards.

"Can't you at least leave the children out of this?" Mama was pleading with Damadianz, who looked more small and pinched than usual.

"Ah, the children!" he said, letting a smile pull the corners of his mouth up in a grimace. "Yet they are hardly children, Mme Romanova."

Mama had been leaning for support on a chair back. But when he said those words, she pulled herself up to her impressive height and looked at him down her long, delicate nose. "They have been brought up to be innocent and pure. They are more like children than many who are several years younger than they."

"Really!" he said. We had arranged ourselves in our OTMA ranks, with Alexei standing protectively to the side of us. His forehead was creased. He was in pain. He would have an attack, and Mama would be wholly occupied with him and not concerned with anything outside his sickroom. I did not wish it on Alexei—how I cried when I was younger to hear his moans that no one could stop. However, if it was not too bad an attack, it would distract Mama long enough for the business of the murder to blow over, for them to decide that it had nothing to do with us.

I was thinking this as Damadianz strolled slowly in front of us, just close enough to make us all feel uncomfortable but not close enough that we could reasonably object.

"There is a rumor that one of you has been dallying with the guards."

"I protest most vehemently!" Mama's voice was sharp and imperious.

Damadianz looked around at her as if she were a fly that had alit on his ear and he wanted to brush off, but it flew just out of reach. I struggled against an urge to cry out and admit to my guilt, so that I would not carry my secret any longer. "I do not credit these rumors, Mme Romanova. None of them are attractive enough to warrant it. Some men will do anything for a taste of virgin flesh, however."

Mother seethed. I could see that she wanted to call for a servant and have the man escorted out of the room. But of course, she could no longer expect help from the guards, so she simply gripped the top of the chair.

"Still, one of you might have seen something," Damadianz said. "The incident occurred in the cellars two floors below your bedrooms."

"My daughters neither saw nor heard anything. They would have told me."

I could feel Mashka's breath quickening. I had drawn her into the lie too. She now guessed what had distressed me so, and she would not be able to carry it off if questioned closely. "Perhaps you are mistaken in your confidence?" Damadianz said, his voice rising at the end. I thought he was going to leave, but instead he wheeled around and, starting with Olga, addressed questions directly to each of us. "Olga Romanova, if I am not mistaken? Did you hear anything last night between the hours of one and three in the morning?"

Olga shook her head slowly from side to side, then said in her melodious voice, "No, Commander."

This respect pleased him. He continued to Tatiana.

"What about you, Tatiana Romanova?" He spoke so quietly that Tatiana couldn't hear him—she hadn't yet fully recovered from the deafness that the measles had caused. She leaned forward and cupped a hand around her ear.

"I said, did you hear anything!" he yelled into her ear, and she jerked backward.

"As you see, I have a hard time hearing at all at present." Tatiana did not repeat Olga's politeness.

He passed quickly on to Mashka, who was by then trembling so violently I feared he would guess everything without having to be told.

"And Maria Romanova? Is there anything you wish to say to me?"

Mashka's eyes were open wide and a light beading of sweat had broken out on her brow. She moved her lips as if she were about to speak, but instead went deathly pale and slumped to the floor in a faint.

I could no longer contain my anger. "Look what you've done!" I flung my words at Damadianz. Mama pressed the bell for a servant. Olga and Tatiana joined me in patting Mashka's hands and face and fanning her to wake her up. "She has been very ill. Her constitution cannot bear any nervous strain. Please leave us." I kept the side of my face with the scratch turned away from him.

To my surprise, he left the room without saying a word.

It was fortunate that at first everyone in the family attributed Mashka's swoon to her convalescence, and once she awoke she had enough self-possession to keep my secret. I prayed that no one would ask her a direct question, certain that she would not have the strength to lie.

I stayed with the family through lunch—a light affair consisting of clear, almost tasteless soup and hard bread, with only a little cold tongue for meat. Mama, as usual, did not touch the meat and barely drank any soup. The bread was too hard for her to bite.

"Mama," I asked, "would it be awfully impolite if I softened my bread in the broth?"

She smiled weakly at me. I took it as a yes, and proceeded to make the bread at least chewable, using my spoon so that I might set an acceptable example for Mama, and she would take a little more nourishment. But she did not seem to notice. Alexei was not at lunch. A bad sign. The pain I had noticed in his face must have become unbearable enough to keep him in bed. Mama left the table as soon as we were done to go directly to his room.

None of us had any spirit for games, so I decided I would go up and sit with Alyosha, perhaps read to him if his attack wasn't too bad.

"Is that you, Nastya?" he said when I entered, his voice high and pinched, as it was when he was speaking through the pain.

"Yes, here I am. Do you want me to read to you? Or just sit?"

"Don't read. Not yet."

I sat down in the chair that was always by his bed. "Where's Mama?"

"I sent her to her room to rest. It's not such a bad attack this time. Nastya," he began, then stopped.

"What, Sunshine?"

"I have a feeling about the murder. I think I may know who did it."

"Oh?" I said, hoping he would hear the lack of interest in my voice and drop the subject.

"Yes. I have bad feelings about that guard, the one with the patch who shoved you in the garden that time. I think he could murder someone."

I forced myself to laugh. "What makes you say that? Just because he has a patch on his eye, like a pirate? Aye, matey! I'll make ye walk the gangplank!"

"No, Nastya. I'm serious. Something about him frightens me. See if he hasn't disappeared now. I bet we won't see him again."

Alyosha's eyes closed and the muscles in his face tightened.

He was having a wave of pain. He had become so accustomed to it that unless the pain was really intense, he didn't make a sound. I stroked his head lightly and watched the attack pass and his face relax into restless sleep. I kissed his forehead and stood just as my mother returned.

"How was he?" she asked, not looking at me, but only having eyes for Alexei.

"Not too bad," I said, "but he was talking some nonsense. I think he's become confused about the murder and it's part of his pain."

Mama nodded. "I'll sit with him while he sleeps."

I went down to the little library, where I hoped I would be alone. It was the first opportunity I had had to think through what had happened the night before. What Sasha had done was horrible, but he had done it in my defense. I owed him something. The first thing was to deflect Alyosha's suspicion. How had he put that together? Sometimes I thought my brother had the wisdom of an angel, as though he had been so close to death that he had taken on some supernatural characteristics. He certainly seemed to be able to see into my heart.

But what more could I do than manage Alexei? In our palace prison I had no power at all. Sasha had said we would be moved. Perhaps it would give us more freedom if we were not in Tsarskoe, where we could so easily reach the Finnish border. Yet if we went to Moscow, or even farther, what then?

Now, the future stretched bleakly before me. Even out in the garden, ogled by the guards, I had had the secret knowledge that he was nearby, and that he would jump to my aid if he had to. And, too, the heart-flipping anticipation of our night-time meetings in the cellar, where he showed me what it was to be a woman, gently and tenderly. I had those memories, but they pained me. What if we never saw each other again?

I knew then that even if we had said our final good-byes last night, I would always love him.

## ⚜ CHAPTER 23 ⚜

Inquiry into the guard's murder eventually quieted down; it was largely assumed that he had startled an intruder while making his rounds, and paid for it with his life. My relief was enormous.

It was late in July when we heard at last that we were definitely going to be moved. Kerensky came himself to tell us. "There are people here who do not want you removed from your current location, but I have persuaded the Provisional Government that your continued safety depends upon this happening as soon as possible."

We all listened closely to the minister of justice, who, as things had become harder for us in Tsarskoe, had become more and more sympathetic. I believed he was sincere in wanting to protect us from the extreme elements in the ranks, and that he would do his best to get us away.

"Where will we go? To Livadia? It would be so good for Baby's health," Mama said. She had warmed a great deal toward

Kerensky over the past months, realizing that although he was passionate about the new order, he was a man of principle and decency, believing that the people would ultimately prove themselves worthy of being entrusted with the government of Russia.

"I cannot tell you that," Kerensky answered, as if he was genuinely sorry, "but preparations must be made in conditions of the utmost secrecy. We do not want the guards to know that you will leave Tsarskoe."

He gave us detailed instructions about what we were to prepare, what we could bring, and who could accompany us. "Any of your suite who are willing to go with you may do so and share the terms of your imprisonment, but your attendant staff must be limited."

He handed Mama a list. She looked it up and down. "It says here that the ladies are to bring furs."

"It is always better to be prepared for anything," Kerensky said, then bowed and departed.

Furs meant we would not be going to the warm climate of the Crimea. I alone dreaded even a removal to Livadia. How would Sasha find us? And how would he gain admittance to the palace, if they suspected him of the murder of a Soviet guard? I held out some hope that wherever we were going would not be as strictly guarded as the Alexander Palace, and that if Sasha came to me, we would be able to meet again. But it was a slender thread of hope that, even at my most optimistic, I found hard to cling to.

We began that very day, quietly and without attracting notice to ourselves, to gather together all the things we wanted or needed to bring. Isa helped Mama make lists, but not long into the preparations Isa fell ill with pneumonia. She kept mainly to her room after that, and Nastinka took over.

Our departure had been set for August 13, the day after Alexei's birthday. About a week before, we all met in the parlor and Papa addressed everyone.

"I do not know where we are going, how long we will be there, or what conditions will be like," he said. "It is clear that if we stay here life will soon become intolerable, and we owe our removal to a safer place to Minister Kerensky. He has said those who wish may go into exile with us, and share our same conditions of arrest. But I must caution all of you that I have no way of knowing what the future holds, and will not think less of any of you if you prefer not to cast your lot in with us."

It was the first time I had heard my father directly address the matter of our future. Everyone's face in the room was grave, but determined. One by one, the members of the suite who remained, our tutors, and Mama's and Papa's valets and personal servants announced their decision. Nastinka, Lili Obolensky, our nanny Alexandra Tegleva, Prince Dolgorukov, General Tatischev, Zhilik, Trina, Mama's physician Dr. Botkin and his family, Alexei's physician Dr. Derevenko and his family, Demidova, Chemodurov, and Volkov would all come with us. Count Benckendorff's wife was too elderly to make the trip, as was our dear Count Fredericks, and Count Apraxin felt he could do more on behalf of the family by staying behind. And

Isa, of course, was still in bed and sick, and would not be well enough to make the journey with us. Mr. Gibbes would have to be asked separately since he had still not been permitted to come into the Alexander Palace. It was settled. That left the matter of the servants. We took what we determined to be a minimum: six chamberlains, ten footmen, a butler, a wine steward, and three of the palace cooks. Papa's barber would also travel with us, and of course, the faithful Nagorny, the sailor who carried Alexei when he was too ill to walk.

It would be a somewhat diminished, but not terribly small group. That Kerensky allowed so many to come made us assume that we would at least be housed comfortably somewhere.

It was difficult to do all the necessary sorting and packing without provoking any comment on the part of the guards, but we did our best. I was surprised to see that Mama cheered up a little. I think our life at Tsarskoe had become so vexing and tedious that she looked forward to a change. The rest of us were not so happy.

That night after we left the suite, Zhilik and Trina in the parlor at their card games, the five of us went to our schoolroom to talk things over before going to bed.

"Do you think we'll ever come back here?" Mashka asked.

Tatiana, as usual, was quick with a reply. "Whether we will or not, we have to pack as though we're leaving for good. That means taking everything that you cannot do without, and all the jewels, certainly."

"May I bring Joy? I won't go without Joy," Alyosha said.

"I don't know," Olga said. "But we'll assume we can take

Joy, Jimmy, Ortino, and Olga's cat. Let them try to wrench away our pets at the last moment!"

"I'll be glad to go," Mashka said. "It's been so strange here. Better to be someplace new where everything doesn't remind you of how life used to be."

I agreed with Mashka, but said nothing. The one familiar person I wanted with me more than any other had already gone away. I suddenly realized that I didn't even have a photograph of him. Why had I never taken any? I wondered then if I would have preferred a picture of him younger, with both eyes clear and uncovered, or now, with the patch hiding his scar, and the memory of our closeness—our transformation from friends to . . . lovers. Yes, we were lovers. I smiled.

"Nastya, what are you thinking?" asked Tatiana.

I quickly wrenched myself back to the present. "I was thinking of all the photographs I want to bring with me, and that I must have my camera."

"Then you can help Mama with the pictures and mementos. Olga, you be in charge of the jewels and icons, and I'll decide with Trina, Zhilik, and Mr. Gibbes about the books." Tatiana was only happy when she was organizing something. I didn't mind. It would help focus our efforts.

"I'll help Papa," said Alyosha.

"The best thing you can do is try to remain well," Olga said.

"I'm glad at least Kolya Derevenko will be with us, so we can play sometimes." The doctor's son was one of the few playmates Alyosha was allowed. He knew about the disease, and took care not to be too rough with him.

"What shall I do?" Mashka asked.

"Clothes," answered Tatiana. "Help Mama decide what she really needs. Demidova will want to bring everything, and that is probably unnecessary. Zanotti will take charge of the important jewels, of course, but she must be persuaded that the court gowns are unnecessary where we're going."

Where we're going. But where were we going? I wished I knew.

I settled into helping Mama as Tatiana had decided.

"At least Kerensky understands how much these things mean to us," Papa said as he watched Mama and me put photographs into two piles. Mama did not answer, only looked around her mauve boudoir with such emptiness in her eyes that it made me want to cry.

"Kerensky says that Kobylinsky and a detachment of the guards will come too," he said.

"I hope they're the nice ones," Mama said, not stopping her sorting.

"He says they'll be handpicked for their loyalty and discretion."

"Loyalty to whom?" I asked.

Papa didn't answer.

I thought again of Sasha. If he had remained, I was certain he would have been chosen as one of those three hundred fifty.

The day approached when we were to leave, and it became harder and harder to disguise our purpose. Drawers were turned out, trunks opened, bookshelves emptied. While Mama and I were working in her boudoir, a guard came in carrying two balalaikas. One was Alexei's—a beautifully decorated instrument he had been given by the villagers at Livadia, and that he loved to play—and the other was Sasha's simple instrument that I had hidden in the back of my wardrobe. I hoped that Mashka had taken it out, and not waited until a maid came upon it, or worse—Zanotti. Pain stabbed my heart to see that token of Sasha's and my first meeting exposed to scrutiny as if it were an ordinary object.

"The commander says you may take these if you wish, although they will occupy much space for their size."

Either Mama did not realize that Alexei possessed only one balalaika, or she chose to ignore that fact when she saw the look on my face. She answered only, "Of course we will take them. The children must continue to be educated in the customs and culture of their country."

I pretended that the matter didn't interest me, but I was so relieved that I would not have to part with my one memento of Sasha that from that moment on, having to leave so much else behind did not feel so terribly unfair.

Obviously, some of the guards knew and took our departure in stride. For those who didn't, we tried to attribute the frenzied activity to cleaning, but I knew many of them—the ones who were not coming with us and who were the most Soviet—looked at us with suspicion and were brewing trouble.

We had no choice but to carry on despite everything. Kerensky came frequently with instructions and news. One afternoon he arrived beaming with pent-up excitement.

"I am pleased to announce that the government has seen

fit to honor me with the position of minister of war." He bowed to Papa when he said it.

"Good, Kerensky!" Papa seemed genuinely pleased. "The war needs a leader like you. Things have been sadly neglected. I had hoped that it was the distraction of an unwanted tsar, and that once matters had been sorted out, the war would again be our first priority. But I hear nothing but bad news about it."

Kerensky nodded. "I have already taken measures to remedy that. I stop here in the midst of my travels to visit all the troops and their officers, and rekindle their zeal in this important effort for our nation."

"Just what is needed, Kerensky. You're a good man."

Although he tried to hide it, I thought I saw Kerensky smile and blush just a little. "I'm also pleased to inform you that my efforts have already produced results. We have accomplished the first advance of the war since the beginning of the Provisional Government."

"It's what I had hoped for," Papa said. His eyes filled with tears and he could say nothing more.

"Won't you stay and have tea with us?" Mama said. Her attitude toward Kerensky had changed dramatically in recent weeks. Perhaps she had some premonition about the commissars and commanders to come.

"Thank you, Madame," he answered with an incline of his head, "but no. I must return to Petrograd immediately."

He left right away. At tea, with all the family and the suite gathered there, Papa could talk of nothing else besides the good news about the war. He looked happier than he had for a long time. "This is precisely why I sacrificed myself for the country, hoping that it would make the difference and everyone would turn their attention to the war, and helping our allies."

"Perhaps this is the beginning of a change for the better," Prince Dolgorukov said.

"Change or not, we still have to leave." Nastinka sighed, and the conversation stopped for a moment as everyone thought about what that might mean.

It was Mama who broke the silence. "Darling, do you suppose they will allow us to have a service of thanksgiving in the chapel?"

"Perhaps, if we do it on Alexei's birthday so that no one suspects it's because we are about to travel." Papa had taken Kerensky's instructions completely to heart. It struck me then that he was much better at being a soldier than a general.

Alexei's thirteenth birthday was August 12, the day before we were scheduled to leave Tsarskoe. I didn't know whether that was coincidence, or whether Kerensky had anticipated this request by my mother, and built an excuse for a religious observance into his plans.

But however clever Kerensky had been, the Soviet, in the end, nearly had their way. We had packed everything, and the moment came when our departure could no longer be hidden from the guards. A mountain of luggage, including our camp beds, linens, kitchen supplies, and much more sat in the courtyard of the palace, waiting to be taken to the imperial train station.

I have replayed the scene of the night we left Tsarskoe so often in my mind, like viewing a film over and over again, the motions devoid of color and sound, like the movies we used to watch at Livadia, the newsreels and bits and snatches of whatever Volkov considered suitable fare for us children. Sometimes I even dream about it. The whole experience was half-lit, nightmarish.

It began in the semidarkness, no candles being brought because we thought we would soon be leaving. We were all gathered in the semicircular hallway, just as we used to gather to go out to take the air, only it was already evening on August 13. Our scheduled departure time was ten o'clock, and we were told to be ready an hour earlier. We wore our traveling clothes, and the trunks and valises with our personal possessions surrounded us. The problem, we were first told, was that there weren't enough servants left to load the luggage. But that apparently wasn't the real reason for the delay.

Damadianz, who had become increasingly surly as we packed in the previous weeks, came in and announced, "The Tsarskoe members of the Soviet are meeting to decide if you will be allowed to go." He folded his arms across his chest, daring us to object. But we knew better. Papa made Mama sit down in her wheelchair, and the rest of us stood or sat as comfortably as we could in the hall, not saying a thing.

Hours passed. My back began to hurt from doing nothing. At 11:30 there was a commotion at the door. The guards unlocked it, and I thought perhaps we were finally being allowed to go, but we were all surprised to see Kerensky enter, accompanied by my uncle, Grand Duke Michael. It was he, my father's dear brother, who had refused to accept the crown from him and paved the way for the Provisional Government to be established.

"Mishka!" Papa said and ran to him. They embraced. I saw tears in both their eyes. Kerensky ushered them quickly away from the hall and into Papa's study. Papa returned a short while later without Uncle Mishka.

"Kerensky was there the whole time," he said in a hushed voice to Mama. "But he apologized and said he wouldn't listen. Mishka wanted to come and bid his farewells to everyone when we were done, but he was not allowed to. It is for me to convey his fondest good wishes to you and his nieces and nephew."

At that moment Damadianz, who had gone away for a while to see what was happening with the Soviet guards, returned. "Your departure, by permission of Kerensky, has been set at midnight." He said it as if he was disgusted with the whole thing. "Had it been my decision, you would not be going, but the men have chosen to ignore me."

So that was the problem. The men alone were not trying to keep us. Damadianz and Kerensky were engaged in a power struggle over the matter. Damadianz was naturally on the side of the Soviet. Having control over us gave him importance he might not otherwise have. He left without a word, possibly to go and stir up more trouble. We waited and waited. Every time someone came in to say we would be going soon, we would once again prepare ourselves, putting on the traveling coats we had removed as the delay stretched on, picking up our small parcels of books and the valises that contained our brushes, combs, and other toiletries, and our jewel cases. And then time would pass and nothing would happen.

Guards streamed in and out in small groups, announcing yet more excuses for the delay: The luggage was too heavy—although mostly it contained bedding and items from the kitchen and pantry, and therefore was all necessary. There would not be enough room for everything. The train was not yet ready to receive us.

The train. I looked forward to the comfort of that rolling palace, so familiar from better times. Train rides had nearly always been happy occasions, as they meant we were going to Livadia or Poland or to the port where the *Standart* awaited us for a cruise to the beautiful waters of Finland. And when we again boarded it after those delightful holidays, it meant that we were returning to the comforts of Tsarskoe Selo or Peterhof.

"Perhaps we should get out the cards," suggested Olga, one eye on Papa who took small, pacing steps back and forth past a window to the courtyard.

"There is no point. We shall be going soon," said Mashka, gesturing her head toward Alexei. Poor Alexei. He was so exhausted that he looked gray. He sat on a trunk, holding Joy's leash, who alternately lay down and slept at his feet, then roused herself when someone came in. Joy acted out what we all felt. Alternate relief and weariness. The other dogs and the cat were in crates with the luggage, and probably felt as confused and tired as we did.

❦

By the time the signal came that we were actually to leave, we almost didn't believe it, and the guards had to practically yell at us to get us going. It was six in the morning and none of us had slept. Mama was paler than I had ever seen her, and Alexei had deep blue circles under his eyes.

We were hurried into small, dirty automobiles. Several of the guards mounted horses to escort us. Mashka and I sat in the backseat of a tiny motorcar, clutching our things. We pulled away very quickly. I turned to look out the back window as the familiar sight of our home became less and less distinct in the gray morning. There were Isa, who was better but still not well enough to travel, Count Benckendorff, and Count Fredericks by the front entrance, leaning against it as if they were not capable of supporting their own weight. Isa would follow us when she was better, but Count Benckendorff would probably return to his own country, Austria, despite leaving his stepson, Prince Dolgorukov, to remain with my father. Count Fredericks would return to Petrograd.

It had never quite been real to me before then. Our captivity, as vexing as it had been, hadn't removed us from the scenes of happy times. And when I wanted to, if I remained on the children's floor where the soldiers rarely ventured, or we spent an hour or two in the Mountain Hall with its wide, built-in slide, I could forget for a while that things were not as they once had been. But now, I somehow knew that I would never see my bedroom, or the schoolroom, or Mama's mauve boudoir again. I had to turn away to keep from crying.

We arrived at the station and boarded a train that was comfortable enough, but I was disappointed to see that it was not the imperial train. That had apparently been requisitioned by the Provisional Government, just like the limousines. And we were traveling incognito, under the guise of being members of the Japanese Red Cross. Were we really in such danger? I wondered. It seemed odd to think we would cut through the countryside, and no one would know it was us.

"You must not reveal yourselves at all when you pass through towns and cities," Kerensky was telling us. "Stops for exercise will be in remote areas. You should have all you need, and Colonel Kobylinsky will manage any requests for papers. Makarov and Verchenin are also traveling with you to take care of any difficulties, should they arise." Makarov was commissar to the minister of the court, and Verchenin was a deputy of the Duma.

We listened to Kerensky, too tired to think. He gave us a short bow, kissed my mother's hand, and said, "Farewell, Sire—you see, I use the old address." There was something very touching about that gesture from someone who believed so wholeheartedly in the new order. But it didn't surprise me. Everyone who really knew Mama and Papa loved them for who they were, instead of wishing they would be different.

We were all shown our compartments, and Kobylinsky explained how the guards would be arranged.

"Tell me, Commander," Prince Dolgorukov said. "Are all these sharpshooters and soldiers here to protect us, or to keep us imprisoned?"

"Both," answered Kobylinsky.

The idea that we needed such protection against the citizens of our country affected me deeply. All my life, even recently, had been passed in isolated security and safety. Now we would travel through a hostile wilderness that was once our country. Somewhere in that wilderness, I knew, were a few who would have done anything to preserve us from harm, but they had no power to reach us.

More important than that, somewhere in all the vastness of Russia was one whose heart held a piece of my own.

The train lurched into motion sometime before seven in the morning. As we picked up speed and the rhythm of the wheels became regular and determined, the thread that bound Sasha and me to each other stretched tighter, and soon my heart ached with longing. He had been a part of that life in Tsarskoe and Peterhof, even as he opened their doors and guided me to a strange outside world.

None of us could say a thing to each other. The government—or rather Kerensky—had obviously taken great pains to see that we were comfortable. The carriages were first-class, and we had a dining car. The soldiers who accompanied us remained largely outside of where we were, so that we had the illusion of being free. We sisters had a carriage to ourselves. Mama, Papa, and Alexei shared one. And what remained of the suite and the servants were distributed among three more carriages. We watched the village of Tsarskoe pass by us, the tower of the cathedral, then the outlying farms. It was the last time I would see any surroundings that belonged to my earlier life.

About an hour outside of Tsarskoe, it became clear that we were traveling east, not south to Livadia, or even Moscow. A Soviet guard came through the train and announced to us where we were being taken.

To the Governor's House in Tobolsk, Siberia.

## ❖ CHAPTER 24 ❖

Our rail journey lasted three and a half days. We stopped each day for half an hour to take walks and get some fresh air. It was always far away from any village, and Papa was told not to get too near the engine because they didn't want the engineer to recognize him. The guards who accompanied us were mostly the kinder ones, and they stayed largely in their own cars. We had our own excellent cook along, Kharitonov, who prepared meals that were much more ample and delicious than those we had lately been receiving at Tsarskoe. And I will never forget crossing the Urals, the massive range of mountains and hills that separates the more densely populated part of Russia from the wild, desolate steppes of Siberia. Every curve revealed a magnificent new vista of forbidding, snow-covered rock rising above the dense fir forests that stretched for miles. Despite the fact that we were little more than captives now, I felt my heart surge at the sight. This was our Russia. This was what Papa had made his sacrifice for. It would always be here, no matter what happened to us.

We passed along gorges that sheered away from the edge of the railway. I would look out and have a thrill in my stomach, imagining what would happen if we failed to round the bend and plunged hundreds of feet to the frothing rivers below.

Not long after the hills flattened out on the other side of the Urals, we arrived at Tyumen, a city on the Tobol River. Tyumen was the nearest station to Tobolsk, but we still had a journey by boat to reach our final destination. We all boarded the *Rus*, a small but comfortably appointed steamboat, to continue on by river for several more days.

For a while, on the *Rus*, it felt as though we were on holiday again. The fresh air blowing across the open, rolling steppes made my lungs feel healthy after the sooty, enclosed train ride. We were given the run of the vessel. They obviously didn't expect us to risk our lives in the swirling waters of the Tobol. And no one objected when we all gathered on deck as we passed the village of Pokrovskoye, the native home of Grigory Efimovich Rasputin.

"He foretold this, you know," I heard Mama say to Papa. "He said, 'Willingly or unwillingly, you will someday pass my house.'"

"We must not dwell on the past. Anything may yet happen."

Mama did not look at Papa when she answered. "He said that after he died our dynasty would be destroyed with violence, and Russia would descend into chaos."

Papa said nothing, only taking hold of Mama's hand and patting it. I couldn't help recalling what I had seen on that macabre night at Tsarskoe, watching while the coffin containing the rotting flesh and bones of Rasputin burned to ashes. Perhaps the starets had been right. Perhaps his existence had been the one thing that bound Russia as it had been together.

When we reached our destination of Tobolsk, Colonel Kobylinsky, Prince Dolgorukov, and General Tatischev went to inspect the house we were to occupy.

"It is not fit for pigs to inhabit," said the prince when they returned. "It has been used as a barracks, and the men obviously took the opportunity to show their disdain for their betters by destroying a fine house." I knew it must have been true, because the colonel did not contradict him.

"I assure you, we shall remedy the situation," Kobylinsky said, and went off to the town again.

We never saw the Governor's House in that state. We remained in our quarters on the *Rus* for another week while the house was cleaned and painted, and our furnishings moved in for us. What we didn't have, they purchased from people in town, we later discovered. And although we were anxious to be settled, we didn't mind staying on the *Rus* a little longer. The weather was glorious, and we had always enjoyed sailing.

"Perhaps now that we are so far away from all the trouble they will forget about us," Mashka said as we went on one of our walks in the beautiful, wild countryside, having steamed some way down the river on a fine day. The guards hardly followed us, only watching from the ship and the shore nearby. After all, where would we escape to? We were nearly a hundred and fifty miles from any other city, and the countryside was bare. We would be seen for miles.

"Perhaps," I said. Everyone seemed a little more relaxed than at Tsarskoe. "Perhaps they will at last allow us just to have a private life in Russia, and life will change, but go on." Even as I said those words, they felt impossible. But for that moment at least, I had the illusion of being free and contented, and so did not listen to the warning in my heart.

The detachments of guards that had traveled with us on the train and on the *Rus* would be augmented, apparently, by others. The prince gave us the information that the balance would not be dissimilar to that at Tsarskoe, with those who were respectful and pleasant toward us, and those who treated us with suspicion and disdain. "They have recruited some from other cities nearby, from Omsk and Tyumen. The anti-tsarist sentiment is stronger there than out in these provincial towns."

Prince Dolgorukov, as an aide-de-camp to Papa, always made it his business to be as informed as possible. I assumed he used his private fortune to bribe people to tell him things, because I could not imagine how he would manage otherwise.

It was as we were disembarking to move into the newly painted and cleaned Governor's House that one of these additional guards, who had not been among those traveling with us from Tsarskoe, approached me. He fell into step beside me and did not look at me, but something in his manner made me think he wanted to tell me something. I was not wrong.

"Comrade Anastasie," he said. "I bring you greetings from one who has been transferred to a regiment not far from here, and who assures you that he will find a way to contact you soon."

As soon as he finished his message, he quickened his pace so that he was no longer by my side.

From that moment, my future opened and I felt my spirits take wing. No longer was I facing more extended captivity with my family, whom I loved with all my heart but who, since one particular night in a pantry at Tsarskoe, were no longer everything to me. There was no question what the soldier meant: I was going to see Sasha again. The blood tingled in my fingers. He was not far away. He had found me. I walked along the street to our new prison, hardly noticing where I went. I ended up walking next to Mashka.

"What is it, Nastya?" she whispered to me.

"Nothing. I'm just glad to be settling at last," I said, and I squeezed her arm.

The Governor's House at Tobolsk turned out to be quite comfortable inside—at least during the summer—thanks to the efforts led by Prince Dolgorukov. We had the entire main floor to ourselves, so that we could see out to the countryside over the high fence that had been built to surround it. But these quarters were not large enough to house the suite as well. They stayed instead at Kornilov's house, a smaller merchant's house across the road from ours.

"I like it here!" said Mashka, the most optimistic of us. "Look! Our beds and everything are all set up, with our pictures and clothes in the chests. And we're all together, just like we are on the *Standart*."

We each claimed our corners in the room that had been

assigned to us. Mashka was right: it was comfortable and companionable. Mama and Papa each had a dressing room and a study or parlor. There was a great hall where we could gather for games and where we would eat our meals. The prince and General Tatischev shared a room on our floor. Zhilik and his servant shared a room on the ground floor, and Demidova, Zanotti, the valets, and Tegleva also had small rooms down below. The other half of the ground floor was occupied by kitchens and maids' rooms. There was a door that was not locked leading out to the yard where we could take our exercise.

It was wonderful to be able to go outside without having to wait for the guards to open the door. The only really vexing thing was how small the space was. It consisted of a tiny kitchen garden plus a barricaded street that ran alongside the house. To make matters worse, the guards' barracks overlooked us, so we never had any privacy when we were outdoors. Still, we had the illusion of greater freedom just because we could go out whenever we wanted to.

And still more surprising, the suite and the servants could come and go as they wished: to visit us, or even to go to the village alone and bring us delicacies and news. This freedom gave me an idea, and I immediately started to concoct a plan to find Sasha, and perhaps to get out of the Governor's House myself to meet him. I had to choose my messenger very carefully, though. None of the valets or maids were to be trusted. They would immediately inform my parents if I did anything untoward, since their loyalty was entirely to them.

And Zhilik too was out of the question. I wished I could

have trusted Dr. Derevenko, who lived in town with his wife and son—they had followed on another train and joined the doctor within a few days of our arrival. But no, I would have to find a lower servant who might be made to trust me, who was neither deeply involved with my parents nor a possible Soviet spy.

I spent a few days not doing anything about my plan, simply observing those who came and went. The servant who built the fires and took out the garbage from the kitchens was a sour older woman named Magda whom I remembered as rather surly in Tsarskoe. We had all decided that she must be a Soviet spy, as she would turn up in places where her work would never have taken her. She would not do. Likewise, a handyman whose job it was to hang pictures and rearrange furniture had the look of someone who only performed his task because it gave him a means of reporting our conversations back to the Soviet. Any of my mother's ladies were likewise not an option: although they could come and go into the town, they were too loyal to Mama.

Finally I decided on a young boy who took out the trash and swept the paths outdoors. I didn't recognize him from Tsarskoe, so I thought perhaps he was a local fellow, the son of a peasant. He had that almond skin and dark, oval eyes of the Siberians that made them seem to belong more to China than Russia. I saw him watching us with curiosity but not contempt, and so one day, when no one was around, I spoke to him.

"What's your name?" I asked.

"Igor," he said, but I could hardly understand him because of his strong accent.

"I'm Nastya," I said. "I have white bread here. Would you like some?"

He opened his eyes wider. I wondered how old he was. Perhaps older than he looked. I held out a crust that I had tucked in my pocket at breakfast. He took it, then nibbled on it like a little bird before stuffing it inside his shirt.

"I'd like to be your friend," I said.

He leaned in a little and looked over his shoulder, checking to see if anyone was there. "But you're a princess," he said.

"Not anymore." I sighed.

"The tsar is always the tsar. A princess is always a princess," he said, with a duck of his head.

I had made a lucky choice. Clearly his family was loyal to the monarchy. "Would you be willing to help me?" I asked quietly. I felt very guilty. If anyone discovered he had taken messages for me, who knew what punishment he would face. He nodded. "You must promise me that if it looks like you are going to get in trouble, you will run far, far away. Don't worry about us." His eyes changed expression. A sadness well beyond his years passed across them. I reached out and touched his cheek tenderly. "I need you to take a letter from me to Alexander Mikhailovich Galliapin. He's a soldier."

Igor looked frightened and took a step back.

"Not a loyalist," I hastily added. "He's with the Soviet." Now the boy's expression changed to confusion. "You must trust me. He is my friend too." I took the tiny, folded piece of paper I had kept in my pocket ever since I had a moment to write a message and pressed it into his hand. "You may find him in the barracks, or someone who knows him. Say a lady friend is looking for him and they will probably tell you where to find him. Do this, and I will make sure there is more bread for you, and perhaps some sausage."

I heard steps approaching and went and sat in a chair, taking up a book someone had left on a table nearby. The house was well stocked with things to read in addition to what we had brought with us, which was a blessing, since once the weather changed we were condemned to more inactivity here than at Tsarskoe. The door to the room opened and I saw that it was only Mashka, who had come in with her knitting. We still made socks for the soldiers, knowing that few of them would ever reach those who fought in the war against the Germans. By the time I had greeted Mashka, little Igor had left so quietly he might never have been there.

# CHAPTER 25

The message I received in return from Sasha came through a very unexpected channel. Perhaps if I had been more aware of what was going on in other parts of Russia, it might not have seemed so surprising. It was one of the guards who never smiled, never spoke, who had not been among the friendly guards on our train. He came over to me after he had escorted Nastinka and Lili into the sitting room. He pretended to glance at the drawing I was doing in pencil of Mama, who leaned on her arm and gazed lovingly at Alexei's head.

"Tonight, at eleven, in the alleyway." He said it so quietly and quickly that I wasn't certain I had heard him properly. But then he dropped something in my lap that made me believe he could be trusted. It was a tortoiseshell pick for a balalaika. No one else but Sasha would have known to give me that signal.

The members of the suite left us after dinner, and Papa and Mama finished their game of bezique early, almost as if by some strange signal the world knew I had an important appointment that night.

It was nearly September, and in Siberia the nights were already cool, the breeze sending a chill down from the distant mountaintops. How different from the balmy evenings at Livadia or the pine-scented nights of Skernevizi—either place one of our habitual dwellings at that time of year. I wrapped myself in a shawl, telling Mashka that I was not tired and would wander through the empty sitting rooms of the house rather than try to sleep. I wondered if I would be able to go down the stairs and walk outdoors without being stopped at that hour of night. I assumed that Sasha, who had always managed to arrange things before, would have known that it was possible or he would not have sent me the message. But practical matters were not at the top of my mind. I thrilled to my secret, a little guilty that I could experience such intense pleasure at a time when everything else was so uncertain for our family. At that time I was still unaware of how much conditions could deteriorate, and I continued to hope that this move to Siberia was the beginning of the end of our captivity, that we would be allowed simply to disappear into the vast wilderness of Russia.

Although nothing in my parents' behavior had given me the hope I nurtured then, all of us, OTMA and Alexei, had been feeling similarly cheerful. Mashka had even said she wished we could remain there in Tobolsk forever, she was so happy. Mama was more affectionate with us than she had ever been, and, if anything, we were closer as a family now that the pressure of the monarchy was not upon us.

In this same fog of false security, I was not surprised to see the guard who had spoken to me earlier standing by the small door that led out to the barricaded road where we were allowed to exercise. He did not say a word to me, turning away as if to imply that if anything happened to me, or Sasha and I were discovered, he had seen nothing and would not come to our defense. But it was mute censure, and easy to ignore.

I slipped noiselessly into the alleyway. There was no moon that night—perhaps that's why Sasha had selected it as the time when we should meet. All the lamps in the Governor's House had been extinguished, and the villagers did not stay up beyond ten. Only the stars above shed the feeblest, illusory light. I had to put my hands out in front of me. The dark was so thick it seemed as if I could touch it, or that it bore down on me and would suffocate me, swallow me into a void so intense I would not be able to climb out again. I felt myself begin to panic, my heart beating fast and my breath coming in short gasps. Then Sasha took hold of my arm and drew me to him, and the dark took on a different quality, one of envelopment and safety, from being enfolded in his arms. His lips, his hands—these I felt rather than saw, and it wasn't until several minutes had passed that my eyes became enough accustomed to the dark to make out his right eye, and distinguish the still darker patch that covered his left.

"Where have you been? What happened to you?" I breathed into his ear.

"I changed my name to Mikhail Alexandrovich. I got false papers, and then reenlisted in the guard. It took some time, but I eventually volunteered to go to Siberia, so they posted me here."

I almost couldn't believe my good fortune. How had he managed it, when so few seemed to have any control over their lives now?

"I—and those who are friendly to your cause and whom I cannot name—are working to get you out of here."

"You mean all of us? I cannot leave without Papa and Mama and my brother and sisters."

He paused for the briefest instant before answering. "Yes, yes, of course. All or nothing, eh?"

"Oh, Sasha! It's been so horrible."

"Are you being mistreated?" he asked, holding me away from him as if he possessed the ability to see in the night.

"No, no. Things are better, really. It's just . . ." I felt a little foolish letting on that what was horrible was not imprisonment or disgrace, but being without him. "It's just . . . not knowing what is to come," I said, deciding against the absolute truth.

"You must not lose heart," he said, pulling me to him again and rubbing his cheek against my hair, which had grown another couple of inches since we had last seen each other. "I am afraid that things might get worse. The Bolsheviks are planning another revolt, and this time they may have the strength to pull it off."

His remark caught me off guard. How could he know what the Bolsheviks were planning? Perhaps he really was a spy for the monarchists, and they were using the extreme faction to create chaos and overthrow the Provisionals. Or what if . . . "What will that mean?" I asked.

"New commanders are coming in September to guard your family."

"You mean new jailers!" I said.

"Ssshhh!" he said, but not in a mean way, and he made me quiet by kissing my lips gently, just as I remembered him doing before the horrible event in the pantry at the Alexander Palace.

"Oh, Sasha! It's really you! I can't believe it."

I squeezed him until he said, "Ouch! Any harder and you'll break my ribs!"

I loosened my grip on him without letting go. He stroked my head. We stayed like that for several minutes, letting the dark take us over.

"I wish you could all just walk out of here and disappear into the steppes," he whispered.

"Why do they care what becomes of us? Why can they not simply let us go, to live in peace and quiet? What harm would we do anyone?"

"You would not do harm, but your father . . . You see how the people here still cross themselves when he passes by to go to the village church. He is a symbol of the old way, the comfortable, safe way. He is the representative of God on earth to these superstitious people." While Sasha talked, he continued to caress me, but absently, his movements keeping time with and adhering to the shape of his thoughts. Something was on his mind aside from me.

"Surely you mean religious, not superstitious." God was a certainty I never questioned. We started every day with prayers and ended it the same way. We had even begun to learn the chanted responses to the Mass.

"Yes, religious. The Bolsheviks, of course, consider them one and the same."

"You seem to have made quite a study of the Bolsheviks," I said, meaning to tease him, but he stiffened perceptibly.

"We don't have long," he said, abruptly changing the subject and making me aware of where we were.

"But you are here now, and we can see each other again." I nuzzled him. I wondered if he would be able to find some private place like that pantry, where we could forget the whole world and be only us, together.

"Yes, but it's more difficult here. There are not so many places to hide in such a small town."

If it had been a few months later, I might have heard the discouragement in his voice. But I had no experience of love and its trials. All I knew was that Sasha had returned. "Alexei and I sometimes practice the balalaika together, and there is a piano here that Mama plays often, although it's not very good. Sometimes some of the officers come and listen in the evening. My sisters and brother and I with the help of Zhilik—M. Gilliard—are thinking we might mount a series of little plays, to pass the time and amuse Papa and Mama and the suite. Perhaps you could—"

He interrupted me with a fierce kiss. "Nothing is certain. Except that you are here and I am here, and that we will be able to meet again, but it must be secret. I cannot become a part of your daily life."

I did not ask why. I did not question anything. I just

reached up and ran my fingers through his fair hair, passed them lightly over the patch on his eye, and tenderly kissed his mouth. "I love you," I breathed.

"You had better return to your room before you are missed," he said, turning me around and giving me a gentle push toward the door, which I could see faintly outlined against the glowing white of the outside walls.

## ❧ CHAPTER 26 ❧

Sasha was right about the new commanders, Pankratov and Nikolsky: they were civilians. Pankratov was reasonable enough and quite polite, but Nikolsky was crude and nasty. One of the first things he did was insist that we all wear identity cards. We had to have our pictures taken, and had to pin our cards to our clothing or wear them around our neck, even though everyone knew full well who we were. "It's time they had to live like the rest of us," he said, referring to us as if we weren't there to a group of guards who had assembled to watch us be photographed and issued our pasteboard cards. Mine said "Anastasia Nicholaevna Romanova." It was my name, but it felt odd to use it in that way, written down.

And then, not long after that we were told that the government would no longer pay the stipend that provided our food, clothing, medicines, and the wages for our servants, but that we would have to live off the interest from our private fortunes.

"We must decide what to do. I confess, I am at a loss," Papa said one evening.

Prince Dolgorukov stood as if he were calling a meeting to order. "Gilliard and I can figure something out, I'm sure. A plan of economy. Like living on rations."

Zhilik rose too. I felt as if we were all about to have a lesson. "It may be necessary, you understand, to make some substantial changes. What is the amount we have to live on for the entire household?"

Papa looked down and pursed his lips. "Six hundred rubles."

"Per week? That is not so bad," the prince said.

"Per month," Papa said, and everyone went quiet.

"Why, that is an absurdly small amount!" Mama looked as if she did not believe it. I had no real idea about how much or little six hundred rubles might buy, and so I could not react.

Papa went to Mama. "We will have to make changes. But it is not so terrible. We shall manage, as long as we're all together."

"If there is any way at all I can help . . ." It was Nastinka. "I have some private funds, but I don't know how to get them." As a maid of honor, she was a salaried employee of the court. "And of course, there is no question of my own compensation. That goes without saying."

She went to Mama and took her hands. I could see the tears well up in Mama's eyes. I realized then that Mama had always been the one to give to others. She had never been in a position of needing material help. It must have been so upsetting to be in her shoes just then.

The prince and Zhilik spent several hours working on our family budget. I was intrigued at the idea of having to count what everything cost, having never thought about it before. I don't think I had ever fully realized that a loaf of bread had a fixed price. When they reported to us later, we discovered exactly what it would mean to have to live on a limited income.

"I am afraid, Your Majesty," Prince Dolgorukov said, "We must dismiss nearly all the servants."

"How can this be?" Mama said.

"There simply isn't the money if you are to continue eating and have money for laundry and heating this house."

"Who may stay?" Mama asked.

"Demidova, Chemodurov, and Volkov, of course. Tegleva may stay to look after the grand duchesses. We can keep one cook, a footman, a maid, and a man to help with the heavy chores. All the others must go."

"We can do more chores, Mama," Mashka said, always the one to try to make things seem better than they were. In this case, though, we all readily agreed.

"I shall speak to the servants myself," Mama said. "Call them here."

Zhilik pressed the bell that rang in the kitchen. A moment later, one of the underservants arrived. "Yes, Comrade Romanova?" she said, clearly annoyed at having been summoned in the midst of preparing some food.

"Bring all the servants to this room. I have to speak with them."

Without saying a word, she left, and a few minutes later

the servants trickled in, until there were about twenty in the great hall.

"I regret to tell you," Mama said, "that our finances will no longer support such a large staff here. I have been informed that we can employ only one maid, a handyman, and a cook. Magda and Yeleni, you will stay, with Kharitonov as cook. The rest of you, I regret to say, are dismissed."

"Oh! So we are to go just like that! What about our families? What about feeding our own bellies? It's all right for you lot!" The young kitchen maid, one of the locals who had been hired when another servant became ill and had to return to Petrograd, threw down the rag she had in her hand and stormed out.

The others looked down at the floor. Several of the servants who had been with us for a long time blushed. One or two wiped tears away from their eyes. Zhilik stepped forward. "There is enough money to give you two months' wages and your travel expenses back to Petrograd, or wherever else you need to go."

At that, eight of those present curtsied or bowed to Mama and Papa and left. There were five or six remaining, aside from the two who had been told they could stay. They looked at each other, coming to a silent agreement before one of them spoke.

"If it's all the same to you," said an older fellow who had been polishing brass and marble and doing other work in our households at Tsarskoe Selo and wherever else we went, "we'd just as soon stay. We need no wages. Our life is with you."

At that, Mama lost the control she had maintained until

that point, and wept into her handkerchief. The servants left quietly.

⚜

A few weeks after our new household arrangements had begun and we were just getting used to our additional chores, we had yet more difficulties to face. We were waiting for the members of the suite to join us after breakfast, and they were late. Papa took out his pocket watch every so often and looked at it. He and Mama exchanged a few glances. Everyone looked up every time there was a sound.

At last, we heard the guard unlock the front door, and the sound of people approaching. It was not the usual happy sound of guests, however, just footsteps. I don't think we were entirely surprised when Nastinka, Lili, the prince, and General Tatischev entered accompanied by Pankratov, Nikolsky, and a guard.

"What is this?" Papa asked.

"New regulations from the Soviet," Nikolsky said, unmistakable glee in his voice.

Pankratov stepped forward, not letting the deputy continue. "I regret to say that the Soviet has found it necessary to require the residents of the Kornilov house to remain in that house unless escorted by guard to this one."

So, it was an end to their being able to go into town and post our letters, to buy us provisions and little necessities. I couldn't help sighing. Things weren't getting better here in Siberia after all. They were getting worse.

That was the beginning of the time when it "officially"

became my task, as it had always been when I was younger, to keep everyone's spirits up. Fortunately, my own mood was practically ecstatic since Sasha and I managed to meet two or three times a week. This made it relatively easy to play the clown and divert everyone's thoughts from our imprisonment and the approaching Siberian winter. I think it was that secret, that joy that I had to keep hidden from everyone else, that gave me not only happiness, but strength. I could take small vexations in stride. Ignore the bad manners and disrespect of some of the guards. Not fall into despondency when Alexei's ankle hurt or some other joint swelled and gave him pain. Play silly songs on the piano and imitate the opera singers we had heard years ago in Petrograd.

Our life settled into a new pattern that had an element of unpredictability at its core. Although our plan of economy had been carefully worked out by Zhilik and the prince, we found we had less and less money, and by the time the first snows came in late October, it was barely possible to heat the open rooms of the Governor's House.

Even my breath didn't feel warm enough when I blew on my hands. All of us wore furs indoors, and gloves without fingers so that we could mend, knit, play the piano, and play bezique. Now that Sasha's balalaika had been revealed to everyone, I took great pleasure in bringing it out in the evening. Alexei and I learned some duets. He strummed the chords and I picked out the tune with the pick that had been part of Sasha's first message to me when we arrived at Tobolsk. I practiced that fast vibrato so typical of the balalaika, and much easier with a pick than with a fingernail. I was happy to note that I became quite good. Our livelier tunes got Olga and Mashka up to dance, and sometimes one or two of the more friendly guards would wander in and take part. They must have been bored themselves, watching over people who were not dangerous or volatile, and who made no attempts to escape or otherwise break the rules of their imprisonment.

The worst days were the ones that were so snowy we all had to stay inside, and no one from the suite could come over to relieve the monotony. Those days weighed on Mama, who would read from spiritual books and pray, her eyes shut. Once a week a priest would come, and initially we were allowed to go to church on Sundays. We could only go to the first Mass in the morning, though, and no people from the town were permitted to be there at the same time. After another month or so, even that privilege was discontinued, but the local priest put a makeshift chapel in the large hall and would officiate at a service for us at the Governor's House. Unfortunately the altar was not consecrated, so we could not receive the sacraments.

One day, everyone was huddled in Mama's sitting room looking miserable. Papa stood up and began to pace rapidly back and forth across the small space. "I must have exercise. I cannot simply spend my days idle and useless!"

I couldn't help thinking that we women always had something to do, even if we didn't want to do it. Either we cleaned or we knitted and sewed. It was tedious and repetitive, but it was something. I realized something about my papa then that had never occurred to me before. He did not have much imagination. I suppose he hadn't had time just to daydream when he was little, but was always kept busy with lessons and sports. Now, when all distractions were at an end, he couldn't abide the unvarying company and see new ways to be occupied or useful. It was Zhilik, in the end, who spoke to Kobylinsky and had them bring logs into the yard so that Papa and Zhilik could saw them for fuel.

We desperately needed that fuel for the stoves in the drafty house. But in truth, the stoves were so old and small that no matter how one kept them fed they could not heat a room. Apparently the mansion had a system of central heating that required a great deal of fuel to run, and the Soviet decided it would cost too much and be too luxurious for us to use, even if it had been in decent repair.

My hands, feet, and even my nose were always cold, but inside, I was so warm I was certain the rest of the family must have felt it when I was around them. In addition to Sasha's and my secret nocturnal meetings, he had become bolder and showed himself more often during the day, even speaking to me in front of others occasionally—pretending we were complete strangers to each other, of course. Instead of notes and messengers, we created our own private code, so that I would know by what he said whether we could meet that night or not. It was a challenge for me to continue to pretend disdain for him, or at least indifference. I yearned to tell Mashka that this was the Sasha from Tsarskoe, but I didn't dare. I realized she might have guessed, noticing the patch on his eye if nothing else. Each time Sasha and I met, he would impress on me the necessity for utter secrecy.

I thought we had succeeded in fooling everyone, until one day Alyosha and I were alone in the great hall, each staring out a window at flakes of snow drifting lazily down to merge into the blanket that covered everything as far as we could see.

"I didn't know that impudent guard with the patch on his eye had come from Tsarskoe with us. I didn't see him there for the last weeks."

I tried to pretend nonchalance. "Didn't you? I think I saw him once or twice. And he must have come on the train and the boat, mustn't he."

"I didn't see him on the *Rus* either." Alyosha came over to stand next to me. "I think that if he didn't murder that fellow in Tsarskoe, he's a spy. I've noticed that the guards who come and go are the ones we can usually tell are watching us and reporting back to the Soviet. Or even the Bolsheviks."

"What do you know about the Bolsheviks!" I ruffled his hair. "You've been sick half the time all these things have been going on."

He took my arm and turned me toward him. His eyes were disturbingly deep and sad. "Being sick gives me a lot of time to think, and I think that guard is a bad man. I don't like the way he acts around you."

"Don't be silly, Baby." I shook his hand off my arm. "He's just a guard like the others. He doesn't 'act' like anything around me."

Alyosha shrugged. "Perhaps. But I shall be watching him."

He left me alone there as the twilight deepened. My heart was beating fast. If Alyosha had noticed something, perhaps the others had too. I was getting careless. I would have to be more cautious.

# CHAPTER 27

By November it had become too cold to spend much time outdoors, except at midday when the sun shone and the wind died away. The hours of tedium were almost unbearable, with only a few rooms to roam in, the same books to read, and lessons I no longer had any interest in doing. Mama made me read unceasingly from the book of Isaiah—I don't know why. All those evil children and sinful cities upon whom God turned his back. Beating swords into plowshares—perhaps she sensed my restlessness, the way I wandered around, unable to settle, longing only to see Sasha but with no one to tell, no one to share my feelings, good and bad. I sometimes satisfied my frustration by reverting to my old tricks. Why not? I thought. Everyone expected it of me. And then, I hit upon something that might at least give me a sight of Sasha, let me drink in everything I could in one glance to take back with me to my solitude.

"I'm bored," I said, after lessons were over and our lunch cleared away. "Let's go see what the guards are doing."

"We can't do that!" Mashka exclaimed.

"Why not? We're allowed to go outside, and the guards' house has an entrance from our yard. We could hardly escape through a building full of people who wish to keep us captive."

To my surprise, it was Tatiana who seconded my plan. "Yes, why not!" she said. "The worst that could happen would be that they'd turn us away."

"But what would we do once we got there?" Olga asked.

I went to the table and picked up the draughts board and pieces. "We'll play," I said.

In the end I convinced everyone except Alexei. "It's too cold to go outside," he said.

"Oh, don't be such a little girl!" I teased. His look held a warning, though. For a moment I thought he saw through my mischief to the real purpose behind it. But I didn't remain there long enough to find out, and the others didn't know anything, or if they did, they hadn't said.

Even if I hadn't wanted to lead the way, my sisters would have pushed me ahead of them when we reached the door of the guardhouse. As I knocked, I hoped they would open quickly—we hadn't bundled up as we would if we were planning to stay outside, and it was already so cold that within minutes our noses would turn blue. Thankfully, our knock was answered quickly by a young guard who stared at us in silent amazement.

"Hello. Would you like to play draughts with us? And can we come in? It's terribly cold out here!" I gambled that his astonishment would overcome any resistance he might have had to fraternizing with us.

And I was right. A helpless grin brightened his face as he opened the door wide and said, "Come in! It's not very luxurious here, but we could do with a change to cheer us up in this weather."

He led us into a sort of common room filled with cigarette smoke, with men huddled around a stove for warmth. A quick glance showed me that Sasha wasn't there. For a moment we all stared at each other, speechless. Then I held up the draughts board, and quickly the guards cleared off a table, pulled up stools for us, and brought out their own draughts boards. Before long, the competition was fierce—and friendly.

I've always loved playing games, and I soon forgot myself in the challenge of trying to win these fast-paced contests. Before long, the room rang with everyone's laughter, shouts of triumph, and groans of defeat. Time went quickly.

I gave up my seat at the board to Mashka, who had initially held back but eventually became caught up in the fun. One of the younger guards came over to me and offered me a cigarette. I took it. It was not one of the ones Papa would give us, elegantly wrapped in colored paper with a gold band around it for your fingers. This was hand rolled, tobacco spilling out at one end. I wasn't prepared for the rawness of it, and the smoke burned my throat. I coughed.

The guard smiled. "A little strong for you?"

I waved my hand in front of my tearing eyes and nodded, then handed the cigarette back to him.

"Tell me," he said. "Point out which of your sisters is which."

I told him who was who.

"Tatiana," he said musingly. "How old is she?"

I had to think for a moment. "Twenty-one."

He looked surprised. "Really? She seems younger."

That was the end of our conversation, but I continued to look around at the guards, many of whom could not take their eyes off my older sisters, who did look especially beautiful in the flush of winning or losing their game.

After I don't know how long, the door opened, and Colonel Kobylinsky entered. Suddenly everyone became quiet. A draught fell on the floor and rolled away, the only sound as we all held our breath, worried that the colonel would punish the men or become angry at us.

"I see you have found a way to pass the long winter afternoons," he said, then smiled. A sigh of relief went around the room. "So long as you don't forget when it is time to relieve your brethren at their duties." He pointed to a wall clock, and in an instant, the guards in the room stood and put their hats on their heads. We also stood, putting our coats and hats back on.

"Thank you," Olga said, and we all followed suit.

"Will you come back tomorrow?" one of the youngest guards asked.

We all looked at Colonel Kobylinsky. "Members of the Romanov family are free to move anywhere in the confines of this area. If they wish, they may come."

No one could suppress a grin.

Before I fell asleep that night, I thought about Olga and Tatiana. If things had been different, they both might have been married by then, perhaps even had children of their own. Would that ever happen now? Some of the guards were quite handsome, and I could tell that my sisters would have liked to be able to flirt with them openly and that they might have had romances like mine with Sasha. I was a little glad they didn't, though, because in the cold weather there were few places to meet in private. I giggled to myself at the idea of us all enacting a sort of imprisoned bedroom farce, like the French plays we put on under Zhilik's direction.

Sasha and I had taken to meeting in a small room in the cellar of the guard's house, which had been built in the old Siberian style, with chambers below the ground that had small windows that just peeked out above. One of these was little more than a root cellar, but again Sasha had done his best to make it comfortable for us. He brought a wool rug down, and cushions, so we could sit and talk and do those other, intimate things that made me feel so alive and free even as in our daily lives we became more and more like prisoners.

It was on a bitterly cold November day that Sasha informed me of something that would have monumental importance for my family, although I couldn't have realized it at the time. We had met as planned, but after our initial greeting he seemed more distant and quiet than usual.

"What's wrong?" I asked him, threading my fingers through his after we had lain together and kissed for a while.

He furrowed his brow, making the patch over his eye dig into the edge of the socket in a way that looked uncomfortable. "There has been news today. It hasn't been in the papers yet, so you mustn't say anything to your family."

I sat up. This sounded serious. "What is it?"

"There has been another Bolshevik uprising in Petrograd and Moscow. This time, they succeeded. The Provisional Government has fallen and the extremists are in control."

I didn't know what to say. "Does this mean anything for us?"

Sasha dropped my hand and a cross look passed over his face. "I see. So nothing is important except insofar as it directly affects you and your family? Well, ex-Grand Duchess, the world is no longer the same. You are not Her Imperial Highness!"

His words stung me. "I—I didn't mean that. I meant you and me."

He shrank visibly, his shoulders drooping, as if all at once the tension in his muscles had let him go. "I don't know. It could."

"Perhaps they will forget about us? Surely they have more important things to worry about than keeping guard over people who are now, as you say, simply private citizens."

"You and your sisters and brother are. But your parents are under arrest. Prisoners of the state. And there is a strong feeling against them among the soldiers."

"But they are so friendly to us, most of them anyway."

"You make a sympathetic group, you four girls and Alexei. But even that, I fear, will soon change. As soon as they hear about the revolution."

There it was again. Sasha knew something that nobody else knew. How could he? Where did he get his information? I wanted to ask him, but I was afraid. I didn't want to change our relationship, take it out of the realm of pure feeling, out of its magical time and place, where only we two existed. I didn't want to know things that would spoil that enchantment. "So, I must truly keep this to myself."

He kissed me. "I know I can trust you. You've always proven that to me. I wish everyone in Russia could know how worthy you—and your family—really are."

When we parted that night I had a heavy feeling in my heart. Where before when it came to Sasha, all was sunshine and light, now I sensed gathering clouds. I did not know how soon those clouds would rip open and hurl lightning bolts at us in our relative tranquility, beset by vexing regulations and constricted in our movements, yet still—for the moment—able to eat and sleep and dream of better times.

## ❧ CHAPTER 28 ❧

We spent a quiet, cold Christmas and New Year in Tobolsk. We had made what Christmas gifts we could for the servants and our friends, using the scraps of this and that we were permitted to keep. With ribbons and cloth we made sachets and cards, and embroidered prayers onto handkerchiefs that we wrapped around beads and paper images of the saints. Mama knitted woolen waistcoats for Zhilik, Dr. Botkin, and Dr. Derevenko, as well as for some of the servants. We even gave presents to one or two of our guards, the ones we saw every day, which I think surprised them. Mama gave a Christmas tree to the servants, but without any decorations it looked sad and somber.

Mama also invited Kobylinsky, Pankratov, and Nikolsky to our Christmas dinner. It was a silent affair, as we felt keenly how different this Christmas was even than our last, as prisoners at Tsarskoe Selo.

We all wrote letters to our friends, to Anya and Isa, to Lili Dehn and others, knowing that they would be read and scrutinized for codes and conspiracies many times before they reached their intended recipients—if they ever did. Anya, at least, was out of prison and living with her parents. This we heard through Mr. Gibbes, who had visited her and taken a photograph of her in her horrible conditions. He had arrived a few weeks before the holiday and was staying with us, whereas poor Isa left only a week or so later and had still not been given permission to visit.

"It took me weeks of effort to get the necessary papers to travel here," Mr. Gibbes said as he sipped his evening tea with us at Christmas.

"Why are they so afraid of letting us have our people around us?" Mama said. "I'm so glad you're here, Syd. Baby's English has become quite bad."

I noticed Zhilik flare his nostrils and turn away a little. I think that was the first time I realized that our two foreign tutors actually disliked each other so much. Mr. Gibbes had refused to share Zhilik's room, and so was given a much smaller room that was barely more than a cupboard.

Although Isa was right across the street in the Kornilov house, Mama never saw her at all in the end, only getting messages to and from her through the others. We all wrote letters to her as if she were still at Tsarskoe. I really wished she could have visited us then. She would have been a comforting person to have around. Always practical, always kind. She would have helped with the accounts and other matters; perhaps she would have been able to prevent the complete destruction of Mama's undergarments by the local laundry. Then it would not have been necessary for our friends outside in Petrograd to deprive themselves by sending her underlinen and warm stockings.

After the New Year, the weather grew as bitterly cold as Siberia could manage. All of us became ill with colds, or in our cases, with German measles. This was not nearly as bad as the measles we had in Tsarskoe, and we recovered quickly. Then it was endless days and nights of ice and snow. Most days we couldn't even get across to the guards' house for games of cards—which Sasha never took part in, I noticed. He knew we were there whenever we came, because he would mention it to me. But he always stayed away. I've come to think it was wise of him. We might not have been able to act as distant as we should, and someone might have guessed what was going on.

I have an image of Tobolsk that I will always carry with me. It is snowing hard, a blizzard, so that the railings that enclose our small exercise area are indistinct. The windows are etched with beautiful, crystalline patterns of frost climbing up them from the bottom, leaving only a small space at the top where I can look out and see. I am standing on a chair so that I can peer through that tiny space. I stay like that for a long time, watching the snow climb up the fence, wondering if that fence will disappear completely and we might have the illusion of not being enclosed, but connected to the town and the rest of Russia by that smooth whiteness. I keep my eyes focused on the swirling snow, until the constant, white movement makes it seem as if the snowflakes are neither falling nor being blown, but suspended in air, suspended in time. In my memory I fantasize that perhaps we too were not only out of the mainstream of life, but had been placed in a bubble of time. If we could only break out of that bubble, we would find that the world outside was just as we had left it before the war: Papa would be tsar and we girls, OTMA, would be thinking about who we might marry. And Alexei would be well. He would not suffer any more. And Sasha . . .

These were just comforting fancies. My other comfort, the warmth of Sasha's arms, had been denied me since the beginning of the year. The heavy snow made it more and more difficult for us to meet, since I could not make the short walk outside at night without anyone noticing. At the very least, opening a door or window let in such a blast of cold and snow that the entire house felt chilled by several degrees, and it often took a long time to clear up the snow that had blown in, requiring buckets and mops and a lot of noise.

During our enforced separation, I composed letters to Sasha in my head, since I did not dare write them down. The letters gradually evolved into poetry. I wanted my mind and heart to leap across the barrier between us. Those twenty or so feet could have been an ocean requiring a long voyage to cross, for all the contact we were able to have during that Siberian winter. I remember some of the poems I wrote. Perhaps they are silly. Here's one:

> A curtain of snow between us,
> Soft, white, and pure.
> That such beauty can separate us
> Makes life impossible to endure.

Silly, yes. But I ached so to see Sasha. The only times I was able to were when he happened to be among the guards who would come in and make what they called a domiciliary visit, which was only a less offensive way to say house search. They would go in pairs and dig through drawers and shake out books, looking for messages or for evidence that we had somehow broken the rules of our imprisonment. They always managed to find something suspicious: a letter Mama was writing in Old Church Slavonic; one of Alexei's few toys, kept more for sentiment than use but that might have been employed to carry a message; books in English and French that they could not understand and were thought therefore to contain counter-revolutionary propaganda. I particularly remember one of the more unpleasant guards picking up a copy of *Martin Chuzzlewit* with his first finger and thumb and dropping it as though it had a bad smell into the satchel full of "evidence" they would bring back to the commander to pore over and sift through. Sometimes the books made their way back to us via Pankratov, but he had less and less influence as time went by.

"The personal life is now of no importance," Nikolsky announced one day, as if by a wave of his hand he could change millennia of human behavior and create a new order in the world. I wondered if he knew how imperious he sounded, and that my father, the supposedly evil tsar, would never have presumed to force his will on his subjects in such a way.

The snow eventually stopped falling, leaving piles and piles of whiteness. In our small space outdoors, we began to build our own mountain to slide down and climb over. We made it quite gigantic. We brought buckets of water out from the house to solidify it. It was so cold sometimes that the water would freeze in the buckets on the way, so it became a game to run as quickly as possible and throw the water, watching some of the droplets crystallize in midair. It was our only project, and all of us with the addition of our tutors and Kolya Derevenko attacked it with determination and concentration. Some of the guards we had played draughts with helped us too. I noticed a few flirtatious gestures, and once thought I surprised a guard trying to give Tatiana a surreptitious kiss. I pretended not to notice, but she blushed so obviously that it was plain enough for anyone to see.

Often we would end by throwing snowballs at each other and competing to build the mountain to its highest point before it was crushed down by clambering feet. When our mountain was done, we made makeshift toboggans out of wooden slats, and passed many hours in the winter sunshine sliding down its slope.

Soon enough, life began to change and shift around us. In February, we learned that many of the guards from Tsarskoe who had become friendly with us were to be sent back to Petrograd, and a new division would replace them. On the eve of the guards' departure, Nikolsky came to pay a visit to Papa.

"The ice mountain must be destroyed," he said.

"Why on earth?" asked Papa, who had enjoyed seeing our progress as much as anyone.

"You and Marie Romanova were seen climbing to the top of the mountain and looking over the fence into the town. This disturbs the townspeople."

"That's absurd!" Papa replied and shook his head. Nikolsky didn't look at any of us. No doubt he didn't want to confront our disappointed faces.

We gathered at the window to watch some of the same

soldiers who had helped us create our whimsical ice slide now hammer it to pieces with picks and shovels. They looked as disappointed as we felt. What startled me most, though, was to see that Sasha was the soldier assigned to watch over the destruction. He stood by passively, only occasionally pointing out a vulnerable place that would undermine the structure and save some work for the men. I couldn't help staring out the window, willing him to look up in my direction so that a silent signal could pass between us. But he didn't. I hoped it was because he couldn't trust himself to do it. I prayed it was not because he no longer wanted to see me, or wanted to forget what we had been to each other.

"It's sad, isn't it?"

Mashka had come up behind me and passed her arms around my waist, resting her chin on my shoulder. "Yes," I answered, knowing that I was responding to more than she probably meant.

"Let's have some music this evening," she said. "Alexei's not feeling well, but you could play the balalaika. Not the sad songs, the lively ones. It always cheers everyone up."

"All right," I said. "After dinner."

"Ah yes, dinner! How many courses will the servants bring us this evening?"

It was a game we played, pretending that the meager rations we now had were in fact sumptuous feasts. "I believe we shall start with the soup."

"A clear soup for the first course, yes. And then a bread roll for the second course," Mashka said, giving me the cue to continue.

"And Papa will carve." This started us laughing at the idea of our father ceremoniously carving up a roll into small portions for our large family, plus the suite and the doctors and the tutors.

"Are you coming to Mama's sitting room? It's so cold in here," Mashka said. I was watching from the one room in the house I knew would be empty just for that reason.

"I'll be along soon," I said. Mashka knew enough to kiss me lightly on top of my head and leave without asking any more questions.

In fact, it was always Mashka who could read the mood of the house. I was too involved in my own feelings to notice the changes in those around me. And I did not feel much like strumming cheerful dance tunes and comic songs on Sasha's balalaika that evening. It would remind me too much of him. When we were seeing each other every second or third night, it used to make me feel as though he were touching me even when I was in the midst of my family. But now it had been almost a month, and he hadn't even looked at me directly, let alone met me or spoken to me or touched me. Now the hollow wood of the balalaika seemed empty and forlorn, not full of unspoken promises.

But Mashka was right. I had to be the one to keep everyone's spirits up. They all expected it of me, and for me to appear hopeless or downcast would make everyone feel worse.

❧

It was while we were playing and singing in Mama's sitting room one evening about a week later that Pankratov and

Nikolsky came in to see us, not wearing uniforms, but in ordinary street clothes.

After some clearing of his throat, Pankratov spoke. "It has been decided . . . we are obliged to . . . well, we wanted to tell you ourselves—"

"We have been asked by the new soldiers to resign, and we are to be replaced by a Bolshevik commissary from Moscow," Nikolsky interrupted, having bristled with impatience at Pankratov's stuttering and stammering.

Papa stood and approached them. We all had our eyes upon him as he walked forward. "When must you leave?" he asked.

Pankratov, having got over the news itself, found his tongue again. "We're leaving tomorrow. We have no desire to be here when the new commissary arrives. Things are so uncertain."

Papa nodded. Then he put out his hand to each of them. "You have been fair, and treated us with respect. I—we— shall miss you."

Nikolsky stood erect, but I could tell even he was affected. Pankratov sank to his knees and kissed Papa's hand.

"No, no, that is all at an end. I am no different from you or from any of the men in the guardhouse. Go with God."

We all felt unaccountably sad about the departure of our principal captors in Tobolsk. They had been the authors of many petty regulations that had made our lives less tolerable. And yet, we knew them, and now once more we had no idea what would happen next.

Mama spoke from her couch just before the two men left. "Will Kobylinsky stay?" He had somehow managed to remain as the commander of the guards, and had become more and more our friend and protector.

"He remains, but will no longer be in command. The soldiers have elected Lieutenant Galliapin to take over the day-to-day operations."

I couldn't help myself, and I gasped aloud. Everyone looked at me. Thinking quickly, I said, "I think he is much to be feared."

"Galliapin? He's a bit severe, but fair nonetheless."

"Which one is he?" Mama asked.

"The one with the patch over his eye. He was wounded in action, at Tannenberg."

Papa nodded. "Then he has sacrificed something of himself for Russia. We shall trust him as much as we can."

I tried not to look at Alyosha, but he sauntered over to where I sat and positioned himself so that he could give me a sharp pinch on the arm. I ignored it.

"I think it is clear that we need to watch what we do. I want you girls to keep your distance from the guards from now on." Papa swept his eyes over us, still lumping us together as a group rather than as individuals. I saw that all my sisters looked down or away from him. Perhaps their hearts had been touched in some way too by the young men who were the only familiar faces we ever saw besides the suite.

But if they had been, what they felt was nothing to what was going through me at that moment. My heart spun around in my chest to hear Sasha talked over like this in Mama's parlor. I wanted to jump up and say, "You don't know him! He is the best, the bravest, most honorable man and I am in love with him!" But I knew I could never admit it now. He had become too visible, too important. I suddenly felt that our love was ruined. How could he meet me now, even when the weather improved?

I was almost grateful that there had been other news to dampen everyone's enthusiasm for music and laughter, because I didn't think I could bear to pluck another string on Sasha's balalaika that evening.

## ❧ CHAPTER 29 ❦

I can hardly bear to think about that month when Sasha and Colonel Kobylinsky shared control of the guards. Sasha distanced himself more and more from us, while Kobylinsky did the opposite. The colonel had become a representative of the old regime to the men, and they paid almost no attention to what he said. He became more and more friendly with us, and I began to realize that he would have liked to do something to help us escape.

In fact, one evening after the members of the suite had been escorted back to their house across the street and Kolya Derevenko had gone home to his mama in the town, Kobylinsky returned to speak with Papa and Mama. We were all on our way to bed, but when I heard the colonel come in, I hung behind, pretending to look at the moon out of the window in the darkened hall.

"There are people on the outside who want to help," he said very quietly to Mama, Papa, Trina, and Zhilik, who still stayed up with them, finishing a long game of bezique.

"What would they do? How could it be arranged?" Papa asked.

"There is not yet a Bolshevik presence here in Tobolsk. The townspeople are on your side. If you would consent to be taken out of the country, to Japan or Afghanistan, you could make the journey before the Bolsheviks get here."

"Would the family remain all together?" Zhilik asked, in his still-not-very-good Russian.

"We might have to separate some of you to avoid suspicion," Kobylinsky answered.

"I'm afraid," Papa said, "that we cannot consent to have our family split up even for a short while."

Silence followed. Then I heard the low voices of Trina and Zhilik earnestly entreating Mama and Papa to consider the plan.

"No." It was Mama. "I know you are trying to help, but our family, and Russia . . . it would mean leaving everything we cared about and fought for. It would be death for both of us."

"I very much fear, Your Majesties, that staying will be death for certain." Kobylinsky clicked his heels together, and I knew from having seen him do it many times before that he bowed to them. He would have to cross the hall to leave, so I ran through it to our bedroom, where my sisters were already covered in blankets and trying to get to sleep.

"What did Kobylinsky come back for?" Tatiana asked.

"I don't know," I said, "I didn't hear what they spoke about."

Tatiana leaned up on one elbow. "I know that's not true, Nastya. You have to tell us."

She was right. I couldn't keep such important matters

from them. They had as much right to know as I did. I repeated the conversation as accurately as I could.

"You mean, we could be free?" Olga said.

"Except Papa and Mama won't agree to it, because they don't want to leave Russia or split us up."

"I would never want to leave Mama and Papa," Mashka said. "I'd rather stay here and face whatever is coming with them."

The three others of us sighed almost in unison. Of course we loved our parents and Alexei and each other, and none of us could imagine being separated. But as conditions continued to worsen for us, we realized that we were all in danger. The soldiers could decide anything any day. Most of those who knew us and felt kindly toward us had gone, and the new ones barely smiled, let alone talked to us.

"Would you ever think of running away if someone helped us?" I asked Tatiana.

She thought awhile before answering. "No. I could not leave Mama. She is too unwell. It would kill her. And Alexei could not do it because of his illness, and it would be unfair to leave him." The analytical Tatiana had thought it all through.

"What about you, Olga?" I asked my oldest sister, who at twenty-three no doubt had imagined quite a different life for herself by this time.

Olga just stared at me with her wide eyes, letting me read her thoughts there. They seemed much like my own: there was no way to choose. Either thing was completely unthinkable. We were doomed if we remained. We would be desolate if we left.

We blew out our evening candle and jointly pretended to go to sleep.

~

The next day was Carnival, the night before the solemn season of Lent began and the world went into a period of mourning for the life of Jesus. Carnival used to be one of our favorite days. We always had performers and acrobats come to the palace, and we dressed up and acted silly. It was a joyous day, even though it ushered in weeks of abstinence and quiet. The city of Tobolsk was no exception when it came to celebrating Carnival. Whatever the Bolsheviks were trying to do elsewhere, in these small, remote Siberian cities, religious life was still strong. When we heard the sound of loud, joyful music and cheers and laughter, we all went to the windows to look out. We watched as beribboned carts went by and the townspeople blew whistles, rang bells, and sang. Acrobats tumbled, jugglers tossed balls and other objects in the air, and the atmosphere of crazy revelry infected everyone—even the soldiers.

Everyone, that is, except those of us imprisoned in the Governor's House. The contrast between what was happening in the town and the quiet monotony of our life was intense. Most other times, we could pretend what we did was normal. We took family photos as though we were on vacation in Livadia: Here's Papa and Zhilik sawing wood; there we all are sunning ourselves on the roof of a greenhouse; there is Mama in her chair, knitting. Except for the sadness that none of us could entirely banish from our eyes, we were simply a family like everyone else. We awaited the photographs just as we always did. Only now, instead of having one of the servants take the roll of film to the palace darkroom, we gave our roll to Kobylinsky and he sent a guard to a local chemist's shop to get it developed for us. We didn't take as many pictures as we used to, now that we were living on such reduced means. But we couldn't give up the practice entirely. Mama kept most of the family photographs when we came to Tobolsk—nineteen albums. She browsed through at least one of them every day.

When I was younger, I would have eagerly taken pictures of the Carnival spectacle as it passed, looking for that moment when the elements would come together and tell a story. The little boy refusing to smile, dressed up like a clown and being tossed into the air by his papa, who has already been at the vodka. The bear on a chain, head hanging down, obviously cowed by his mean owner, who pretends for the sake of the crowd that the bear is a fierce and dangerous animal. And if I caught just the right moment, you would see the look in the bear's eyes that says he knows he is stronger than that oaf who feeds him or denies him food at his pleasure, and that he is waiting for the day he will turn on the man and destroy him.

Like the Bolsheviks and Papa. But Papa wasn't mean. Not intentionally. Yet the people must have had some feeling that it was he who caused famine and privation. Or they had been told that, anyway, by those who wanted to seize power.

The shouting and singing went on into the night. The guards themselves had been given an extra ration of vodka, and we could hear the laughter from the guardhouse all through the day, while we ate our quiet dinner and as we were preparing for bed.

It was then, just before I put on my nightgown, that we heard a disturbance outside our window.

"Oh, princesses! Let us sing you to sleep!" Variations of these words were yelled, chanted, screamed in the small yard so that it would be impossible for anyone to sleep. "Come on! Come out and dance with us! We won't hurt you!"

"I wish they would go away," whispered Mashka, who was always rather fearful of the soldiers.

"Don't pay any attention to them and they will stop," Tatiana said in her practical way.

But then I heard mixed in with the yelling an occasional shout of "Nastya!" as the noise became more and more wild and impossible to ignore. "I'll go and tell them to go away," I said, pulling on the heavy sweater I had just taken off and wrapping myself in a warm blanket.

"Nastya, don't!" cried Mashka, but I pretended that the sound of the door shutting behind me drowned her voice out.

*I knew he would find a way!* I thought with barely suppressed joy as I ran through the darkened house to the door that led out to the back. Without hesitating, I threw the door open.

There in front of me were about twenty of the guards, all looking red-eyed and disheveled. I had never seen a group of men leer like that before, and suddenly realized how unwise it had been to go charging outside just because I thought I heard Sasha among them. I scanned the faces, and could not see his. The men began to inch forward toward me. I tried to run back through the door, but someone slammed it shut before I had a chance. "It's not the tall one, but she'll do." "She's a pretty little thing." "Come here and make me feel good." "Give us a kiss." I shrank back until I was pressed against the door. I didn't know what to do. I was on the verge of screaming, not caring that I would awaken the whole house for something that I had brought upon myself, when I heard a familiar voice in the back.

"Stand aside! This is not what we agreed upon. Let me through."

I had never been so relieved to hear Sasha's voice. He pushed through the crowd, pulling on his heavy jacket, his hair mussed as though he had been awakened from sleep. So it hadn't been Sasha who had called my name. The blood in my veins turned to ice.

He took me a little roughly by the arm and pulled me away from the door, which he opened. "Get back to your quarters, all of you!" Even though officers were a thing of the past in the new regime, Sasha's tone of command sent everyone scurrying. He pushed me inside and closed the door behind us. We stopped in the dark. He took hold of my shoulders and held me arm's length away. "What were you thinking! They might have torn you to shreds!"

"I—I thought I heard you," I murmured.

"You think I would do such a thing as rouse this rabble to an unlawful action?"

"I—I thought . . ." I couldn't continue. I couldn't tell him that I thought he had engineered a situation where we could meet in the most logical way possible, given the times. Clearly, he had planned nothing of the kind.

"You have to understand. I'm doing all I can to protect you, and right now, that means being harsh and distant and making the soldiers and those who are coming soon to take over command believe that I have the same goals as they have."

Sasha's arms had relaxed, and we gradually drew closer to one another, until he let his hands drop from my shoulders and twine around me and I passed mine around his back, and rested my head against his shoulder, tucked safely under his chin.

"I've missed you so much," I whispered.

"You have to understand, more is at stake than a schoolgirl romance. It is your life, and the lives of your family."

"You think my feelings for you are childish? How can you say that, after all we've done. I don't want to live without you!" I cried. He hushed me by putting his finger on my lips.

"You are so young. You are beautiful. There will be many others, some one of whom might deserve you. But there will be no one if you do not live to meet them."

I knew in my heart that what he said was true. But I didn't want to hear it. I knew I was being selfish wishing only for his love, because to continue as we had could have some terrible effect upon my entire family. I had seen how they dealt with anyone who showed obvious softening toward us. Kobylinsky would be the next to go, no doubt.

"Nastya? Are you there?" It was Olga, coming through from our bedroom. She hadn't seen us yet.

Sasha kissed me hard and fast, then slipped out the door. I leaned against it and let the tears flow. Olga found me like that. "We were worried, we heard the men disperse, but then you didn't come back. Why are you crying?" She put her arms around me and stroked my head.

"Because, nothing . . . no one . . . we can't ever . . ." I couldn't continue.

"Hush, darling. I know."

Together we went back to our room where Mashka and Tatiana sat up, wide awake, and flooded with relief when they saw us. "Let's try to get some sleep," Olga said, taking on her role of mother to us, as she was accustomed to doing when Mama was too overwhelmed with Alexei's illness, or too unwell herself to do anything. I wondered if it was easier or more difficult to be Olga, who had been able to see more of life and the world before our imprisonment. I suspected it was equally difficult for all of us—a thought that did not comfort me as I fell asleep that night.

# ✦ CHAPTER 30 ✦

It was in April that the new soldiers arrived in the town, some from Omsk, some from Yekaterinburg. They supposedly were there to ensure that the Bolshevik regime was carried out exactly, meaning no one had more than a certain amount of space to live in or retained any luxuries, or was entitled to anything more than the meanest rations. The two bands were not friendly with each other, though, and we heard stories about looting in the town, and random arrests of lawful citizens. Oddly, we were protected from all of this by our guard, but they could easily have been overrun or turned on us themselves, and I didn't understand how Kobylinsky managed to keep control.

Then one day, orders came from Moscow to arrest comrades Hendrikova, Dolgorukov, and Tatischev. The countess, the prince, and the general all moved into the Governor's House with us, with Trina as well, who until this time had had the comparative freedom of the suite. The countess and Trina brought their maids with them, and suddenly we were very crowded indeed. It was a little warmer, so we could once again use the large hall to gather together, but we had almost no privacy, and the demands on our already limited sanitary facilities were extreme. Worst of all, Alexei had caught whooping cough from Kolya, and burst a blood vessel coughing.

Although I teased and tormented him when he was well, Alyosha's bad illnesses put me under a pall of despair. It was as if there were two Alexeis: the impish little brother with too acute an eye for what was going on around him, and the shriveled creature who embodied pain so completely that everyone near him felt it. This time was one of the worst ones. It reminded me of the time in Poland, first at Skernevizi then at Spala, when we thought he would die. He recovered then, but it was hard to imagine him well again when he was in the grip of such terrible pain.

Dr. Derevenko called us all into Alexei's room. We sisters stood clutching each other for comfort. Mama and Papa were at Alyosha's bedside, looking on helplessly as he moaned in wordless agony, his eyes glassy and his face beaded with sweat. He was the color of the heavy sky before a blizzard.

The doctor spoke. "We must all be prepared for the worst. I cannot get the usual medicines to relieve Alexei's pain, and his fever remains very high."

"Is there nothing you can do for Baby?" Mama's voice was barely above a whisper.

"There is a new treatment, very experimental. I have what I need to try it, but there is no guarantee it will have any effect at all, and it could make him worse."

Mama turned and looked at all of us, as if to say, "What are you doing here? This is a nightmare world I inhabit with my son alone." Papa took the cue and nodded to us, and we all filed out slowly and quietly.

I was with Papa in his study later when Dr. Derevenko came in to speak with him. "I cannot persuade the tsaritsa to make a decision about Alexei's treatment." He looked exhausted and pained himself. "I fear that if I do not do something his body will not stand the pain, and he will die."

Papa sighed. "My poor boy. Yet is death the worst? He has suffered so much in his short life already, more than most people ever do."

The doctor was silent for a moment. When he spoke, it was quietly, gravely. "This treatment I spoke of. It might work. But I must caution you that it could be dangerous."

"If I had only myself to consider, I would say let the boy expire and rest at last. But my wife. Sunny." He paused, then looked up at the doctor with resolve. "You must do whatever you can."

The doctor bowed to him and left. Papa turned his attention to me. "Little Nastya, I know I can count on you never to repeat what you heard me say. If Alexei were still the heir, it would be different. But he is just a boy with more than his share of sorrow and pain."

I went to him and kissed him on the cheek. He patted my arm. I'm not sure he ever really forgave me for being a girl, especially since Alexei had turned out to be so ill. But the more I understood about what it must have been like to have to rule a country as vast as Russia, the more I forgave my papa anything.

We held our breath for the next twenty-four hours, and

gradually our mood lightened as Alyosha's terrible moans subsided. To everyone's surprise and relief, Dr. Derevenko's remedy worked. Alexei did recover, but was extremely weak after his attack.

Outside our little world, which was centered on Alexei's condition, changes and upheavals continued. The soldiers from Yekaterinburg had gone off to raid a small city to the north of Tobolsk. Others came to take their place. But disaster struck on April 22, when a train that had been shrouded in secrecy along its route arrived in Tyumen, its passengers disembarked, and carts and horses navigated the rough roads down to Tobolsk. The mysterious official was a special envoy from Moscow, sent to shatter our world.

Kobylinsky came to tell us the news. "I'm as surprised as anyone. I had no idea he was coming, and have still not been told the reason for his arrival." The colonel paced up and down the hall. Our eyes followed him back and forth.

"Perhaps they will take us to Moscow and put us on trial once and for all," Mama said.

"I don't know. But the fellow addressed the guards, showered them with praise for carrying out their mission to keep you imprisoned."

"Does he have any real power, this one?" Papa asked.

"As much power as anyone could have. His orders were signed by Sverdlov himself, and Sverdlov has a direct link to Lenin. This fellow can have anyone he chooses executed without a trial."

A chill ran through me. I thought of Sasha and the good colonel, who had been secretly trying to help us escape, even if their efforts had come to nothing so far.

"You'll have a chance to judge him for yourself tomorrow. He will visit you," Kobylinsky said.

We were all anxious about this strange new development, and few of us ate much of our meager dinner.

The next day, three official-looking men came to see us. We were all gathered together in the hall. The men were Yakovlev, Khokhriakov, and Rodionov. Yakovlev was the leader. Very well spoken and courteous. He asked us our names and inquired about our health. They even went to Alyosha's room to question him, as he was still unable to sit up, let alone get out of bed.

"I am here to inform you that your guard and Colonel Kobylinsky have been relieved of their posts."

For an instant, I wondered if they could be setting us free. Had they at last decided that we were no threat to anyone, and might be allowed just to live in peace somewhere in the wilds of Siberia? My hope was short-lived.

"My men will take over the guard. They have strict orders not to harass you, but will deal with any breach of security in the harshest way. I need not tell you what that is."

I shuddered again for Sasha. What could this mean for him?

I soon discovered that I should have been much more concerned about what it meant for us. Yakovlev returned a day or so later with his two assistants. They looked serious and arranged themselves in a row in front of the door as if they wanted to prevent us from running out.

"Nicholas Romanov, I have orders to remove you from Tobolsk."

Mama cried out and clutched her throat. "No! You cannot take him from his family!"

"Comrade Romanova, I can do whatever I want, and the ex-tsar is to come with me under guard. I will give you a few hours to arrange your affairs and decide whether anyone will accompany you."

"I refuse to leave my wife and children!" Papa said.

"If you persist in this unwise attitude, you will be forcibly removed, as would anyone who defied the orders of the Bolshevik government."

Yakovlev never changed the tone of his voice. He was clearly a man not accustomed to being defied in any way. He simply turned and walked out with the other two men.

Mama retired to her sitting room, unable to face anyone. Demidova went with her. The rest of us sat and stared at one another, uncertain what to do or think. At last the members of the suite scattered into other parts of the house, perhaps to be alone with their thoughts.

I could hear Mama pacing back and forth across the floor of her bedroom. It was unlike her to be so restless and disturbed.

"We must talk this through," Tatiana said, calling us all from our private musing.

"Papa cannot go alone. We cannot let him," Olga said. "I shall accompany him."

"No!" I said. I couldn't bear the thought of sensitive Olga, who was prone to sickness and still coughed from the German measles, being the only defense for Papa against heaven knew what. Besides, she was so lovely, she could put herself in danger just by traveling with him. "Perhaps I should go," I said.

"You are too young," Tatiana said.

"I am nearly seventeen," I said. "I am of age!"

"Mama must go with Papa. It is the only way." This was Mashka. Mama was weak too, but we all realized that she would never forgive herself if she allowed him to go away without her, remembering those anxious times when he abdicated and could not get back to Tsarskoe Selo. "And I will go with them too, since I am the strongest of us. Tatiana must stay and nurse Alexei. Olga, you are the oldest so you can run the household and deal with the guards." As usual, Mashka—plump, gentle Mashka—had seen exactly what had to be done, not so much on a practical level as Tatiana would see it, but on a level that went deeper and got at the truth.

"And me?" I asked. "What about me? Am I to have no task when everyone else is allowed to be helpful and strong?"

Olga answered. "You have the most difficult task of all, Nastya. You must ensure that we do not become too sad and hopeless."

They still thought of me as the clown. The one who would always find a way to make everyone laugh. Roller-skating on the *Standart*. Throwing snowballs. Changing the words to songs to make them funny. Well, I supposed, it was something anyway. I realized they assumed that, because I was the youngest sister, I could be cheerful because I didn't understand fully what was happening to us. But I had more experience of love, at least, more than they did, and knowledge they could not imagine concerning our imprisonment, which I had gained through Sasha. It comforted me to know that. I had developed a very realistic view of life, and deep experience of love and distance and sorrow and abandonment. Even though I knew that Sasha was acting in our best interest at that time, I still could not help feeling abandoned by him. And I knew, better than the rest of them, that clowns are often the saddest people of all.

"I'll go talk to Mama," Tatiana said. She was the right person to do it. She had always been closest to Mama, and Mama trusted her with Alexei's care.

&

Tatiana stayed with Mama and helped her decide what to bring with her, which photographs were too precious and important to leave her possession. She had already sewn as many of her private jewels as she could inside her clothing, or covered them with cloth to disguise them as buttons. She brought her Bible and several icons. We all gathered at the little chapel in the hall to pray before dinner.

Everyone came together for dinner, but hardly anyone could speak. Only small pleasantries, and questions about whether Mama and Papa had remembered certain necessities.

They would leave sometime that night. It was all so sudden, after the weeks it had taken for us to prepare our departure from Tsarskoe Selo. Things were different. We stayed up with them. We all wanted to spend as much time together as we could. We clung to Mama and Papa, saying that soon we would be joining them wherever they were going.

Mama's good-byes to Alyosha were the most difficult of all. Although he was becoming a young man, in his illnesses he became totally dependent on her. I could hear his sobs from the hall where we waited to see them off.

At three in the morning, the carts pulled up to the gate. They were springless, uncomfortable vehicles, designed to cope with the rough conditions of the roads from Tobolsk to Tyumen, which at this time of year would be especially awful. They could not go by boat, the more comfortable alternative, because ice still clogged the Siberian rivers.

Mama's cart had a hood at least, but there were no seats in any of them. Someone brought some straw from a pigsty and wool rugs to cover it, so Mama could at least be cushioned. Anna Demidova went in another cart, so she would be with her to see to her personal needs, and Chemodurov went to help Papa. Dr. Botkin took his case with him, insisting on going with his patient, Mama. In a way, it was hardest for me to bid adieu to Mashka. We had spent almost every moment of our lives together, sharing a room, playing, taking care of one another.

"Take this icon with you," I said, giving Mashka a little ivory locket I kept with me all the time. "May it protect you on your way. And write to me every day—you must promise, even if you cannot post the letter. I want to know what you're thinking, how your journey goes, what you eat, how they treat you—everything." Mashka got in next to Mama, and Papa had to ride with Yakovlev. I tried hard for the sake of Alexei and my parents not to cry. They did not want to leave us unprotected without them, I knew. The new guards hadn't been there long enough for them to know if they could be trusted.

We watched the small party go in their horse-drawn carts, not knowing where, not anticipating just how horrible their journey would be, and how Yakovlev's intention of taking them all the way to Moscow would be undone by the Ural Soviet.

# ❧ CHAPTER 31 ❧

After two tense days, a telegram arrived for us. Tatiana opened it and read it aloud.

"Arrived safely in Tyumen, all is well. Boarding the train tomorrow."

"Still no word about where they're going." Olga sighed. "We must write to them and hope they can receive our letters."

"Alexei seems a little better today, so that is some cheering news we could send, once we know where to send it," Tatiana said.

The house felt utterly empty without Mama, Papa, and Mashka, as well as the prince, Dr. Botkin, and the three servants who went with them. Even though Nastinka and General Tatischev were still with us, I had not realized how much it mattered for us all to be together. And I was nearly as desolate without Mashka as I was at the idea that Sasha—who had maintained his distance recently—would abandon me.

But although he was distant, he was still there, which seemed a miracle. Almost all of the Tsarskoe Composites had been sent away, replaced with unpleasant Bolshevik guards. Only one or two familiar faces remained. I caught sight of Sasha occasionally, leaving the guardhouse to stand outside the palings of our prison. Once, he looked at me, and I thought I saw him nod, as if to reassure me that he had not forgotten. Yet what would happen?

Two more days passed before we had any further word from Mama, Papa, and Mashka. Apparently they had gone in the direction of Omsk at first, but had turned back and stopped at Yekaterinburg. I shuddered when I heard. Papa had said once that Yekaterinburg was the one place he would not want to go, knowing how extreme the Bolsheviks were in that city full of factories. Mama's letter said that they were taken off the train, and the three of them, Dr. Botkin, and the servants had been installed in a merchant's house, much smaller than the Governor's House in Tobolsk, and quite filthy. She didn't want to worry us, but they weren't certain how long they would remain there, and Prince Dolgorukov had been taken to the local prison.

"To prison!" Olga turned pale.

"We have all been prisoners for more than a year now," I reminded her.

"Yes, but it is different. In a house, we can walk from room to room. There are no bars on the windows. A prison is—a prison! Think of poor Anya, and all she suffered at Peter and Paul."

I couldn't contradict her. Everything was confusing and out of our control. That was the moment I decided that I had to talk to Sasha, however I managed it. Since he appeared to have some position of power among the guards, inexplicable though that was, I thought I was within my rights to request that he come and explain what was happening, or that I have a meeting with him.

A meeting. How different it sounded in this context than it had before. We didn't "have meetings," we *met*. We were together. We joined one another, physically and emotionally. This meeting must be neither of those; I must engage only my mental faculties, get answers, find out. And it was not just for me, it was for all of us.

"I shall speak to the head guard and ask him what we can expect," I said.

"Nastya! It shouldn't be you," Tatiana said.

"Why not? Knowing will be better, make everyone more cheerful, and wasn't that my job? My noble task? To keep everyone's spirits up? Because I, as the baby girl, am not capable of anything more?" Tatiana and Olga stared at me. I suppose I was rather angry at being dismissed all the time, like an extra sock, having everyone assume I didn't know what was going on when it was clear to anyone with eyes and a brain that the situation was desperate.

"I need to check on Alexei," Tatiana said.

"I'll see about the day's meals," Olga said.

I put on my light coat and let myself out into the small yard that adjoined the guard's house. Before I had a chance to lose my courage, I rapped sharply on the door. After a moment, a guard in an unbuttoned jacket and with a crumpled, hand-rolled cigarette dangling from the corner of his mouth opened the door. "What is it, Comrade?" he asked, not unkindly.

"I wish to speak to someone in charge. That fellow with the patch over his eye seems to be the one." I lifted my chin and stared him down. I would not be denied this.

He closed the door and left me standing there. The weather was much milder now that it was April, but the snow and ice had melted, leaving the yard and the alley a sea of mud. My shoes were already clogged up, and would take a long time to clean.

I concentrated on that fact so that I wouldn't become too nervous waiting for Sasha to appear. When he at last opened the door, I thought I would be perfectly calm. But at the sound of his voice, I began to tremble.

"Can I help you, Comrade Romanova?" he said, not really looking directly at me, more over my shoulder.

I cleared my throat, trying to control my voice so it would not shake. "We—my sisters, brother, and I—would like to know what is going to happen. Why have the rest of my family been stopped in Yekaterinburg, and when will we join them?"

The mention of Yekaterinburg made the pupils of his eyes widen and his face pale almost imperceptibly. "Come in out of the mud where we can talk without interruption," he said.

The guardhouse was familiar to me from those earlier times when we would visit during the bad weather and play draughts and cards with the Tsarskoe guards. We now realized they had been the embodiment of kindness and leniency compared to the Bolsheviks, who spit on the ground in front of us and sometimes even called out rude epithets when they saw us in the yard. Sasha led me past the common area, where a few off-duty guards lounged and smoked, and into a small room that had a desk and two metal chairs. He closed the door behind us, then grasped me so quickly I hardly had time to realize what he was doing. He whispered hurriedly in my ear, "Listen very carefully. Yekaterinburg is in the control of ultra-red Bolsheviks. They have stopped your parents and their party there, but they were supposed to go to Moscow. I doubt they will ever reach Moscow now."

"Will they let them stay in Yekaterinburg then? When will we go to join them?" Sasha's tone frightened me. If they didn't get to Moscow, where would they go?

"You had much better wish that you never see them again. But there are plans to send you, your sisters, and brother in a month or so, as soon as Alexei is well enough to travel, I believe, and as soon as permission can be secured from Moscow. If you do as I say, you will be safe. You must not leave Tobolsk!"

"What do you mean?" I asked.

Sasha opened his mouth to tell me, but we were interrupted by a sharp rap on the door.

"Comrade Galliapin! The Commissar wishes to see you immediately."

"Yes, Medvedev," Sasha called out. "Tell him I will come right away." And then he turned to me and spoke in a loud voice, "I am afraid, Comrade Romanova, that you may have no extra rations of milk for your brother. He has no rights beyond any of us."

"But he is ill!" I shouted, taking the cue from Sasha.

"Nonetheless, that is my final word." He opened the door as he said this. The fellow called Medvedev was immediately outside the door, and there were also one or two others who had gathered as well, probably curious or suspicious about what I was doing alone with their superior. I suddenly hoped that my actions had not endangered Sasha.

"See that this girl gets safely back to the house, and next time, don't let her in!" Sasha brushed past me. I had no trouble acting indignant. How dare he treat me like that, even if he was a Bolshevik guard!

&

As I sat cleaning my shoes before going in to talk to my sisters, I thought over what little I had gleaned from Sasha. Everything I had thought about Yekaterinburg was true. The extreme elements were in control there, and they now had the ex-tsar and tsaritsa in their hands. Sasha said it would be better if I didn't go to join them, but how could I not? How could I leave Mama and Papa and Mashka to face whatever it was alone? We belonged together. If nothing else, this forced separation, our first ever aside from when Papa was at the front with Alexei, had taught me that. Surely as a family we had more claim to the Bolsheviks' sympathy than Mama and Papa alone?

I decided to tell Olga and Tatiana only that we might be going to join the rest of our family at Yekaterinburg in a month, once Alexei was better.

"Thank heavens!" said Olga. Yes, there was comfort in that, whatever else lay ahead.

&

Alexei's health waxed and waned. At times he seemed quite well, at others his fever would rise again and we would be very anxious about him. Tatiana was the best nurse of all of us, seeming to have a sense for what would soothe and nurture him. He took comfort from her presence, and we did what we could to make him comfortable.

But there was more than Alexei's illness to make us anxious. With Kobylinsky gone, now Yakovlev's deputy, Rodionov, had become commander. He was a horrid man. He came in every morning, and we all had to stand at attention in front of him.

"Are you Olga Nicholaevna?" he would say.

"Yes," Olga would respond.

"And you," he would say, moving a step along to where Tatiana stood. "You are Tatiana Nicholaevna?"

She always bristled, but bit back her words. "Yes, Comrade Rodionov."

Then he would come to me. "That leaves only Anastasie Nicholaevna. Is that you?"

"Yes." I could not bring myself to say anything else.

"There are so many of you, I have to be certain none of you have fled away." And then he would start on what was left of the suite. We also had to leave all the doors open, day and night, so that we wouldn't be able to plot and scheme. Zhilik argued about this, pleading that it was unsafe for young women to be exposed to possible insult, but was told he would be shot if he did not comply.

And then, worst of all, the soldiers who had taken Mama, Papa, and Mashka to Yekaterinburg came back to Tobolsk, bringing news of their condition and how they were being treated. Yakovlev's guards, still not the worst of the lot and linked to much more moderate Bolsheviks, had apparently been imprisoned for a while themselves before being released to return to their homes.

"They don't even trust their own," Olga said as we sat knitting in what had been Mama's dressing room.

General Tatischev, who looked as though he had aged ten years since we arrived in Tobolsk, had yet more information. "It seems your family has been allowed only three rooms in the Ipatiev house. The doors have been taken off the hinges, and they follow everyone right to the toilet, even. Their meals are brought in from a local restaurant and arrive at odd hours, after the guards have had what they want of them."

"Mama eats little enough as it is. She must be starving," I said.

"Shh!" said Tatiana. "You've upset Olga."

Olga was the one who could become sad at the smallest things, and when I looked over at her, she had buried her face in her hands and I could see the tears seeping out from under them.

Nastinka approached her with a lace handkerchief. "There now, Olga, dear, perhaps the soldiers exaggerate. Soldiers do sometimes, you know."

Soon after that day, we began to have sentries posted inside with us, so that no conversation could be private. We had to speak Russian all the time: no more English or French. Even our prayers in the makeshift chapel were listened to. I always made a point of adding a supplication for the guards, who committed the sin of trying to come between us and God by interfering in our worship. This usually made them at least back away a little. Olga became more and more agitated by the constant presence of the guards, while Tatiana was still too busy caring for Alexei to notice it much. I kept hoping that Sasha would be one of the sentries to watch over us, but that didn't happen, at least not at first.

Although I had wished for it, I was terribly unnerved the first time I saw Sasha inside the Governor's House in the middle of the day. He tried very hard not to look at any of us, and had to join in the occasional snide comments the guards usually made, just so he didn't seem to be showing us any favor. I caught his eye every so often, and I could tell that he was trying to convey a mute apology.

# CHAPTER 32

It was Alexei, in the end, who determined what was to happen to us next.

"Alyosha wants to sit up for a while. His fever is down. Do you think it wise if I let him?"

Tatiana rarely consulted Olga or me about Alexei's care, but we were all so unsettled by the way things had changed since the others had left, that I could understand her doubt.

"What does Dr. Derevenko say?" I asked.

"He says it would not hurt for him to sit up for a little while, but that he is still very weak. The commissar said that as soon as he could sit up, he would be moved, and the doctor does not think he should be."

I looked around and through the doors. Sasha was the sentry that day, and he was by the front door. It seemed safe enough. "Perhaps for just a little while, if it would cheer him and make him feel better."

We quickly went to Alexei's room and prepared a chair for him to sit in. Then Dr. Derevenko lifted him gently out of his bed and placed him in the chair. He smiled. I hadn't seen him smile for such a long time. But he was so thin! And pale. Always, after a bleeding episode, he was extremely pale from loss of blood. "I feel so much better," he said. "Soon we will be playing our balalaikas together again, Nastya!" he said.

"You'll have to practice hard to catch up with how good I am now," I said, ready to resume teasing him. We were all so thrilled with his improvement that none of us heard the footsteps behind us. Even Joy, who was usually so watchful over her master, calmly wagged her tail and licked the hand he let hang down just for that purpose.

"So! Alexei Nicholaevich is well now. Good! The ice is gone from the river, and the *Rus* has arrived. You leave tomorrow."

It was Rodionov. What had made him come just then? For an instant, I had a horrible notion that Sasha had gone to get him. Why would he do such a thing?

"I cannot allow my patient to travel! You see how weak he is?" The good doctor risked much to stand up to Rodionov.

"Hah! He is sitting! I see him. Tomorrow it is."

"Please—a word with you in private, Comrade Commissar," Dr. Derevenko said. Rodionov nodded and the two of them went into the next room.

After that scene, Alexei was so pallid that, rather than wait for the doctor's return, Tatiana and I lifted him ourselves and put him back in bed. He felt as light as a snowflake, lighter than the hunting dogs Papa used to have. I felt as if he could melt away, as if there was nothing I could do to keep him with us.

The doctor came back after a few moments. "He will give us one more day, that is all."

"One more day, and we will be on our way to join Mama and Papa and Mashka!" Olga said, stroking Alexei's hair away from his forehead. "Don't worry, Alyosha. We'll all take care of you. Won't we?"

"Of course," said Tatiana and the doctor. I don't know why, but I couldn't add my voice to theirs. I didn't know how to take care of such a fragile creature as my brother.

"It's all because of the guard with the patch, isn't it!" Alexei turned his accusing eyes on me.

"Don't be silly!" I answered. "It was Yakovlev who came from Moscow who made all this happen, and instructed them about you and us." I couldn't think of anything else to say to take the attention away from Sasha.

"He's evil! I hate that man! He's bewitched you!" Alexei started to cough, and then the tears came. The doctor rushed to his side and took his pulse.

"You'd better go," Dr. Derevenko said to me. I looked to Olga and Tatiana for help, but they stood in shocked immobility, staring at me as if I were a stranger who had just been dropped in their midst.

I left slowly and quietly. Olga and Tatiana remained behind to comfort Alexei. I wondered what else he might tell them. He had seen so much, and I never realized it. Or at least, what little he'd seen was enough for him to draw conclusions that were all too close to the truth.

❦

Because of the constant presence of the guards we couldn't talk to each other about the scene in Alyosha's room for the rest of the day, but I felt my sisters' eyes on me wherever I went. We would have to talk later, somehow.

I went into my room in the afternoon to fetch the book I was reading, and I wasn't completely surprised to find a message from Sasha waiting for me tucked beneath my pillow. I didn't know how he got it there, but he must have written it as soon as he found out what was to happen.

Be ready tomorrow night before you are to sail. Bring only the barest necessities. A boat will take you up the river to a small town, where a band of loyal whites can ensure that you get across the border safely.

What did he mean? Just me or all of us? And how could we go without our parents and Mashka?

And what would happen to the others in the suite if the four of us managed to escape the night before we were going away? Would they still travel to Yekaterinburg, or would they be punished? Perhaps shot? And was the danger for us in escaping really any less than the danger of going to Yekaterinburg?

The four of us. How could we care for Alexei and flee in secret? He could barely sit up, let alone walk.

The time had come, I realized, to be honest with my sisters. Our only time to talk without guards listening in would be after we had gone to bed. Tatiana still slept in our room, even though she spent most of her time with Alexei. During the night, the doctor kept watch over Alexei in case he became ill again.

☙

The hours crept by more slowly than any day I had ever known. We had to sit through supper, and then the countess read aloud, until finally Olga yawned—the signal that we should all go to bed. Dr. Derevenko, who had spent the evening in our company, went to Alexei's room to relieve Tatiana.

When at last Tatiana came into our bedroom, I crossed to Olga's bed on the pretext of kissing her goodnight, and whispered, "We need to talk. Come over to my bed when the lights are out."

They did as I asked, probably knowing that I would not suggest such a thing if it wasn't important. Once we were all within whispering distance, I spoke quickly.

"We have a chance to escape. But we must be ready to go tomorrow night."

"How?" Tatiana asked. "How can you know this? Alexei too?"

"I cannot say, but there is one guard here who is friendly toward us, and he has planned this. It is very dangerous for him."

"Sasha," said Olga.

I stopped and stared at her in the darkness. "How did you know?"

"You murmur his name sometimes in your sleep. Mashka

tried to convince us it was nothing, but it happened often enough that I never believed her."

"He's the one with the patch over his eye. That Alyosha was talking about. The one who was in Tsarskoe, isn't he?" Tatiana said.

I was glad it was dark so that they could not see me blush. "Yes, I know him. But he is just a guard who is loyal to us and will help us escape." I hoped they would simply figure that Alexei knew this and was upset only because he was afraid.

"What have you been doing, Nastya?" Olga asked the question I most dreaded. I would have to lie, for their sakes as much as mine.

"I have only been doing what I can to save us, ever since I realized that things were not getting better here."

"But you knew this guard before. When did you meet him?" Tatiana sounded a little piqued. After all, she was the beautiful one.

I paused before I answered. "We met when I was just a little girl. He has been my secret friend all these years. He has looked out for all of us. He wants to help us." I was determined to steer the conversation to the urgent matter at hand. Talking about Sasha made me ache with sadness and tempted me to tell them everything about our love, our magical times together. But there would be no point.

"What about Mama and Papa and Mashka? How can you even think I would leave them?" Tatiana again asked a question I did not want to answer. Nothing had changed since that time we had first mentioned the idea of escape. It was, truly, unthinkable to go away without them, not knowing if they would be safe or if they would eventually be able to join us, or if our last farewells had been just that, and we would never see them again.

"And you heard what Dr. Derevenko said about Alyosha. He is barely able to travel with a little bit of comfort, let alone rushed and secretly. How could we manage it?"

"Perhaps that was why he was so angry about Sasha, even if he didn't know who he was," Olga said. "I sometimes think he senses things none of the rest of us can, because he has come so close to death so often. He knows that if an escape is planned, he will either slow everyone down or be left behind."

She was right. Alyosha's sad, wide eyes swam before me. I had to shake my head to dispel the vision. "Well," I said, not certain what to say that would not send us around in a circle again, "I want to live. I want to be free again. Don't you think the others would want it for us, if we had that chance? Even Alexei? I intend to be ready with my stoutest shoes and layers of clothing at eleven tomorrow night. If you choose, you may all come with me. Alexei too, if he wants. I'll carry him myself."

I felt the severity of my words and wished them immediately unsaid. Perhaps Olga might take a chance with me, but Tatiana wouldn't. She had been entrusted with Alexei's health and safety, and she would do nothing to break that trust.

Before I knew it, my sisters and I embraced one another in

a huddle of silent tears. I wished we had one bed large enough so that we could all sleep close to each other, drawing comfort from our familiar warmth. But we gradually untwined ourselves and each went back to our narrow camp beds and tried to sleep.

# CHAPTER 33

The next day, the commissar and a few guards came to tell us what we could bring with us and what we couldn't.

"The house you will stay in is smaller than this. You may bring camp beds and linens, blankets, some of the household items you brought, and one bag of personal possessions. These must be inspected before you leave, to ensure that you are not stealing any of the items that belong to the Governor's House."

Our mouths dropped open at this suggestion. It was Nastinka who first managed to speak. "The grand duchesses and the tsarevich were not brought up to steal!"

"To whom do you refer, Comrade Hendrikova?" Rodionov said, his face reddening to an even deeper hue. "There are no such things as grand duchesses. I see before me only individuals with an unfortunate alliance to the monarchist counterrevolutionaries."

The countess was about to speak again, but Olga went

over and took hold of her arm. "Comrade Commissar is right, Madame. We are all the same."

"Might I bring my balalaika?" Alexei asked. He was again sitting up, since the journey was settled on, and the doctor thought he had better try to get a small amount of exercise. There had been no more outbursts. He didn't mention Sasha. But he also would not meet my eyes when we spoke.

He alone of all of us saw the coming change not as laden with fateful significance, but as a reunion with Mama, Papa, and Mashka. It was his joy at looking forward to that which made my own decision stick in my heart. Olga and Tatiana kept looking at me with beseeching eyes. I could hardly bear the thought of leaving, going off to the unknown without my family, the dearest friends I had known for all my life.

Sasha had managed to get another brief message to me, telling me to meet him in the alley where we used to meet, what seemed like years ago but was only a few months. In those days, I had the thrill of love to give me wings. Now my feet were like leaden weights, and my heart like a lump of dry bread. My only remaining hope was that Sasha would come with me. Surely he would not send me off by myself, to face uncertain dangers? Yet what if he did? Could I go alone?

I kept my clothes on underneath my nightdress and waited until the house was asleep. I knew that Olga and Tatiana would not be, that they were waiting for me to go because they would want to give me their blessings, but I couldn't bear to take leave of them. I was afraid it would break my resolve. I slipped out of bed quickly, trying to get out of our room before they realized I was gone, but Olga was just as fast. She caught me and gave me a fierce kiss and embrace. "I love you, darling Nastya!" she whispered. A moment later Tatiana was there.

"Forgive me!" I felt a sob force its way into my throat. "I have to go!"

They released me, and I left the room, slipping silently with my small bag through the house, letting myself out the door and around the side to the alleyway, feeling as if my life drained away as I went. I could hardly see for tears.

As I turned into the alley, I nearly collided with Sasha.

"What's wrong?" he asked, wiping my face with his hand-kerchief.

"How can you ask? I am about to leave my family, everything I have ever known, for a long, long time!"

"You are about to leave so that you can live the rest of your life!" He sounded angry. "Do you know how dangerous it was for me to plan this escape? Do you have any idea what they will do to me if they discover I helped you?"

"Aren't you coming with me?" I asked, shocked into tearlessness.

He threw his hands up in exasperation. "No! I shall have to lead the hunt to find you. Only then will I be able to take them the wrong way, so you have a chance to reach your destination."

So, I was to be alone. I had never done anything, traveled anywhere, alone. Going away always meant an army of people: sisters, brother, parents, servants, maids of honor. Even coming from Tsarskoe Selo had been the same in its way. All at once I felt much younger than my almost seventeen years.

"How can you hesitate? Do you have any idea what you may well face in Yekaterinburg? The reds will take no pity on you because you are young. You and your family represent everything they hate with an irrational hatred that lusts for blood."

"You frighten me," I said. Sasha had never spoken to me like this.

"I mean to frighten you!" he said, then held me to him in a crushing embrace. I felt his tears on my head.

"Will I never see you again either?" I asked, feeling as though I was about to jump off a high mountain peak and hoping to land without hurting myself. That's how impossible everything seemed at that moment, no matter what I did.

"Perhaps we will meet again," he said, softening his voice. "But you must see that it does not matter. You have so much ahead of you. It's your choice now. Choose the future! Choose life!"

He pushed me toward a gate that led out of the alleyway. I could see someone standing beyond it, clearly waiting to conduct me on the first stage of my journey. I took two steps toward it, then turned.

"No."

The word felt solid. Secure. This—this furtive flight in the dead of night—was not what I wanted. I wanted to stay, I wanted to see my mama and papa again, to go through whatever my sisters and brother would go through. I had no choice. I could not choose nothing, which is what leaving would be. "No," I repeated.

Sasha let his arms fall to his side. He shook his head. "I

don't know if I can ever do anything again to help you. You're not thinking clearly. Just go, Nastya! Go!"

Even as he said it, he walked toward me, and before I knew it, we were in each other's arms, and he was kissing me as he used to. I closed my eyes and imagined for a moment that we were back in Tsarskoe, before the killing, only we were in the garden, in the open air, not underground at night, hidden away from everyone.

When we stopped kissing we continued to hold each other. I couldn't bear the thought of letting go of him. I looked up into his face, seeing there an expression that meant love. He loved me, in all my awkward imperfection. As I loved him. "I want to see your scar," I said, realizing that I must look at it if I were to know him as he was then.

Sasha slowly let go of me, felt for the edges of his eye patch with his left hand, and lifted it to his forehead. It was dark enough that I couldn't see every detail of the ridges that converged where his eye used to be. For a moment, I imagined the young boy I met when I was just a girl, with mischief dancing in both eyes. I stood on my tiptoes and kissed the hardened spot tenderly, then gently slid the patch back down to cover it again.

"I could never go away without you," I whispered. Sasha took my face between his hands and kissed me gently on the lips.

"That heart of yours has undone you, sweet Nastya," he said. He backed away, holding my gaze. After a few steps, he turned away from me and walked in the same, slow pace toward the guardhouse. I watched him go, half expecting him to turn around, grab my hand, and run with me out of the gate.

But he didn't. He opened the door of the building where his quarters were, and then shut it behind him. For a moment I stood shivering, alone, before I too turned and went back into our prison.

I was still in a daze, not quite certain what I had just done. I passed through the darkened rooms to the bedroom I had shared with my sisters for eight months, and crawled in between the sheets I had left only a few minutes earlier, knowing that something had changed in me forever.

"I knew you wouldn't do it," whispered Olga. "I'm glad you're staying, darling."

It felt odd to leave the Governor's House by any door other than the one to the yard. The archbishop had sent a horse and carriage to take the four of us to the dock, so that Alexei would not be too uncomfortable, and I could see the horses pawing the street, impatient to be gone. The carriage was simple and black, but at least it had springs, unlike the rough carts that had taken Mama, Papa, Mashka, the prince, and Dr. Botkin to Tyumen the month before.

We all had to leave in order, our names checked off as we went. Rodionov and his men were coming along to guard us on the voyage. We three sisters stood in the hall and waited. I had little sensation of time passing, still not fully in the moment after the night before. Alexei sat in a wheelchair. Nastinka, General Tatischev, Dr. Derevenko, Zhilik, Trina, and Isa—who all this time had not been permitted to stay with us but was to be accompanying us now—all went out and ascended the carts that were to take them and a few possessions to the *Rus*. Once they had gone, a few servants,

But he didn't. He opened ⟨...⟩
his quarters were, and then shut ⟨...⟩
I stood shivering, alone, before I ⟨...⟩
into our prison.

I was still in a daze, not quite certain ⟨...⟩
I passed through the darkened rooms to ⟨...⟩
shared with my sisters for eight months, and ⟨...⟩
the sheets I had left only a few minutes earlier ⟨...⟩
something had changed in me forever.

"I knew you wouldn't do it," whispered Olga. ⟨...⟩
you're staying, darling."

felt odd to leave the Governor's House by any door other than the one to the yard. The archbishop had sent a horse and carriage to take the four of us to the dock, so that Alexei would not be too uncomfortable, and I could see the horses pawing the street, impatient to be gone. The carriage was simple and black, but at least it had springs, unlike the rough carts that had taken Mama, Papa, Mashka, the prince, and Dr. Botkin to Tyumen the month before.

We all had to leave in order, our names checked off as we went. Rodionov and his men were coming along to guard us on the voyage. We three sisters stood in the hall and waited. I had little sensation of time passing, still not fully in the moment after the night before. Alexei sat in a wheelchair. Nastinka, General Tatischev, Dr. Derevenko, Zhilik, Trina, and Isa—who all this time had not been permitted to stay with us but was to be accompanying us now—all went out and ascended the carts that were to take them and a few possessions to the *Rus*. Once they had gone, a few servants,

But he didn't. He opened the door of the building where his quarters were, and then shut it behind him. For a moment I stood shivering, alone, before I too turned and went back into our prison.

I was still in a daze, not quite certain what I had just done. I passed through the darkened rooms to the bedroom I had shared with my sisters for eight months, and crawled in between the sheets I had left only a few minutes earlier, knowing that something had changed in me forever.

"I knew you wouldn't do it," whispered Olga. "I'm glad you're staying, darling."

# ❧ CHAPTER 34 ❧

It felt odd to leave the Governor's House by any door other than the one to the yard. The archbishop had sent a horse and carriage to take the four of us to the dock, so that Alexei would not be too uncomfortable, and I could see the horses pawing the street, impatient to be gone. The carriage was simple and black, but at least it had springs, unlike the rough carts that had taken Mama, Papa, Mashka, the prince, and Dr. Botkin to Tyumen the month before.

We all had to leave in order, our names checked off as we went. Rodionov and his men were coming along to guard us on the voyage. We three sisters stood in the hall and waited. I had little sensation of time passing, still not fully in the moment after the night before. Alexei sat in a wheelchair. Nastinka, General Tatischev, Dr. Derevenko, Zhilik, Trina, and Isa—who all this time had not been permitted to stay with us but was to be accompanying us now—all went out and ascended the carts that were to take them and a few possessions to the *Rus*. Once they had gone, a few servants,

mostly locals who had been hired by the Soviet to do the things we were either not allowed to do or incapable of doing ourselves, started walking to the same dock.

Rodionov took a roll call one more time before leading us out the door, as if he could not simply count to four and know we were all there. Once outside, eight guards surrounded us. I drew in my breath sharply. At the front of the group was Sasha. Sasha. He had his back to me. I could see his sandy hair beneath his cap, recognize the set of his shoulders. His way of walking was still the same. I wondered if he could feel me staring at him, if he too thought about the previous night, my near escape, our last embrace.

I was rudely shaken out of my thoughts after we had taken only a few steps when all at once the two houses we had occupied erupted with sounds of tramping feet and smashing glass. The guards from the guardhouse and the barracks—some three hundred of them—swarmed into the Governor's House and the Kornilov house where the suite had been lodged. It seemed only seconds until they poured back out again, carrying clocks, books, furniture, and icons—anything that was not fixed in place. Six men even mounted the carriage we were supposed to ride in and whipped the horses to a frenzy, so that they took off at a gallop, scattering dust all over us.

"Those are our things! That was Mama's icon!" Olga said.

"That was the carriage we were supposed to take!" Tatiana yelled.

"There is no personal property now. You are fortunate you are being allowed to take anything other than the barest necessities." Rodionov's smug expression made it evident that far from condemning the actions of his men, he fully condoned them. I saw Sasha's neck go red. At least he did not—

"Oh!" I cried out, seeing a man struggling to get out of the door with an armload of booty from the Governor's House that included Sasha's balalaika. I had begged to be allowed to take it, but they would not let me, and now it was being stolen.

The thief staggered quite close to us so that Sasha could not avoid seeing the instrument. Sasha couldn't acknowledge that the balalaika was his, or he would risk exposing his connection to me. I thought I saw the vein in his neck pulse and his jaw tighten, but he could do no more than just watch the fellow take it away.

"Well, it appears you will have to walk to the dock," Rodionov said, once the looting had stopped. Tatiana kept a firm hold on the handles of Alexei's wheelchair. For a moment I thought the commissar was going to insist that Alexei also walk, but no one who saw my brother would have thought him remotely capable of such a thing at that time. He hardly had the energy to react to the thievery of the guards, other than to sigh and look down at Joy, who was curled up in his lap.

The streets were lined with curious people. No one said anything or made a move to approach us as we passed—I supposed the armed guards were enough to prevent that. And unlike our earliest days in Tobolsk, no one made the sign of the cross as Alexei passed either. Nowadays, people were likely to be shot on the spot for such displays of counterrevolutionary zeal.

*We'll see Mama and Papa and Mashka soon*, I kept repeating to myself. *We'll all be together again. We can be strong together. Sasha will find a way to help us all escape.* I had to believe it. I had to persuade myself that I hadn't given up my only chance of freedom.

Single file, with Tatiana pushing Alexei, we walked onto the gangplank to the *Rus*. I couldn't help remembering what hopes we'd had on the way to Tobolsk. Rather than constricting, the journey had felt freeing. We had started out with a sort of pattern of life that didn't disagree with us. It was only over time that things had changed so much for the worse. Our circumstances had been strangled around us so slowly that each added restriction merely adjusted my sense of what was normal, until it was almost impossible to imagine living any other way.

Now, I think it's the going back, the retracing of our steps, that reveals how far we have fallen. We are confined and kept out of sight, with only small portholes through which we can see the Siberian countryside passing by. Rodionov told us it is for our safety, but he said it with such glee that I didn't believe him. And we have been told we cannot lock our doors at night, while Alexei and the tutors and suite must lock theirs. What can it mean?

And what about Sasha?

I only see him when he happens to be among our immediate guards. When the others aren't looking, our eyes meet now and again in a way that gives me hope. We cannot speak to each other, and so I try to put as much as I can into every shared glance without looking for very long, willing him to see the love I have for him. I begin to understand how much he risked for me. Perhaps if I were someone else, I might have taken the chance. But in a life like mine, where the only bonds of affection are to my family and to a man who has been one of our captors almost as long as he was my friend before that, there is no choice. Without those people, I am only a tiny fraction of myself.

But I still hold out hope that in this frightening world where anything bad could happen any moment, something good might just as easily occur. Sasha almost succeeded in getting me safely away. Maybe he will think of something else in Yekaterinburg, for all of us.

Spring in Siberia is breathtaking. Even the small view we have from our cabin windows can't entirely shut it out. Delicate flowers blanket the meadows, and the wind smells sweet coming down from the Urals. I wish I could change us all into the wind, so that we could blow away where no one could harm us, and mingle together, not separate but one, forever.

It is night now, and tomorrow we reach Tyumen, where we will board a train. One day on the train, and then we will be with the rest of the family again. We will be whole, we will be OTMA.

My sisters are asleep. One of the guards is playing a balalaika. I wonder for a moment if it is Sasha, if he reclaimed his simple instrument and brought it onto this boat to serenade me, to sing us to the end of our journey. I know from all I have heard that life in Yekaterinburg will not be easy. But I am ready. Right now, as the waters of the river rock me in my bunk, I cannot believe that I do not belong to Russia, like the soil itself. There will be a solution, one that will keep us all together and keep us in Russia. I hear the tune and I recall a nursemaid singing me to sleep.

May God protect us. May God protect Sasha. I will dream of him every night for as long as I live.

The imperial family remained together under terrible conditions in Yekaterinburg for nearly two months, from May 23 until July 16, 1918, when Yekaterinburg was on the point of being retaken by the Whites—the resistance loyal to the tsar—aided by Czech troops. The official report stated that the family, their suite, and their attendants were awakened and told to dress, that they were going to be moved again but first to go to a basement room for a photograph. Once they were all assembled, the guards opened fire on them and assassinated the tsar, the tsaritsa, Olga, Tatiana, Marie, Anastasia, and Alexei, along with Dr. Botkin, Chemodurov, Anna Demidova, and possibly one other servant. All the children had sewn jewels in their clothing, and the bullets apparently glanced off them, making it necessary for the guards to fire repeatedly and use their bayonets before they perished.

For many years it was not known for certain where or how the remains of the family were disposed of. In 1991, after the fall of the Soviet Union, an amateur archeologist told the authorities about a mass grave he had discovered in the 1970s and kept secret—perhaps because he suspected whose remains were there and didn't want anyone to disturb them. DNA tests confirmed that the nine people in the grave included five of the Romanovs and four retainers, but that still left two family members unaccounted for.

A second grave was discovered nearby in 2007. It had the remains of two more Romanov family members, which were analyzed and determined to belong to the tsarevich and either Marie or Anastasia.

Despite this seemingly conclusive evidence, some people doubt the validity of the tests. They assert that the finding of the second grave was a little too convenient, and with such fragmented and scattered remains, some have argued that it's impossible to say for certain that every member of the tsar's family was in those two graves—especially since distinguishing among the sisters using DNA evidence is very difficult.

Nonetheless, the Russian Orthodox Church declared the entire Romanov family saints in 2008.

As for the other members of the family and the suite, Prince Dolgorukov and Countess Hendrikova had been imprisoned and shot long before, as had Nagorny, Trina, and a young servant who attended the grand duchesses. The valet Volkov managed to escape. Baroness Buxhoeveden—Isa—perhaps because she was not of Russian descent, was also given her freedom, and Lili Dehn survived as well. Pierre Gilliard and Mr. Gibbes escaped execution, returning to their native countries. However, the Bolsheviks did not spare the other members of the imperial family that they could find, including the tsaritsa's sister

Elisabeth, widow of one of the tsar's uncles, and a devout and selfless nun in a convent. She, along with several others, was thrown into a well while still alive. The Bolsheviks threw hand grenades after them to finish the job.

The only living being known to have survived that night in Yekaterinburg was Joy, Alexei's spaniel. Sidney Gibbes found her wandering lost and forlorn around the yard by the house, crying for her master. She was taken to England to live out her days and is buried in Westminster Abbey.

Despite the massacre, a few members of the imperial family and the nobility managed to escape to foreign countries. Anya Vyrubova lived a long life in Finland. Grand Duke Cyril, a first cousin of Nicholas, had a court in exile in Paris. Vyrubova, Volkov, Gilliard, Buxhoeveden, Lili Dehn, and Count Benck-endorff all wrote memoirs of their time with the Romanovs.

An aura of mystery persists, however, concerning the execution of the imperial family. For years, a woman named Anna Anderson tried to pass herself off as Anastasia, but she was discovered to be a fraud. In all, two hundred people have claimed to have descended from the murdered Romanovs since that night in 1918. None of their stories have held up to scrutiny.

Did Anastasia survive beyond that fateful night? Was there a Sasha to protect her and help her get away? That is a question that may never be answered. Whatever and however it happened for Anastasia, I like to think she had a full life and experienced love in her seventeen years of documented existence.

## ❧ Author's Note ❧

I was pretty scared to write in the first person from the point of view of a real historical character, especially one who has ignited the imaginations of so many people since that tragic day in 1918. But something about Anastasia called to me. Maybe it was that she has always been referred to as "one of the children" when in fact, although she was the youngest daughter, she was seenteen years old when she died. Her oldest sister was twenty-three—no longer a child by any standard. The thought of what it might have been like to have the real emotions of an adolescent at such a turbulent time took hold of me and would not let go.

While putting myself into the mind of a privileged, sheltered, lively, and intelligent adolescent proved to be a rewarding challenge, I felt a deep obligation to adhere as closely as possible to the events as they occurred at the time. The almost overwhelming amount of first-hand documentation of the lives of the imperial family was a boon to my research. Having said that, I found ample areas of doubt and shadows, especially in regard to Anastasia and her sisters. These accounts tended not to focus on Anastasia very much, as if all there was to know about her was that she was part of that ill-fated family.

In the process of constructing a novel (which is, after all, fiction), it is important to consider the pace and structure of the story. I have tried to follow the actual historic events but have taken the novelist's prerogative of creating scenes that might have happened when they serve to illustrate an important point: the sullen mob at the train stop near the beginning, Anastasia and Mashka's visit to the village near Mogilev. The girls did visit villages when they went to see their father, but I have not been able to discover which ones or what they did there.

The months of Anastasia's captivity were dreary and difficult, the bonds gradually tightening around her family as events in Russia led inexorably to their conclusion. For the sake of my plot, I have gently rearranged one or two things that occurred during their time at Tobolsk so that they make more sense to the story. Most of what I detail did actually happen according to the remaining accounts, just not in the exact order. Where different versions of the facts contradict each other, I simply chose what worked best in my story.

Sasha and one or two servants are the only characters who came entirely from my imagination. Everyone else—including the pets—had documented roles in the family's life.

For anyone wishing to dig more deeply into this fascinating time period, I can do no better than to recommend The Alexander Palace Time Machine, a wonderful Web site that includes the full text of several of the existing memoirs, a wealth of pictures, detailed descriptions of the Alexander Palace—even an accounting of all the possessions confiscated by the authorities when they finally took over the palace. It's an incredible labor of love and a testament to an enduring fascination with the doomed imperial family. Visit www.alexanderpalace.org and prepare to spend hours looking at what Bob Atchison has made available to anyone with an interest in what happened or might have happened to the Romanovs.

Finally, do I think Anastasia survived the massacre at Yekaterinburg? Very unlikely, given the circumstances. And even if by some miracle Anastasia had survived the massacre, she would be 108 years old by now. Nonetheless, I will always allow myself to hope that something happened to preserve her from the terrible fate the rest of her family suffered. I can't bear to think of her suffering, and I hope she's up there enjoying the romance I gave her in the pages of this book.

## ⁂   ACKNOWLEDGMENTS   ⁂

Many thanks to my personal family and my writing family, who always support and nurture me through this process—especially Charles and Sue, but also Cassie and Chloé.

Of course, without my agent, Adam Chromy, and my editor, Melanie Cecka, this book would never have come about. I'm very fortunate to have two incredible cheerleaders in this difficult business.

I'd like to say a special thank-you to Raina Putter, my copyeditor, whose keen eye and expert knowledge of Russian history helped me polish the manuscript.

And finally, to all the others whose personal accounts and research helped me discover the world of the Romanovs in captivity, including Bob Atchison and Robert K. Massie, I say thank you.

I didn't expect it to be so easy to get on a coach. All it took was a few shillings. Maybe that was because I asked for the cheapest fare and found myself sitting on the top, shivering in the drizzle that had begun to fall. As a result, I still had some money left from what Will gave me. Even with that, I feared what was left wouldn't be enough for a ticket on the Boulogne Packet.

Dawn made the gray sky pale when we left Charing Cross and set off over the river. The horses' breath puffed out in little clouds as they clopped first over cobbles, then echoed on the wooden planks of the bridge, and after that thudded in the packed mud of country roads. I'd never been outside of London, so in spite of almost no sleep and my stomach tied in a knot, I just kept drinking in the sight of rolling fields with hedgerows cutting them up into neat parcels, brown now and dead after the harvest, stubble showing where hay had grown. At least I thought it was hay, for all I knew about farming. Whatever it was, the air smelled clean and earthy, not sooty like London. The wind up top made it too noisy to talk, and I was glad. I just kept my eyes turned away from the others up there with me, all men.

We drew into Folkestone late in the afternoon, my backside bruised from bumping on the wood plank seat. The man who sat next to me hopped down and lifted me off like I was a sack of potatoes, but then set me gently on my feet and tipped his hat to me.

I took my valise and set out to find the docks. Folkestone was so small I could walk across it in a half hour. Just a little ways in I saw the tops of the masts bobbing up and down on the waves and set my course toward them.

The channel was chopped up with whitecaps. *Must be a rough journey across,* I thought. I couldn't see to the other side. To France. If all went like I hoped, I'd be in a foreign country soon. Someplace where they didn't speak the Queen's English. I shivered, even though the rain had stopped.

I strolled back and forth on the docks like someone taking the air, while really looking for a place I could buy a ticket. All I saw were dock workers, though. I watched them bend and lift, muscles tensing and sweat streaking their cheeks, even though it was cold enough that I could have worn an extra cloak and been grateful for it. *Boulogne Star.* I made out "Star" and guessed the first word, since she was the only boat that wasn't a fishing boat, with deck chairs and a cabin where passengers could sit.

What if I couldn't get a ticket? If there were none left? Or if they were more costly than the few shillings I had in my pocket? I had to suss out if I could get aboard some other way.

Where we lived in the East End, near the docks, I used to play with my brother Ted before the littlest one came along and I had to stay home and help. We'd go and see if we could sneak aboard the finest and biggest ship, and usually we managed it. We pretended we were going to sail off to the South Seas, but of course we never did. As soon as we heard the sailors cry that the tide was on the turn, we'd get off as quick as we got on, sometimes by swinging from a rope to the dock, sometimes we'd just scamper down the gangplank when no one was minding us. There were always children running around on the docks in London, begging or playing or thieving.

Not here, though. What I saw of the town was neat and quiet. No one was begging or thieving that I could see, not even on the docks. And there was only one narrow gangplank leading to the deck. It'd be hard to pass unnoticed. I put my best face on and walked right up to a man on the dock; he was official looking, with a uniform, but not a policeman. I thought he might tell me about the fare for the packet.

"Beg pardon, sir," I said, and I added a little curtsy just for good measure. "Can you tell me where I might purchase a ticket on the packet boat to Boulogne?"

"Fancy a jaunt to France, eh?" he said. He smiled with his lips closed. I stared right back at him and waited for his answer. "The purser'll be coming by soon. You can get your ticket from him. If you've got six shillings, that is." He turned his back on me when a gent walked up to him and asked him a question.

How did I know what a purser looked like? It didn't make a bit of difference though. I only had two and six left. I couldn't buy a ticket. I'd have to think of another way.

I was no longer a little urchin who could squeeze by everyone quick and invisible. Some of the dock workers stared at me as I walked, one or two calling out things I wouldn't repeat to my mum. I ignored them and pretended I was going into the town. Back to the train station. Perhaps I'd meet the train Miss Nightingale and her nurses were on.

I joined a queue of people at a kiosk. When it was my turn I said, "Excuse me, but what time's the train from London?"

"From London? Don't get in until morning," he said and looked behind me to the next person, dismissing me before I'd even stepped aside.

Morning! What would I do with myself all night? I didn't have money for lodgings. And after dark they probably locked up people just wandering around. It was that kind of town. Like the nicer areas in London. So now I'd have to find someplace I could hide, somewhere to put myself out of view all night, and where I'd be safe too.

As I suspected, even though Folkestone was a prospering town, the harbor had its secrets. I wasn't the only one lurking there waiting for daily business to stop. There were lots of nooks to tuck myself away behind crates and great coils of rope. I just hoped the weather wouldn't turn against me, or some thief set on me. Little chance of that, since anyone with something worth stealing would likely have a room at the inn. No, my only difficulty would be managing to keep dry all night long and still look decent in the morning.

So, stomach rumbling and hands now numb from cold, I wandered until the to-ing and fro-ing stopped and the dock workers went home, then found a corner to hide myself in and tried to sleep, sitting on a crate with my back against some sacks of grain.

———⊗⊗⊗———

The train's whistle woke me. My back and neck ached. I wiped a little drool from the corners of my mouth and stretched, straightening my clothes. At least I was dry. And no one made off with my valise—which had nothing valuable in it anyway, but I'd seem even odder aboard a packet with no luggage.

I hurried to the station, arriving just in time to see the London train come steaming in, great puffs billowing from the smokestack in the front. The whistle blew again and again so loud I had to cover my ears.

As soon as the train screeched to a stop everyone flew into a tizzy. Porters and vendors bumped into me, all crowding up at once to help passengers with their luggage or sell them cockles and tea if they were continuing on to France. I wished I could make myself invisible in the crowd so I could watch for the group of women to get off the train. I assumed it would be a large number and easy to see. The newspaper said a hundred would go.

The first-class compartment emptied. Only eight people got out, dressed very fine and one lady carrying a small dog with a squashed-in face. At the same time, all manner of men and women tumbled out of the third-class carriages, some smoking pipes or carrying bundles tied up with paper and string on their shoulders. Still no one who looked anything like a nurse, and no Mrs. Bracebridge.

It was beginning to look like I would have to walk all the way back to London because I didn't have enough for a coach when a second-class carriage door opened, and I recognized the gentleman who'd been introduced to me as Mr. Bracebridge getting down. He cast his eyes up and down the platform as if he was expecting someone. I turned away quickly, hoping he wouldn't recognize me, but kept sight of the carriage door out of the corner of my eye.

Soon they streamed out, one by one. There were two different sorts. One had uniforms, or something like them, like the nuns we sometimes saw in the poor neighborhoods bringing food. The others were dressed in ordinary street clothes. I counted them. Twenty-eight, not a hundred. Was one of them Miss Nightingale? Then Mrs. Bracebridge stepped down from the train, and by the way they all queued up behind to follow her, it didn't seem like any could be the lady herself. Perhaps she was one of the others I'd seen get down from the first-class compartment.

I stuck close to the nurses but out of sight, my only hope

being I could somehow blend in with the lot and sneak aboard as if I was part of the group.

They all stopped at an inn, most likely for a bite to eat. Lucky for me, they didn't stay long. In twos and threes they came out after a bit and gathered on the cobbled street where other people also stood round in groups. I kept my distance but followed them again to the docks.

Passengers already had their tickets out and were filing aboard the packet up the gangplank, all looking like they were on holiday. A man in a uniform, I guessed he was the purser, scowled at each ticket. He stopped people and looked carefully at their papers. My heart dropped like a stale roll to my stomach. How would I pass? There was no hope I'd get by unnoticed. After all this trouble, it looked as if I'd get no farther than Folkestone, and with not enough left over to make my way back to London either. I watched the nurses get their tickets out, ready to take their turn, wishing so I was one of them. I clenched my jaw to stop the tears I feared might start any moment.

Just as I was about to give up hope, a fat man wearing a sash like he was the mayor or something came bustling up to Mrs. Bracebridge with a handful of police officers scurrying behind to keep up. At first I thought the whole crowd of nurses would be arrested.

"Are you Mrs. Nightingale?" he asked Mrs. Bracebridge in a booming voice.

"No, I am afraid *Miss* Nightingale has gone ahead from Dover."

The broad smile on the man's face faded and he started to bow and turn away.

"But these are her nurses, whom I am to accompany to Turkey," Mrs. Bracebridge added, touching his arm to stop him. His smile full of teeth returned and he kissed Mrs. Bracebridge's hand.

By this time a small band had formed. A cornet, a clarinet, and an accordion. At a signal from the mayor—or whatever he was—they struck up "The Girl I Left Behind Me." Everyone watched the nurses. Even the sailors and dock workers stopped what they were doing and swayed a little to the music.

My blood of a sudden rushed into my fingers and toes. Here was my chance! Before I lost my nerve, I slipped up the gangplank all the while sure the whole crowd would see me and I'd be stopped and thrown in gaol. But I made it to the deck. Then, instead of hiding like I would have done when I was younger, I sauntered past the other passengers like I belonged there, forcing myself to move slowly. I even leaned on the rail looking down at the fuss on the dock. I had to be calm, but my heart thumped. I gripped the rail so no one would see how my hands shook.

The mayor made a short speech—time was getting on and the boat had to sail—and then all the nurses and the Bracebridges climbed aboard.

What next? I had got on the packet, but the hardest part was still ahead of me. How would I convince Mrs. Bracebridge to let me go along with them as if it was always the plan?

As soon as we were far enough away from the shore, and the wind picked up and the waves began to rock us, I looked for her, hoping she'd not gone below with so many of the others to escape the bitter wind.

I found Mrs. Bracebridge sitting toward the stern in a sheltered place, her eyes closed. She looked very tired. I felt bad that I was going to trouble her but I had no choice, now I'd got this far. "Excuse me, Mrs. Bracebridge." I hoped my voice didn't quake too much.

She looked up, startled. She shaded her eyes from the sun and narrowed them before talking. "Do I know you?"

"We met at Mrs. Stanley's house. My name is Molly Fraser."

"Molly Fraser . . . yes, I remember. You weren't qualified. How do you come to be on this boat?"

"The truth is, I was waiting for you, ma'am. See, I don't half want to be a nurse and go with your lot to Turkey." Now that I'd got it out, everything was in her hands. She had a kind face. I kept my eyes fixed on her, hoping she'd see how desperate I was and how much I meant what I said.

The frown on her brow creased deeper. "But I explained to you that Miss Nightingale requested only trained, mature nurses."

I'd practiced what I was going to say to her over and over to myself, but now that it came out it all sounded hollow and flat. "I learn things fast. I know I can prove myself. I know about healing. Please just give me a chance." I talked too fast. My lips felt like India rubber.

"It's not my decision to make," she said.

"But Miss Nightingale trusted you to choose the other nurses, didn't she?"

She let out a short laugh. "Yes, but if I bring her an inexperienced girl, what will she think then?"

"If you don't tell her, she won't know. I'm here now and I went to a great deal of trouble to get here. Won't you please just let me try?" I was afraid I might cry if I went on. I was so tired after my night on the docks and all the planning and hoping of the last few weeks.

She sat silent for a moment, looking out over the water. I could almost hear her tossing the idea back and forth in her mind. What would she decide?

"Do you realize that you have taken a terrible risk? I could have you arrested by the purser as a stowaway—unless you have a ticket? Not to mention that you need a passport once we arrive in France."

I shook my head. "No, I don't have neither one of them."

She was silent again. She put two fingers to her forehead and rubbed it a little, like it would help her think. At last she folded her hands in her lap. She looked steadily at me. "All right, Molly. I won't turn you over to the authorities. But this deception does not add to your scanty recommendations. You will have to prove yourself or you will be sent home. We shall have to see to the passport in Paris. But it will be up to Miss Nightingale whether you may continue with us to Turkey. And you must obey me and Miss Nightingale in everything. This is not a pleasure trip. I doubt you can truly know what you are signing up for. Not a wisp of that beautiful hair must show beneath your cap. If you so much as look at a wounded soldier with those big gray eyes I'll send you packing even if Miss Nightingale doesn't notice. And if she agrees to keep you, you mustn't expect the same wages the trained nurses will receive."

She meant to discourage me. But I was so happy I could've thrown my arms around her. I didn't though. I didn't want to do anything that might make her doubt me. Instead I tried to keep a straight face and control the trembling that I thought might overpower me at any time. "You won't be sorry, I promise." I put out my hand to shake hers. She took it and smiled.

SIGRID ESTRADA

SUSANNE DUNLAP graduated from Smith College and later earned a PhD in music history from Yale University. She is also the author of *The Musician's Daughter*, *In the Shadow of the Lamp*, and two historical novels for adults. She divides her time between Brooklyn, New York, and Northampton, Massachusetts.

www.susannedunlap.com

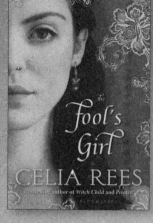

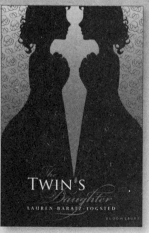